THE PURRFECT CRIME

A Claw and Order Mystery

By M. Tucker Cunningham

Published by Fire Storm Press

Printed in the United States of America

ISBN: 978-1-972539-02-6 (Paperback)
ISBN: 978-1-972539-03-3 (Hardcover)
ISBN: 979-8-2957-6763-0 (EBook)

For information, contact the author:

authormtucker@gmail.com

mtcbooks.com

Dedication

To my family, whose love is my foundation.
And to the cats who made this series possible —

Trouble,

Who crossed the rainbow bridge with the same quiet
grace she brought to every room she entered.
Cancer took her body. Nothing could take what she
taught me — that paying attention is its own kind of
love.
I wrote a detective in your image, sweet girl. I hope I got it right.

Mayhem,

My beautiful, ridiculous, unrepentant boy.
You are every knocked-over glass, every stolen
scrunchie, every twenty-pound demand for attention.
Loyal, loud, and worth every dollar in damaged
upholstery.
Never change.

And Moxie — my real-life Chaos —

Whose name changed on the page but whose spirit
didn't.
Thank you for reminding me that the world
is worth investigating, every single day.
You are the curiosity this story runs on.
Every purr in these pages is yours.

Table of Contents

Prologue

The woman sitting across from Amaya Storm in the third booth at Estrella's Diner had been lying for eleven minutes.

Not about everything. Her coffee order was honest—black, no sugar, a choice that matched the no-nonsense set of her jaw and the way she'd hung her coat on the hook without preamble. The woman's name was probably real too. Diana Cuevas. She'd said it with the easy rhythm of someone who'd been answering to it her whole life, not the half-beat hesitation of a person trying on something borrowed.

But the story, the reason she'd called Amaya's office number at six-thirty on a Tuesday morning and asked to meet before the breakfast rush. That was built on sand.

"He said he was working late." Diana turned her coffee cup between her palms, a slow rotation that had worn a damp ring into the paper placemat. "Three, four nights a week. Started about two months ago."

"What does he do?"

"Assistant manager at a tire shop on Jerome Avenue. They close at six."

Amaya didn't write that down. She didn't need to. The detail that mattered wasn't the tire shop or the hours. It was the way Diana had said "assistant manager." A slight press on the first syllable, emphasis people used when they wanted you to understand that a title was the best version of the truth. He was the assistant manager the way a line cook was a sous chef. The job was real. The framing was generous.

"And you want to know where he's going instead."

Diana nodded once, her dark eyes fixed on a point somewhere past Amaya's left shoulder. "I don't think it's another woman. I know that's what people assume when a wife walks into a PI's office, but that's not—" She stopped. The coffee cup stilled. "I think he's in trouble."

Now they were getting somewhere.

Amaya leaned back against the booth's cracked vinyl, letting the silence do its work. Estrella's was half-full at this hour—construction workers fueling up, a couple of nurses from Montefiore wrapping up their overnight shifts, an old man in the corner booth reading the Daily News with the focused disapproval of someone who'd been disappointed by headlines for decades. The diner sat on Kingsbridge Terrace, not far from Amaya's duplex, and she'd been eating here since she was twelve years old. The coffee was bitter and the eggs were perfect and Estrella herself—now seventy-three and still working the grill on weekends—had once told Amaya's grandmother that the girl asked too many questions.

Grandma Eleanor had said, "Good."

Diana's hands tightened around the cup. "Six weeks ago, he came home with cash. Not a lot, maybe eight hundred dollars. He said a friend paid back an old loan. I didn't push it. Then it happened again. And again." She finally met Amaya's eyes. "Last week, he bought our daughter new sneakers. The expensive ones, the Jordans she'd been asking about since September. Paid cash. And when I asked him where the money came from, he looked at me the way he used to look at his mother when she caught him cutting school."

"Scared."

"Terrified."

Amaya studied the woman across from her. Mid-thirties, hands that worked for a living, nails kept short and clean. A small gold cross at her throat that she touched without realizing it, the gesture of someone who prayed about practical things. Diana Cuevas wasn't here because her husband was cheating. She was here because her husband had gotten himself tangled in something, and she loved him enough to be angry about it and frightened by it at the same time.

The lie wasn't about the facts. The lie was the composure. Diana was holding herself together with the precision of someone who'd practiced in the bathroom mirror that morning, and the cracks were showing in the spaces between her words.

"I charge four hundred a day plus expenses," Amaya said. "Minimum three-day retainer. I'll need his full name, the tire shop address, his vehicle information, and a recent photo. I work alone, I don't carry a weapon, and I'll tell you the truth even when it's not what you want to hear. If I find something that suggests criminal activity, I'll advise you on your options, but I won't suppress evidence and I won't help anyone obstruct an investigation. Are we clear?"

Diana blinked. The rehearsed composure flickered, replaced by something raw and immediate—relief so acute it almost looked like pain. "You'll take the case?"

"I'll look into it. That's not the same thing as taking a case. If what I find in three days points somewhere I can help, we'll talk about next steps. If it points somewhere you need a lawyer instead of a PI, I'll tell you that too."

Diana reached into her bag and produced an envelope. The bills inside were twenties, counted and folded with the care of someone for whom twelve hundred dollars was not a casual sum. Amaya took the envelope, wrote a receipt on a diner napkin, and slid it across the table.

"I'll be in touch within seventy-two hours."

Diana stood, pulling her coat from the hook. At the door, she turned back. "Ms. Storm—my friend who recommended you. She said you were the only PI she'd trust with something personal. She said you'd be honest."

"Your friend has good taste in diners, too," Amaya said, glancing at the envelope. "This is where she hired me."

The trace of a smile crossed Diana's face—brief, involuntary, and then she was gone, the bell above the door chiming her exit into the gray morning.

Amaya finished her coffee and settled the check. Estrella's daughter, Marisol, waved off the tip. "Mami says you eat free on Tuesdays."

"Since when?"

"Since always. You just never come on Tuesdays."

Amaya laughed, a genuine sound, warm and surprised, and left a twenty under the sugar dispenser anyway.

Outside, the Bronx was waking up in layers. The early shift had already passed through—buses pulling away from stops with the hydraulic sigh of something resigned to its route, shop gates grinding upward, the distant clatter of the 1 train crossing the Broadway Bridge. Now came the next wave: school kids in clusters, their voices sharp in the October air; dog walkers navigating the narrow sidewalks with leashes tangled like rigging; a man on the corner of 231st selling tamales from a cooler, his breath steaming as he called out to regulars by name.

Amaya walked north toward Fieldston Road, her stride easy, her mind already sorting Diana's story into columns: *confirmed, unconfirmed, worth pulling.* The husband's pattern— cash appearing in increments, the fear in his eyes, the detail about the Jordans—pointed away from gambling and toward something transactional. Someone was paying him for something. The question: what, and whether he'd walked into it willingly or been walked into it.

Three blocks from her duplex, her phone buzzed. She checked the screen.

Grandma Eleanor, 6:47 AM. A text, not a call—unusual for a woman who considered text messages the domain of people too cowardly to use their voices.

Saw a cat on the news that solved a crime in England. Yours still freeloading?

Amaya grinned and typed back: *They prefer the term "consulting."*

Three dots appeared and disappeared twice before Eleanor's reply landed: *Tell Trouble I said she's getting soft.*

The duplex was quiet when Amaya let herself in—quiet in the way that means everyone was present and nobody was behaving. She knew this silence. It was the silence of a household full of cats that had been doing something they shouldn't and had frozen at the sound of the key in the lock.

She found the evidence in the kitchen.

The fruit bowl, a heavy ceramic piece she'd bought at a street fair in Fordham—lay on its side on the counter, one banana liberated from its bunch and deposited on the floor with a single puncture wound. A ginger tabby sat beside it with an expression of theological innocence.

"Chaos."

The cat looked up at her. His green eyes communicated nothing except a profound and unbothered calm, as if bananas routinely threw themselves onto kitchen floors and he had simply been the first to discover this particular casualty.

From the living room, the sound of claws retracting hastily from upholstery.

"Mayhem, get off the couch."

A pause. A thud. The heavy black cat appeared in the kitchen doorway with the injured dignity of someone who had been falsely accused despite overwhelming physical evidence. A thread of couch fabric clung to his right paw. He shook it off without breaking eye contact.

Trouble was exactly where Amaya had left her two hours ago: at the upstairs window in the office, gold eyes tracking the street below. She acknowledged Amaya's return with a slow blink, the feline equivalent of a nod between colleagues, and resumed her surveillance.

"Anything to report?"

Trouble's tail moved once. Left to right. Definitive.

"Noted."

Amaya cleaned up the banana, righted the fruit bowl, and carried her laptop to the office. She had seventy-two hours to trace the source of Diana Cuevas's husband's cash, and the first step was always the same: build the frame before you fill in the picture.

She sat down, opened a fresh document, and started with what she knew.

The work was quiet, methodical, and completely absorbing, a focus that made hours compress into minutes and turned the world outside her window into background noise. It was the part of the job that no one saw and everyone benefited from: the patient assembly of facts into structure, the slow emergence of a pattern from what had looked like random points.

Her grandmother had called it "building the case before you knock on the door." You didn't approach a subject, interview a witness, or run surveillance until you understood the structure of the situation. Who were the players? What were the connections? Where did money flow, and where did it pool?

Eleanor Storm had spent thirty-two years building houses like that for the NYPD. She'd retired as a detective first grade out of the 4-4 precinct in the Bronx, one of the few Black women to hold that rank in her era, a fact she acknowledged with the same flat pragmatism she applied to everything else. "I was good at the work. The work didn't care what I looked like. The department often did. I outlasted them."

She'd taught Amaya to observe before she could spell the word. Sitting on a bench in Crotona Park when Amaya was eight, Eleanor had pointed to a woman walking past and said, "Tell me about her."

"She's carrying groceries."

"What else?"

"She's... walking fast?"

"Why?"

Amaya had squinted. "Because she's in a hurry?"

"Look at her shoes."

The woman's shoes were mismatched, one sneaker, one flat. She was walking fast because one shoe had a higher sole than the other, and her gait was compensating.

"She's not in a hurry," Eleanor had said. "She's in pain. Left ankle, probably a sprain. She couldn't get both sneakers on, so she grabbed what she could. Now—" she'd turned to Amaya with those eyes that missed nothing, "—what does that tell you about her morning?"

It told you she was alone. No one had gone to the store for her. No one had helped her with her shoes.

Amaya had been building structures ever since.

The afternoon passed in research and phone calls. By four o'clock, she had a framework for the Cuevas case: the husband's name was Rene; the tire shop was a franchise location with modest revenue, and Rene's social media— mostly dormant—showed a recent burst of activity in a neighborhood Facebook group focused on local car meets. Nothing incriminating, but the group's membership list overlapped with a few names that had shown up in Bronx auto-theft reports over the past year.

A thread. Thin, but worth pulling.

She closed the laptop and stretched. Downstairs, Mayhem was asleep on the couch—back on it, naturally, the moment he'd calculated she was too absorbed to notice. Chaos had wedged himself into a bookshelf between a dictionary and a James Baldwin paperback, his ginger fur barely visible. Trouble hadn't moved from the window, though her position had shifted subtly. She was watching the front door now instead of the street, as if she'd known Amaya was about to come downstairs before Amaya knew it herself.

The duplex held the amber light of late afternoon, warm and close, the sounds of the neighborhood filtering through the walls in soft layers. Someone was cooking—garlic and onions, the universal signal of a Bronx kitchen getting serious. A school bus groaned past. Two kids argued over something critically important on the sidewalk below, their voices rising and falling with the drama of people who hadn't yet learned that most arguments resolve themselves.

Amaya stood in her living room and let the moment settle. This was the part of the day she'd learned to protect, the interval between cases, between demands, between the needs of other people's crises. It was small and it was hers and the cats understood it instinctively, which was one of the reasons she loved them.

Tomorrow, she'd start pulling the thread on Rene Cuevas. She'd drive past the tire shop, run the plates on any vehicles that didn't belong to customers, and cross-reference the car meet group with the NYPD's auto-theft database. If Rene was running stolen parts, or worse, helping move stolen vehicles, the evidence would surface. It always did, if you knew where the clues were and how to interpret them.

But that was tomorrow.

Tonight, the duplex was warm, the cats were fed, or at least Mayhem had convinced her he was starving through a performance of pathetic meowing that deserved some kind of award, and the Bronx was settling into its evening hum.

Amaya poured herself a glass of wine, sank into the armchair by the window, and opened the Baldwin she'd been meaning to finish for three weeks. Chaos had vacated the bookshelf and was now draped across her feet like a ginger heating pad. Trouble watched from above. Mayhem snored.

This was the life she'd built: steady, purposeful, and shared with three animals who understood her better than most people. It wasn't glamorous. It wasn't lonely either. It was a private investigator's life in the Bronx, and she'd chosen every piece of it.

She read until her eyes got tired, and then she sat in the dark for a while, listening to the city breathe.

Chapter 1: The Storm Before the Storm

The Rourke file was finished.

Amaya sat at her desk in the morning light, the corkboard above her cleaned of its web of pushpins and red thread, the final report printed, signed, and sealed in an envelope addressed to Mrs. Rourke's attorney. Thomas Rourke, Westchester orthodontist, had hidden $14,200 a month in an LLC registered to his brother-in-law—textbook asset concealment, documented across forty-six pages of bank records, merchant processing discrepancies, and three afternoons of patient counts that didn't match his books.

She'd courier it by noon. Mrs. Rourke's divorce attorney would have what she needed, and Thomas Rourke's careful lies would unravel on someone else's schedule. Amaya's part was done.

She capped her pen and leaned back. The duplex was quiet insofar as early mornings in Riverdale allowed. Not silent, but muted, the neighborhood holding its breath between the first dog walkers and the school-rush traffic. Through the office window, the trees along Fieldston Road were deep in their October turn, the maples going copper and the oaks holding stubbornly to green. A jogger passed below, breath pluming.

Trouble was not at her usual post on the windowsill. This was notable. Trouble's morning routine was as fixed as a train schedule—windowsill by six, monitoring the street until something worthy of her attention appeared or she decided nothing would. Her absence meant she'd found something more interesting downstairs, which in Amaya's experience meant either Mayhem was doing something destructive or someone had left a cabinet open.

She found the answer in the kitchen: Trouble perched on the counter beside the fruit bowl, watching Chaos with the focused patience of a tenured professor observing a student make a predictable mistake. The ginger tabby had somehow gotten the bread bag open and was nosing through it with the delicate concentration of a sommelier, occasionally pulling out a slice and batting it across the tile.

Three slices were already on the floor. A fourth was in progress.

"Chaos. That is a whole-grain loaf and it cost me four dollars."

Chaos looked up. A crumb dangled from his whiskers. He did not appear to feel the gravity of the situation.

Amaya rescued the bread, swept the casualties into the trash, and set the coffee maker going. Mayhem appeared at the sound of the grinder. He always appeared at the sound of the grinder, materializing from wherever he'd been sleeping with the urgency of someone late for a meeting. He wound around Amaya's ankles, his solid body bumping her calves with the subtlety of a small bulldozer.

"You already ate."

He meowed. The sound was low, resonant, and entirely unconvincing in its desperation.

"An hour ago. I was there. I watched you eat."

He sat down and stared at her with his green eyes, employing what Amaya had come to think of as his "Dickensian orphan" face, a look of such manufactured deprivation that it bordered on theater. She held firm for approximately eight seconds before dropping a treat on the floor.

"Don't tell the others."

He crunched it with visible satisfaction and padded away.

The coffee was strong and the morning was hers. She poured a cup, settled into the living room armchair, and allowed herself the rare luxury of an hour with nothing scheduled. The Rourke case had been her sole active file for the past two weeks, and its completion left her calendar open, a state she found both restful and faintly unsettling. Amaya didn't idle well. Her mind was built for pattern recognition, and without a case to direct it, the machinery turned inward, cataloging small domestic mysteries with the same rigor she applied to fraud investigations.

Why did Chaos prefer whole-grain bread to white? Where did Mayhem go during the two-hour window each afternoon when he vanished entirely from the duplex? What, exactly, was Trouble watching on the street every morning with such intensity?

These were not, she reminded herself, billable questions.

She was halfway through her coffee when her phone buzzed against the side table. Unknown number, 212 area code. Manhattan.

She let it ring twice.

"Amaya Storm."

The voice on the other end was measured—carefully so, like a person speaks when they've rehearsed the first sentence but not the second. "Ms. Storm, my name is Lydia Brooks. I'm the executive director of the Studio Museum in Harlem."

Amaya set down her coffee. She knew the Studio Museum by reputation, a landmark institution on 125th Street, dedicated to artists of African descent, recently relocated to an architecturally striking new building that had drawn national attention. It was a place that mattered to Harlem the way a cathedral matters to its parish: not just a building, but a statement of identity.

"I was given your name by a mutual acquaintance," Lydia continued. "I have a situation that requires discretion, and I'd prefer to discuss it in person."

"Can you give me the broad strokes? Helps me prepare."

A pause. The sound of an office in the background—muffled voices, a phone ringing at a distance. Lydia was calling from work, which meant either she couldn't wait or she didn't want this conversation on her home phone.

"We've experienced a series of thefts. Artwork, taken during our exhibition openings." Lydia's voice dropped, and the careful rehearsal gave way to something rawer underneath. "Three pieces in the past six months. Each one more significant than the last."

Amaya reached for the legal pad she kept on the side table. Old habit. She thought better with a pen in her hand. She wrote: *3 thefts / 6 months / during events / escalating value.*

"Reported to the police?"

"The first two, yes. Understaffed, under prioritized. You know how it goes." A trace of bitterness surfaced and was quickly controlled. "The third piece was taken ten days ago. A mixed-media installation valued at over five hundred thousand dollars. That got more attention. A detective has been assigned, but the board—my board—is concerned about the pace."

"You said during exhibition openings. Controlled events?"

"Invitation only. Vetted guest lists. Staff-managed access to all exhibition areas." Lydia paused again, and Amaya listened to the silence as her grandmother had taught her. Not as absence but as content. "Every theft required inside knowledge, Ms. Storm. Someone who knows our security protocols, our storage layouts, the timing of our staff rotations."

"You think it's someone on your team."

The silence stretched longer this time. When Lydia spoke again, the rehearsed composure had thinned to gauze. "I think I'm running out of people I trust."

Amaya underlined *inside* and drew a circle around it.

On the kitchen counter, Trouble had abandoned her post over the bread situation and was sitting in the doorway between the kitchen and the living room. Her amber eyes were fixed on Amaya. Not on the phone, not on the window, but on Amaya herself, with the unblinking focus the cat reserved for moments when the atmosphere in the room shifted. Amaya had learned not to dismiss that look.

"I can come to the museum tomorrow morning. Nine o'clock work?"

"Yes." Relief flooded the word—too much for a woman who'd merely scheduled an appointment. Lydia Brooks had been carrying this weight for a while, and the prospect of sharing it, even partially, had loosened something in her. "Thank you, Ms. Storm."

"One thing. Don't mention my visit to your staff. I'd like to see the space before anyone knows there's something to see."

A beat. "I understand."

The call ended. Amaya stared at the legal pad, her pen tapping a slow rhythm against the paper. Art theft from a cultural institution. Inside access. Escalating boldness. A director who suspected her own people but couldn't bring herself to name names.

She tore the page free and carried it to her office, pinning it to the empty corkboard. One sheet of paper on a blank board. Tomorrow, there'd be more.

The Studio Museum. She sat down at her laptop and began to build the house.

The museum's website was polished and thorough— recent press coverage, board of directors, exhibition history, donor acknowledgments. Lydia Brooks had been executive director for nine years. Under her leadership, the museum had completed its long-awaited new building on 125th Street, expanded its permanent collection, and deepened its community programming. The press loved her. The art world respected her. She'd been profiled in The New York Times, ArtNews, and Essence, each piece painting the portrait of a woman whose dedication to the institution was personal, almost familial.

Amaya noted the board members: a mix of corporate executives, philanthropists, and arts professionals. She scanned the staff directory—small team, maybe thirty people total. A head of security. A registrar responsible for collection management. An assistant to the director whose name appeared in nearly every event credit: Emily Dawson.

She cross-referenced the theft dates with the museum's event calendar. Each theft aligned with a major opening—high-profile, high-attendance, high-energy events where attention would be on the art and the guests, not on the back rooms and storage areas.

Whoever was doing this understood the museum's rhythms the way a musician understands a song. They knew when the chorus hit and the audience looked up. And they moved during the bridge, when nobody was watching.

Amaya pulled up a map of the area surrounding the museum. 125th Street and Lenox—Adam Clayton Powell Jr. Boulevard. The Apollo Theater a few blocks west. Sylvia's. The Schomburg Center. This was Harlem's cultural corridor, a stretch of blocks where history pressed close to the surface and the present hummed with energy. Stealing from the Studio Museum wasn't just property crime. It was taking something from a community that had built and defended its cultural identity against decades of erasure.

That bothered her. Not in the abstract way that all theft bothered her, but specifically, a specificity that made her jaw tighten and her pen press harder into the paper.

She worked through the afternoon, building a preliminary framework: key personnel, event timelines, security questions, financial angles to explore. By five o'clock, she had three pages of notes and a mental map of the museum's organizational structure.

Her phone rang at seven on the dot. Not the office line, her personal cell. She didn't need to check the screen.

"Hey, Grandma."

"You sound like you're chewing on something." Eleanor Storm's voice carried the clarity of a woman who'd spent three decades giving commands in noisy precincts. Even through a phone speaker from two thousand miles away, it landed in the room like she was sitting across the table.

"I'm thinking."

"What's the case?"

Amaya hesitated. She hadn't decided yet whether to take the case—tomorrow's visit was preliminary, an assessment. But Eleanor had a way of cutting through the static to the load-bearing question, and Amaya had learned long ago that talking to her grandmother was the fastest way to find out what she actually thought about something.

"Art thefts at the Studio Museum. Three in six months, all during private exhibition events. The director thinks it's someone on the inside."

A beat of silence. Amaya could hear the faint chime of a slot machine in the background. Eleanor liked to take her Sunday calls at the casino bar, where the drinks were free and the ambience noise gave her something to do.

"She think, or she know?"

"She didn't name anyone."

"Mmm." The sound Eleanor made when she was sorting information. "Three thefts in six months is a pattern, not a spree. Somebody's patient. Somebody's got a system."

"That's what I'm seeing."

"During events—so they're using the crowd as cover. That means they understand the operation well enough to know when the attention is pointed elsewhere." The slot machines chimed again. Eleanor's voice didn't waver. "You said the director called you directly. Not her board, not her security team. Her."

"Yes."

"Then either she doesn't trust her own people to handle it, or she's afraid of what they'll find. Maybe both." A pause that carried the weight of experience. "Who controls the guest list?"

Amaya glanced at her notes. Emily Dawson's name sat in the middle of her personnel chart, connected to every event on the theft timeline. "The director's assistant. She runs the events."

"Start there. Not with accusations, just with her calendar. See who she is when she's not performing for her boss." Eleanor let that settle before adding, "And check the money, Nhoma. Art people like to pretend it's about beauty and legacy, but somebody's always getting paid. Find where the money moves and you'll find your thief standing next to the register."

Nhoma. The word Eleanor had used for Amaya since she was small, a name from their family's history that meant something close to "artist" in the language their ancestors had carried across the water. Eleanor used it sparingly, and only in moments when she wanted Amaya to remember that the work she did, the careful observation, the patient assembly of truth from fragments—was its own kind of creation.

"How's Vegas?"

"Hot. Boring. I took forty dollars off a retired cardiologist from Scottsdale last night. He kept bluffing with middle pairs." A dry chuckle. "Some people never learn to read a room."

"Sounds like you're doing fine."

"I'm doing better than fine. I'm doing excellent. But I didn't call to talk about me." Eleanor's voice shifted, gaining the texture it always carried when she was about to say something she'd been holding. "This museum case. If it's inside work, the person doing it has been watching that director for a long time. Studying the museum's patterns, learning the blind spots. That kind of patience means they feel entitled to whatever they're taking. And people who feel entitled get careless eventually, but they also get dangerous when they get cornered. You hear me?"

"I hear you."

"Good. Now go feed those cats before Mayhem stages a coup."

"He already tried. I held firm."

"For how long?"

"Eight seconds."

Eleanor laughed, a full, warm sound that made the two thousand miles between them feel like a hallway. "You're getting soft, Nhoma. Call me after the museum meeting."

"I will."

"And wear comfortable shoes. Museum floors are murder on the knees."

"Goodnight, Grandma."

"Goodnight, baby."

The line went dead, and the duplex felt both emptier and warmer for the call. Eleanor Storm had a way of doing that—filling a room with her presence and then leaving behind exactly the questions Amaya needed to sit with.

Who controls the guest list. Where does the money move. And what kind of person studies someone's blind spots for six months?

The duplex had settled into its evening quiet. Mayhem was asleep on the couch, his muscular body sprawled across two cushions with the territorial confidence of a cat who'd decided the furniture argument was settled in his favor. Chaos had curled up on the hallway rug, his ginger fur vivid against the dark runner, eyes closed with the absolute commitment of a cat who'd burned through his daily energy reserves. Trouble had returned to the office windowsill, her vigil resumed, her gaze tracking something outside that only she found worth monitoring.

Amaya closed her laptop and stretched. Tomorrow, she'd take the 1 train down to 125th. She'd dress professional but not corporate. She needed to read as someone who belonged in a museum without looking like she was auditioning for the part. She'd bring Trouble; the cat's reactions to people and spaces had proven useful before, and a "comfort animal" was an easy enough explanation. Chaos was too unpredictable for a first visit, and Mayhem had a talent for drawing exactly the attention a discreet assessment couldn't afford.

She stood in the doorway of her office, looking at the corkboard. One sheet of paper. Three thefts. A woman running out of trust. And Eleanor's questions still circling: *Who controls the guest list. Where does the money move. What kind of person studies someone's blind spots for six months?*

Amaya looked at Trouble. Trouble looked back, gold eyes steady, tail perfectly still.

"Tomorrow," Amaya said.

The cat blinked once—slow, deliberate, a gesture that in Trouble's vocabulary meant something between agreement and *obviously*.

Amaya smiled and went downstairs to make dinner.

Chapter 2: 125th and Lenox

The 1 train deposited Amaya at 125th Street just before nine, and Harlem met her as it always did, with noise, movement, and the unshakable sense that every block had opinions about its own history.

She descended from the station into a morning already thick with commerce. A vendor on the corner had set up a table of incense, shea butter, and essential oils, the bottles arranged with the precision of a chess opening. Across the street, a woman in a bright yellow head wrap unlocked the gate of a hair salon, nodding at a passing deliveryman who was navigating a hand truck loaded with produce toward a bodega. The smell of coffee from a cart near the subway entrance competed with the yeasty warmth drifting from a bakery half a block south, and somewhere above it all, a speaker in an apartment window was playing Fela Kuti at a volume that suggested the listener had made a philosophical decision about how mornings should begin.

Amaya walked east on 125th, Trouble tucked into a soft-sided carrier slung over her shoulder. The cat was still. No fidgeting, no protesting, just her eyes visible through the mesh panel, scanning the street with the quiet efficiency of someone clocking in for a shift. Amaya had debated bringing her. A cat at a museum meeting was unusual. But Trouble's ability to read a room, to react to tension, dishonesty, or concealed emotion in ways that Amaya had learned to trust—made her more useful than any recording device. And "emotional support animal" was a phrase that opened doors without requiring further explanation.

Inside the carrier, Trouble didn't just see Harlem; she felt it. She registered the low vibration of the A train three blocks away, a hum that traveled through the soles of Amaya's shoes and into her paws. To her, the morning air wasn't just thick with commerce. It was a chemical map: the scorched-sugar scent of the bakery, the unpleasant bite of exhaust, and the strident, mineral static of the coming rain. She was Amaya's early warning system for a city that never stopped.

The Studio Museum's new building came into view as she crossed Adam Clayton Powell Blvd, and Amaya slowed her pace to take it in. The structure was a deliberate statement, a modern glass-and-steel design that managed to feel both bold and respectful of the neighborhood surrounding it. The façade caught the morning light and threw it back in fragments, a visual echo of the Harlem Renaissance murals that still adorned older buildings nearby. At ground level, wide glass doors opened onto a generous entry plaza where a few early visitors lingered, studying the banners announcing the current exhibition: *Reclamation: New Works by Artists of the African Diaspora.*

The name alone told her something about Lydia Brooks. This wasn't a museum trading on safe choices. The work it championed carried political weight, cultural stakes, and a significance that made theft more than a property crime.

Amaya adjusted the carrier strap and walked in.

The lobby was open and airy, the ceiling high enough to accommodate a suspended sculpture that rotated slowly above the reception desk—metal and glass, catching the light from the windows and scattering it across the polished concrete floor. The space hummed with the controlled energy of a place that took its mission seriously: staff moved with purpose, a small group of docents were huddled near the gift shop reviewing notes, and a security guard in a pressed navy uniform stood at the entrance to the main gallery, his posture suggesting he considered the post a responsibility, not a chore.

Amaya approached the reception desk and gave her name. The young woman behind the counter made a quick call, then directed her to the administrative offices on the third floor. "Ms. Brooks is expecting you. Elevator's to your left."

The third floor was quieter—carpeted hallways, framed exhibition posters from past shows, and the muted sounds of phones ringing and keyboards clicking behind closed doors. The air smelled faintly of linseed oil and paper, the particular scent of a place where art was not just displayed but handled, documented, cared for.

Lydia Brooks met her at the door of her office.

In person, Lydia was taller than Amaya had expected—five-nine or five-ten, with the upright carriage of someone who'd learned early that posture communicated authority before words did. Her hair was natural, close-cropped and silver at the temples, and she wore a tailored charcoal blazer over a cream blouse that managed to look both professional and artistic. Her handshake was firm, her smile practiced, and her eyes—dark brown, nearly black—carried the exhaustion of a person who'd been simulating composure.

"Thank you for coming, Ms. Storm." She gestured toward a chair across from her desk. "Can I get you anything? Coffee, water?"

"I'm fine, thank you." Amaya settled into the chair, setting Trouble's carrier on the floor beside her. Through the mesh, the cat's amber eyes were already fixed on Lydia. Not with hostility, but with the focused attention Trouble reserved for people whose energy didn't quite match their words.

Lydia glanced at the carrier. "You travel with company."

"She's better at reading people than I am. I just won't admit it."

The ghost of a genuine smile crossed Lydia's face—there and gone—before the weight of the conversation ahead pulled her features back into careful neutrality. She sat behind her desk, a large mahogany surface that was meticulously organized: files in labeled folders, a laptop angled precisely, a single framed photograph of a woman Amaya assumed was Lydia's mother positioned where only Lydia could see it.

"Where would you like to start?" Lydia asked.

"With the building. I'd like to see the exhibition spaces, the storage areas, and the security setup before we talk about specifics. I think better when I can see the layout."

Lydia nodded and rose. "I'll take you through myself."

They started on the ground floor. The main gallery was a generous open space with movable partition walls that could be reconfigured for different exhibitions. The current show—*Reclamation*—featured large-scale paintings, mixed-media installations, and sculptural pieces arranged in a flow that guided visitors through a narrative about identity, displacement, and cultural reclamation. The work was striking. Amaya wasn't an art critic, but she could feel the intention behind the curation—each piece in conversation with the ones around it, building toward something larger than any single canvas.

"The stolen pieces," Amaya said, pausing in front of a mixed-media installation that incorporated fabric, found objects, and painted panels. "Were they displayed in the main galleries or in other areas?"

"Two were in the main galleries. The third, the most valuable—was in the lower-level exhibition space, which we use for larger installations and immersive works." Lydia's voice tightened. "That space has its own entrance for deliveries and installation, which connects to the building's service corridor."

"Show me."

As they descended to the lower level, Trouble stirred in her carrier. She'd been calm through the main galleries—alert but settled, her body relaxed against the carrier's base. But the moment the elevator doors opened onto the lower level, her posture changed. She rose to her feet inside the carrier, her weight shifting forward, her nose pressing against the mesh panel. The air down here was different—cooler, denser, carrying the inert scent of concrete and the faint traces of conservation materials. Whatever Trouble was registering, it had engaged a gear that the galleries above hadn't touched.

The lower level was a different world from the airy galleries above—lower ceilings, industrial lighting, concrete floors designed to support heavy installations. The delivery entrance was a reinforced steel door that opened onto a loading dock at the building's rear. Amaya examined the door, the lock, and the security panel beside it.

"Keycard access?"

"Yes. The system logs every entry and exit."

"How many people have active keycards for this door?"

Lydia counted mentally. "Seven. Myself, Emily, the registrar, the head of facilities, two installation technicians, and Derek—our head of security."

Seven people. Seven potential access points, each one a thread to follow. "Were the logs reviewed after each theft?"

"Yes. The first two times, nothing appeared out of the ordinary, all entries corresponded to scheduled staff activity." Lydia hesitated. "After the third theft, the logs showed a keycard entry at eleven-fourteen p.m. The event had officially ended at ten. The card belonged to our registrar, Thomas Yeboah, but he was at home, his wife confirmed it."

"Cloned card."

"That's what the police concluded. Which means—"

"Someone had physical access to Thomas's card long enough to copy it." Amaya ran her fingers along the doorframe, feeling for anything unusual—scratches, tool marks, signs of tampering. The frame was clean. Whoever had used this door hadn't forced anything. They'd walked through it like they belonged. "Where are the keycards stored when staff aren't carrying them?"

"In the security office, in a locked cabinet." Lydia's jaw tightened. "I know how that sounds."

"It sounds like someone with access to the security office." Amaya let the implication sit without naming names. "I'd like to see that office."

The security office was a compact room on the ground floor, adjacent to the lobby. Banks of monitors showed feeds from cameras covering the galleries, the loading dock, the service corridors, and the public areas. The equipment was decent but not state-of-the-art—good enough for a museum of this size, not good enough to catch someone who knew where the cameras pointed and where they didn't.

A man stood as they entered—mid-forties, broad-shouldered, with close-cropped hair and the attentive posture of someone who'd been expecting this visit and had decided to meet it head-on.

"Amaya Storm, this is Derek Osei, our head of security." Lydia's introduction carried a note of something Amaya couldn't immediately place—protectiveness, or perhaps preemptive defense.

Derek extended a hand. His grip was measured—firm enough to convey confidence, calibrated enough to avoid aggression. "Ms. Storm. I'm glad someone's taking this seriously."

The emphasis on *someone* landed squarely on the police investigation without Derek needing to name it. Amaya filed the observation.

"Walk me through your camera coverage."

Derek turned to the monitors with the fluency of a man who'd memorized every angle. "Sixteen cameras total. Full coverage of the public galleries, the lobby, and the main entrances. Partial coverage of the service corridor. The loading dock has one camera—here—" he pointed to a grainy feed showing the steel door from above, "but the angle only captures the door itself, not the approach from the alley."

"Blind spots in the service corridor?"

Derek's expression shifted, a flicker of frustration surfacing through the professionalism. "Two. One near the east stairwell, one at the junction where the corridor turns toward storage. I flagged both in a memo to the director's office eight months ago." He paused, his eyes cutting briefly to Lydia. "Before the first theft."

The silence that followed had context. Lydia's posture stiffened almost imperceptibly. Derek held his ground, his expression carefully neutral but his point made.

"Was the memo acted on?" Amaya asked, though she already knew the answer from the gap between the question and anyone's willingness to fill it.

"Additional cameras were approved as part of next fiscal year's budget," Lydia said. Her voice was steady but the words were chosen with the precision of someone who'd rehearsed this particular defense. "We're a nonprofit. Every expenditure requires board approval."

Amaya didn't push. The dynamic between Lydia and Derek had told her more than either of them intended, a security chief who'd seen the vulnerability and raised the alarm, and a director who'd let budget cycles and institutional inertia delay the response. Negligence wasn't malice, but it created opportunity for people who were paying attention.

"I'd like copies of the access logs for the past six months," Amaya said. "Every keycard entry on every secured door. And the staff schedule for each event where a theft occurred."

"I can have that for you by end of day," Derek said, with the readiness of someone who'd already compiled it.

"You've been keeping your own records."

It wasn't a question. Derek met her eyes. "I've been doing my job, Ms. Storm."

She respected that. His directness, his frustration, his refusal to soft-pedal the institutional failure that had made his job harder. It all pointed toward a man who cared about the museum and was angry that caring hadn't been enough to protect it.

But she also noted as his shoulders carried tension even at rest, and as his eyes tracked Lydia when the director wasn't looking. Derek Osei was loyal to this institution, but loyalty and trust weren't the same thing, and right now, his trust was fractured.

They continued the tour. Lydia showed her the storage vaults—climate-controlled rooms on the lower level where the museum's permanent collection and loaned works were housed between exhibitions. The vaults required both keycard access and a four-digit code, which was changed quarterly. Amaya noted that the code changes were managed by Emily Dawson.

Emily's name kept appearing. She was the person who arranged events, managed guest lists, coordinated with security on access protocols, handled the code changes for storage vaults, and processed the paperwork for loans and acquisitions. She was the connective tissue of the museum's operations, and connective tissue, by definition, touched everything.

Amaya didn't mention this to Lydia. Not yet. Observations gathered weight through accumulation, not declaration, and she was still in the gathering phase.

They returned to Lydia's office. Through the carrier mesh, Trouble had been still for the entire tour. No agitation, no restlessness. But Amaya had noticed the cat's attention sharpen twice: once in the security office when Derek and Lydia's tension surfaced, and once outside the storage vaults when Lydia had mentioned the code-change protocol. Trouble's reactions weren't supernatural. They were the heightened sensory awareness of an animal attuned to changes in vocal pitch, body chemistry, and the electromagnetic atmosphere of a room. But Amaya had learned to note what the cat noted, even when she couldn't yet articulate why.

"Ms. Brooks," Amaya said, settling back into the chair across from Lydia's desk, "I'll take the case."

Relief moved through Lydia's features like a wave—too fast to hide, too genuine to fake. "Thank you."

"I'll need full access to the building, the staff, and your records. Financial, operational, personnel. Anything I ask for, I need it within twenty-four hours. And I need your word that you won't discuss my investigation with anyone. Not your board, not your staff, not the detective assigned to the case."

Lydia hesitated at the last condition. "The detective. Jackson, I think his name is—he's been thorough. Shouldn't we coordinate?"

"I'll handle that relationship. But I work better when information flows through me, not around me. If Detective Jackson needs something from the museum, he can request it through official channels. My investigation runs parallel."

It was a firm boundary and Lydia recognized it as such. She nodded once. "Understood."

Amaya stood and collected Trouble's carrier. The cat shifted inside, resettling her weight with the deliberate economy of a passenger who'd reached her stop.

"One last question. Your assistant. Emily Dawson. How long has she been with you?"

If the question startled Lydia, she didn't show it. "Seven years. She was one of my first hires when I became director. She's been instrumental in building this museum into what it is." A pause, heavier than the others. "She's family, in every way that matters."

Amaya held the pause without filling it. Then: "I'll be in touch tomorrow."

She rode the elevator down to the lobby, crossed the plaza, and stepped back onto 125th Street. The morning had deepened, the sidewalks fuller now, the energy higher, the neighborhood settling into its midday rhythm. A group of teenagers spilled out of a corner store, laughing and shoving each other with the harmless violence of friendship. A woman pushed a stroller past a mural that covered an entire building wall—bold figures in vivid blues and golds, faces turned upward, hands reaching toward something just out of frame.

Amaya stopped in front of the mural for a moment, Trouble's carrier warm against her hip.

Seven keycards. A cloned access card. Two blind spots in the service corridor flagged eight months before the first theft. A security chief who'd raised the alarm and been answered with a budget timeline. And a director who described her assistant as "family, in every way that matters", with a pause afterward that suggested the words cost more than they used to.

Eleanor's questions from last night circled back: *Eleanor's questions still circled. Access. Money. Patience. The architecture of the crime mirrored the architecture of the museum, turned inside out.*

Amaya turned toward the subway, her mind already building the next layer of the house.

Chapter 3: The Loyal Lieutenant

Amaya returned to the museum two days later, having spent the intervening time doing what she did best: reading paper.

Derek Osei had delivered the access logs and staff schedules within hours of her visit, organized chronologically and cross-referenced by door location, the work of a man who'd been building his own case long before Amaya arrived. She'd spread the printouts across her dining table, weighting the corners with coffee mugs and cat toys, and spent an evening mapping the patterns.

Trouble had supervised from the table's edge, her body curved around a stack of event schedules like a furry paperweight. The cat's presence during research sessions had become routine. She positioned herself near whatever Amaya was reading and remained there, occasionally shifting her gaze from the documents to Amaya's face as though checking that the human was reaching the correct conclusions. Whether she was actually reading the room or simply preferred the warmth of paper stacked under a desk lamp was a question Amaya had stopped asking. The results were the same either way: Trouble stayed alert when the work was productive and wandered off when it wasn't, and her departures had proven to be a surprisingly reliable indicator that Amaya was chasing a dead end.

Mayhem had contributed to the research by knocking a stack of financial printouts off the table at eleven p.m., which had forced Amaya to reassemble them in chronological order, a process that, accidentally, revealed a gap in the invoicing sequence she'd missed on the first pass. She'd scratched him behind the ears and told him he was a genius. He'd nipped her thumb and gone to sleep on the couch.

Chaos had eaten a Post-it note. His contributions were less consistently useful.

The logs told a clean story. Too clean. On each of the three theft nights, every keycard entry corresponded to a named staff member performing a documented task. No anomalies. No unexplained entries. No gaps in the timeline that would suggest someone had been where they shouldn't have been.

Except for the cloned card on theft night three— Thomas Yeboah's keycard, used at 11:14 p.m., seventy-four minutes after the event ended and while Thomas himself was home in bed. That single entry was the only crack in an otherwise seamless record, and its isolation felt deliberate. Three thefts, and the system only glitched once. Either the thief had gotten sloppy on the third attempt, or they'd wanted that particular entry to be found.

Amaya circled the 11:14 entry and wrote beside it: *Why this card? Why this time? What changed?*

The staff schedules were more revealing. Emily Dawson's name appeared on every event where a theft occurred. Not unexpected, since she managed the events. But the schedules also showed that Emily was consistently the last staff member to leave the building after each event, responsible for the final walkthrough and the security handoff to the overnight guard.

That meant Emily was alone in the building, or nearly alone—during the window when each theft most likely occurred.

It didn't prove anything. The person who closed the building was naturally the last one there. But it established opportunity, and opportunity was the first indicator in any case worth building.

The financial records Lydia had provided were a different texture entirely—messier, less organized, the work of a nonprofit that had grown faster than its administrative systems. Amaya found the line items she was looking for scattered across three different budget spreadsheets: payments to an outside firm called Whitaker Art Advisory for appraisal and consulting services. The amounts were modest individually—$3,500 here, $5,000 there. But they accumulated to nearly $40,000 over the past eighteen months. Each payment had been requisitioned by Emily and approved by Lydia.

Amaya pulled up Whitaker Art Advisory online. The website was polished, a sleek single-page design showcasing services in art appraisal, authentication, collection management, and private sales. The founder was listed as Calvin Whitaker. His photo showed a man in his early forties with an easy smile and tasteful grooming that communicated money without flaunting it. His client list included galleries, private collectors, and institutional clients across the tristate area.

She bookmarked the page and closed her laptop. Forty thousand dollars in consulting fees over eighteen months. Not outrageous for a museum of this size, but worth understanding in detail—what services had been provided, what deliverables existed, and whether the relationship between the museum and Whitaker Art Advisory extended beyond the invoices.

Eleanor's voice: *follow the money, Nhoma.*

Now, on a Thursday morning that smelled like rain, Amaya sat in the museum's staff break room across from Emily Dawson and let the woman talk.

Emily was good at talking. She was good at most things that involved managing other people's perceptions, her posture was open; her eye contact steady; her smile calibrated to convey warmth without overfamiliarity. She wore a fitted blazer over a silk blouse, pearl studs in her ears, and a thin gold watch that she glanced at once during the first ten minutes—quickly, almost unconsciously, the gesture of someone who tracked time as a professional habit rather than a sign of impatience.

She was thirty-four, had studied arts administration at NYU, and had been with the museum since its early days in the old building on 125th. She spoke about her work with the museum as people spoke about founding a company, with proprietary pride and the recall of someone who remembered every obstacle overcome.

"When I started, we had a staff of nine and a budget that would make you cry," Emily said, her hands wrapped around a cup of green tea. "Lydia had the vision, but the infrastructure was held together with duct tape and good intentions. I built the event programming from scratch, the galas, the donor cultivation series, the community open houses. That first year, I think I slept in this building more than I slept at home."

Amaya nodded, listening with the half of her brain that processed content while the other half processed delivery. Emily's narrative was smooth. Not rehearsed exactly, but curated. She was telling the story of the museum in a way that centered her own contributions without explicitly diminishing Lydia's. The technique was subtle enough that most people wouldn't catch it: every sentence about Lydia's "vision" was followed by a concrete detail about Emily's execution, the implication being that vision without execution was just talk.

"That's a lot of trust Lydia placed in you early on," Amaya said.

"She took a chance on me. I was twenty-seven, no museum experience, just a degree and a lot of nerve." Emily's smile shifted. Something warmer, almost nostalgic, followed immediately by a tightening at the corners that could have been fondness souring into something else. "I like to think I've earned it since then."

"Tell me about the event structure. Walk me through a typical opening night, who does what, and when."

Emily straightened, sliding into operational mode with visible comfort. This was her territory. "I manage the full production. Guest list, catering, AV setup, programming—speakers, performers, whatever the exhibition calls for. I coordinate with Derek's security team on access and crowd management. I handle the VIP lounge setup personally. On event night, I'm essentially the stage manager—I'm in the building from noon to midnight, sometimes later."

"And after the event ends?"

"I supervise the breakdown. Catering out first, then AV. Once the vendors clear, I do a walkthrough of the public spaces with whoever's on overnight security—check the galleries, confirm the installations are undisturbed, lock the lower-level access points." She took a sip of tea. "Then I hand off to the night guard and go home."

"That walkthrough. You do it personally every time?"

"Every time."

"Has anyone ever joined you? Another staff member, a board member staying late?"

Emily considered this. "Occasionally Lydia stays for the walkthrough, but that's maybe one out of five events. Most nights it's just me and the guard."

Amaya made a note. Not on paper, which would signal what she found significant, but mentally, adding it to the architecture she was building. Emily alone in the building. Emily with access to every secured space. Emily controlling the schedule that determined who was where and when.

"The three stolen pieces," Amaya said, shifting the register of the conversation. "Can you walk me through what you noticed on each of those nights? Anything unusual—timing, guest behavior, staff movements."

Emily's composure held, but her hands adjusted around the tea cup, a micro-movement, fingers repositioning by millimeters. "The first theft was in April. A painting by Nkechi Adeyemi—emerging artist, first major museum show. Powerful piece, very personal. It was displayed in Gallery Two on the main floor. The event ran from six to ten, roughly two hundred guests. Everything ran smoothly. No disturbances, no complaints. I did the walkthrough at ten-forty-five and the painting was in place. The next morning, it wasn't."

"The walkthrough was normal. Nothing caught your eye."

"Nothing. I've replayed that night a hundred times." Emily's gaze dropped to her tea for a moment, a brief retreat from eye contact that could read as either genuine anguish or performed vulnerability. Amaya noted it without assigning meaning. Not yet. "The second theft was in July. A bronze sculpture from the permanent collection, a William Edmondson piece, incredibly rare. Same pattern:

successful event, clean walkthrough, piece gone by morning."

"And the third?"

Emily's jaw tightened. "Three weeks ago. A mixed-media installation by Rashida Okonkwo—large-scale, anchored to the floor in the lower-level gallery. That one should have been impossible to move without equipment and at least two people. It was valued at five hundred and thirty thousand dollars."

"But it moved."

"It moved." Emily set her tea down. "And that's when I stopped sleeping through the night."

Amaya studied her across the break room table. Emily Dawson was either a woman devastated by the systematic dismantling of an institution she'd helped build, or she was one of the best performers Amaya had encountered in a decade of investigative work. The difficulty was that both scenarios looked nearly identical from the outside.

What separated them were the margins, the moments when control slipped by a fraction and something unscripted surfaced. The pride that edged into resentment when she spoke about Lydia. The hands readjusting on the cup. The dropped gaze that lasted a beat too long.

"Emily, I need to ask you something directly, and I'd appreciate a direct answer."

"Of course."

"Is there anyone on staff you suspect?"

Emily's response was immediate—too immediate, arriving before the question had fully settled. "No. Absolutely not. Everyone here is dedicated to this museum. I'd stake my career on it."

The conviction was genuine. The speed was not. People who'd truly considered the question agonized over it; people who'd already decided what their answer would be delivered it like a line.

Amaya let a silence open. She'd learned from Eleanor that silence after a definitive statement was more effective than a follow-up question. It created a vacuum that people filled with whatever they'd been holding back.

Emily filled it. "I know how the optics look. I know my name is on every event schedule, I know I'm the last one in the building, and I know that if you're building a case based on access and opportunity, I'm the obvious person to look at." Her voice had hardened, the warmth replaced by something steelier. "But I've given seven years of my life to this museum. I've turned down three job offers from larger institutions because I believed in what we were building here. If someone is stealing from us, I want them caught as badly as anyone."

The speech was good. Well-structured, emotionally calibrated, with just enough edge to convey indignation without tipping into defensiveness. It was a statement a smart person prepared when they knew scrutiny was coming.

It was also, Amaya noted, the first time Emily had said "I" more than "we" in an extended response.

"I appreciate your candor," Amaya said, keeping her tone neutral. "One more thing—can you tell me about the museum's relationship with Whitaker Art Advisory? I noticed some consulting invoices in the financial records."

The shift in Emily's expression was minute but unmistakable, a flicker behind her eyes, there and gone in less than a second, like a card player catching a glimpse of their opponent's hand. She recovered smoothly.

"Calvin Whitaker. He's been our appraisal consultant for about two years. Lydia brought him on initially. He came recommended by one of our board members. He handles valuations for insurance purposes, authentication for new acquisitions, that sort of thing." Emily's voice had returned to its professional register, but the ease wasn't quite the same. She was choosing words now instead of letting them flow. "He's very well regarded in the field."

"Do you work with him directly?"

"I manage the invoicing and scheduling, but the consulting relationship is between Calvin and Lydia."

A clean partition. Emily handled the logistics; Lydia owned the connection. It was an answer that sounded like full disclosure while actually drawing a boundary around what Emily was willing to discuss.

From the carrier on the floor, Trouble shifted. The movement was slight, a resettling of weight that made the carrier rock almost imperceptibly. But Amaya felt it against her ankle. She glanced down. Through the mesh panel, Trouble's eyes were fixed on Emily with the unwavering intensity the cat usually reserved for closed doors and suspicious sounds.

Amaya didn't know what Trouble was registering. She rarely did in the moment. But she'd learned to catalog these reactions the way she cataloged evidence—without interpretation, without judgment, filed for later review when the picture became clearer.

"Thank you, Emily. You've been very helpful."

Emily stood, extending her hand with the polished grace that seemed to accompany her every movement. "Anything you need—schedules, records, introductions, just ask. I want this resolved."

"I know you do."

They shook hands. Emily's grip was firm, her palm cool and dry. She held eye contact for exactly the right amount of time—long enough to convey sincerity, short enough to avoid the intensity that sometimes signaled its opposite.

Amaya watched her walk back toward the administrative offices, her heels clicking a steady rhythm on the hallway floor. Poised, capable, controlled. A woman who ran a museum's operations with the precision of a Swiss watch and who, when asked if she suspected anyone, had answered "absolutely not" before the question stopped echoing.

In the carrier, Trouble had gone still again. Not relaxed, but watchful. The distinction mattered.

Amaya left the museum through the lobby, nodding to Derek as she passed the security office. He returned the nod—brief, professional, the acknowledgment of someone who recognized a fellow traveler in the business of watching things carefully.

On the sidewalk, she pulled out her phone and typed a note to herself: *Emily Dawson — 7 years, NYU arts admin, manages events/access/codes/invoicing. Controlled, prepared, articulate. Answered "absolutely not" too fast. Flicker on Whitaker question. Trouble alert. Follow the consulting relationship.*

The afternoon had turned overcast, the threatened rain arriving as a fine mist that softened the edges of Harlem's buildings and made the sidewalks gleam. Amaya walked toward the subway with Trouble's carrier against her hip, the cat's warmth a familiar anchor.

She had two threads now. Emily Dawson and her uninterrupted access to every system the thief would need. And Calvin Whitaker, an outside consultant whose appraisal fees flowed through Emily's invoicing and whose name had produced a reaction Emily thought she'd hidden.

Two threads. One building. And somewhere in the space between them, a pattern that was beginning to take shape.

Chapter 4: Opening Night

The museum transformed for its openings the way a theater transformed for a performance, the bones stayed the same, but the light, the energy, and the intent shifted into something heightened.

Amaya arrived at seven, an hour after the doors opened, timing her entrance to blend with the mid-event crowd rather than the early arrivals who tended to draw more attention from staff. She wore a fitted navy dress and low heels—professional enough for a museum gala, understated enough to avoid being memorable. A silk scarf at her throat added a touch of color without making a statement. She'd left the cats at home. Tonight was about observation, not investigation, and three cats, even one cat—would anchor her to conversations she needed to move through freely.

The ground-floor gallery had been reconfigured for the evening. The partition walls that normally directed foot traffic through the exhibition had been pulled back to create an open flow, allowing guests to circulate between the art and the social spaces without bottlenecks. A string quartet played near the entrance, two violins, a viola, and a cello working through something by Dvořák that felt both classical and unexpected for the setting, which Amaya suspected was the point. Waitstaff in black circulated with trays of champagne flutes and small plates of food that looked too pretty to eat but smelled extraordinary.

The crowd was a blend of Harlem's cultural establishment and the broader New York art world—gallery owners, collectors, critics, academics, community leaders, and a handful of the kind of people whose wealth was evident in the casual perfection of their clothing rather than its conspicuousness. Amaya estimated two hundred guests, give or take. The noise level was a steady hum of conversation punctuated by laughter, the occasional clink of glass, and the quartet's patient persistence beneath it all.

She accepted a champagne flute from a passing tray—holding a drink was social camouflage, the quickest way to look like you belonged at a party, and began her circuit.

The exhibition was titled *Convergence*, featuring twelve artists working across media: painting, sculpture, photography, textile work, and digital installation. Amaya wasn't here for the art, but she found herself stopping in front of a large-format photograph of a Harlem brownstone, shot from below so that the building seemed to lean toward the viewer like a confidant about to share a secret. The photographer had caught the light at the precise moment when the setting sun hit the upper windows and turned them to copper. It was beautiful in a way that felt personal rather than decorative.

She moved on, cataloging the room as she went. Emily Dawson was everywhere and nowhere—visible at the edges of the event, checking in with catering, exchanging words with the quartet leader, directing a security guard to adjust the velvet rope near the VIP area. She moved with the efficiency of a person who'd choreographed the evening down to the minute and was now executing the performance in real time. Amaya noted that Emily's expression shifted depending on who she was speaking to: warm and deferential with board members, brisk and precise with vendors, and, when she thought no one was watching—tight with a private tension that surfaced in the set of her jaw and the speed of her steps.

Lydia Brooks held court near the center of the main gallery, surrounded by a rotating cast of patrons and supporters. She was luminous tonight, a midnight-blue gown that complemented her silver-templed hair, her posture relaxed, her laughter generous. This was the version of Lydia the public knew: confident, commanding, the embodiment of the institution she'd built. Amaya could see the director's energy drawing people in, creating a gravitational center for the room.

She could also see the cost of the performance. Each time Lydia turned from one conversation to the next, there was a half-second gap, a fractional pause where her smile dimmed and her eyes went flat before reigniting for the new audience. It was the face of a woman running on will, and the fuel was getting low.

Derek Osei was stationed near the entrance to the lower-level gallery, his navy uniform crisp, his posture alert without being aggressive. He'd positioned himself where he could see both the main gallery floor and the corridor leading to the service areas, a choice that told Amaya he was thinking about sight lines, not just crowd control. Two additional guards were visible in the room, and Amaya suspected at least one more was covering the loading dock entrance downstairs.

The security was better than what she'd seen on her first visit. Derek had tightened things up, and she wondered whether that was a response to her assessment or something he'd already been planning. Either way, anyone attempting a theft tonight would find fewer gaps to exploit.

Which didn't mean the gaps had disappeared entirely.

Amaya was studying the corridor that led to the storage vaults—noting the camera positioned above the junction, confirming that the blind spot Derek had flagged was still uncovered, when a voice beside her cut through the ambient noise.

"You're looking at the architecture instead of the art. That's either deeply practical or deeply sacrilegious."

She turned. The man who'd materialized at her shoulder was tall—six-one or six-two, with the lean build of someone who worked out regularly. His skin was a rich umber, and his hair was cropped close, emphasizing a face built around sharp cheekbones and a wide, expressive mouth that seemed perpetually on the verge of amusement. He wore a charcoal suit with no tie, the top button of his shirt undone, projecting an ease that felt practiced but not false. A drink. Something amber, neat—rested in his right hand with the casualness of a prop he'd been holding all night.

"Depends on the architecture," Amaya said.

His smile widened. "Calvin Whitaker." He extended his free hand. "I consult for the museum. And you are clearly not a regular at these events, because I would remember."

The line was delivered with enough self-awareness to acknowledge its own smoothness, a man who knew he was charming and offered the charm openly, without pretense. Amaya took his hand. His grip was warm, his palm dry, and he held the shake a beat longer than professional courtesy required.

"Amaya Storm. I'm a friend of Lydia's."

"Lydia has excellent taste in friends." Calvin released her hand and shifted to stand beside her, angling his body so they were both facing the gallery, a positioning that created a sense of shared perspective, two people observing the same scene rather than facing off across it. The move was subtle and practiced, and Amaya recognized it as the technique of someone who spent a lot of time making other people feel at ease.

"What kind of consulting do you do for the museum?" she asked.

"Appraisals, mostly. Authentication, valuation for insurance purposes, the occasional acquisition advisory." He took a sip of his drink. "Art is a beautiful thing, but it's also an asset class. Someone has to make sure the numbers match the beauty."

"And do they? Match?"

Calvin turned to her with an expression of genuine interest, or a flawless approximation of it. "That depends on who's asking and why. Art valuation is part science, part storytelling. A piece is worth what someone will pay for it, and what someone will pay depends on what story they've been told about why it matters."

It was a clever framing, and Amaya noted the implicit philosophy: value was constructed, not inherent. For a man in the business of appraising art, that was either refreshing honesty or a convenient justification for flexibility with numbers.

"Sounds like a field with a lot of room for interpretation."

"All the best fields are." His smile was easy, inviting her into a shared understanding, a look that made people feel like they'd been admitted to an inner circle. "Are you in the art world yourself?"

"Adjacent. I work in research."

"Ah. The behind-the-scenes people who make the rest of us look smart." He raised his glass in a small salute. "What are you researching tonight?"

It was a pointed question wrapped in casual packaging. Amaya held his gaze and smiled. "The architecture."

Calvin laughed, a warm, unhurried sound that drew glances from nearby guests. "Fair enough. But if you're interested in what's actually happening in this room, you should talk to the artists. They're the ones with the real stories. The rest of us are just the support system."

He excused himself with the grace of a man who understood that leaving a conversation at the right moment was more memorable than overstaying. As he moved through the crowd, Amaya watched him pause at three separate clusters of people, each time adjusting his energy to match the group—more animated with a cluster of younger artists, more measured with a pair of older collectors, solicitous with a woman Amaya recognized from the board of directors list.

Calvin Whitaker was a chameleon. He read rooms the way Amaya read people—quickly, accurately, and with purpose. The question was what purpose.

She was turning back toward the gallery when a disturbance near the entrance caught her attention. Not a loud one. No shouting, no alarm. But a shift in the energy that rippled outward from the door like a stone dropped in still water. Several heads turned. A security guard took a half-step forward. Emily Dawson appeared from somewhere to the left, her expression sharpening.

A man had entered the gallery with the specific energy of someone who'd come to make a point. He was young— late twenties, maybe thirty, with a closely trimmed beard, thick-framed glasses, and an intensity that radiated from his posture like heat from pavement. He wore paint-stained jeans and a dark blazer that might have been ironic or might have been the only blazer he owned. His eyes swept the room with the hunger of someone looking for a face they intended to confront.

He found Lydia's.

Amaya watched him cross the floor toward the director, his stride purposeful enough to part the crowd without him needing to ask. Lydia saw him coming, her social smile faltered, replaced by a guarded expression that suggested this encounter was not unexpected but also not welcome.

"Ron." Lydia's voice carried the diplomatic warmth of a host managing an uninvited guest. "I didn't see your name on the list tonight."

"Didn't realize I needed an invitation to visit a public museum." His voice was low but carried an edge that turned nearby heads. "Especially one that's supposed to represent artists like me."

Lydia's composure held. "This is a private event, Ron. But you're welcome to visit during public hours. We'd love to have you."

"You'd love to have me walk through and look at other people's work hanging where mine should be." He didn't raise his voice, but the anger in it was compressed, pressurized. "Three submission cycles, Lydia. Three times my portfolio crossed your desk and three times it came back with a form letter. Meanwhile you're showing artists with half the community connection I have, because they went to the right schools and know the right people."

The exchange was drawing attention now, the quiet, magnetic kind that made people stop mid-conversation and angle their bodies to watch while pretending not to. Emily had moved closer, her hand reaching for her phone, ready to call security. Derek, still at his post by the lower-level entrance, had shifted his weight forward but held his position—watching, assessing, not yet intervening.

Lydia lowered her voice, stepping closer to Ron. "This isn't the place for this conversation. If you'd like to schedule a meeting—"

"A meeting." Ron's laugh was short and bitter. "Right. Another meeting where you tell me the curatorial committee values diverse perspectives while the same twelve artists rotate through your galleries."

"Ron—"

"My work is about this neighborhood, Lydia. Not about it, from it. I paint the people who walk past this building every day, the people this museum is supposed to serve. And you keep telling me it's not ready." He caught himself, the anger flickering into something rawer—hurt, maybe, or the frustration of someone who'd confused persistence with entitlement and couldn't tell the difference anymore.

Amaya observed the exchange from ten feet away, close enough to read faces, far enough to avoid being drawn in. Ron Devane. She'd seen his name in the museum's submission records during her research. He was not performing. His anger was genuine, rooted in a grievance that had fermented over time. But genuine anger didn't disqualify him as a suspect; it provided motive.

A rejected artist with a grudge against the institution. Access to the building during public hours, potentially familiar with its layout. Emotionally volatile enough to make a scene at a private event.

Or: a rejected artist with a legitimate complaint, showing up because he'd run out of quieter ways to be heard.

Both readings fit the available evidence. Amaya filed both.

Emily reached Ron's side and placed a gentle hand on his arm, a practiced gesture, firm enough to steer, soft enough to avoid escalation. "Ron, let me walk you out. We can set up a time for you to meet with the curatorial team next week."

Ron looked at Emily's hand on his arm, then at Emily, then back at Lydia. Something in his expression shifted, the anger banking into embers, not extinguished but controlled. "Next week," he repeated flatly.

"I'll personally make sure it happens," Emily said. Her voice had dropped into a register of warm authority that Amaya recognized from the interview, the mode Emily entered when she wanted someone to feel handled without feeling managed.

Ron allowed himself to be guided toward the door. As they passed Amaya's position, his gaze swept across her face without stopping. But something in his expression caught, a brief flicker of recognition or curiosity, as if he'd clocked her watching and filed it away.

The room exhaled. Conversations resumed. The quartet, which had never stopped playing, seemed to grow louder as the ambient noise recalibrated. Lydia turned back to her circle of patrons with a smile that cost her visibly.

When Emily returned from escorting Ron, she leaned in close to Lydia, her voice a sharp whisper Amaya caught over the quartet. "The Board Oversight Committee meeting is Friday morning, Lydia. If we don't have a suspect or a recovery by then, they're going to freeze the endowment and call for a management overhaul." They didn't have weeks. They had seventy-two hours before the museum's future was signed away by men in suits.

Amaya stayed another ninety minutes, circulating, listening, watching the machinery of the event operate. She observed Emily return from escorting Ron and resume her choreography without missing a beat. She watched Calvin work the room with the fluid ease of a man who understood that social capital was a renewable resource if you invested it correctly. She noted the moments when Calvin and Emily were in the same part of the room. Not together, exactly, but proximate, and the moments when their eyes met briefly across the crowd before looking away.

Those glances were fast. Professional, if you were being generous. Coordinated, if you weren't.

At nine-thirty, Amaya slipped out through the lobby. The October air hit her face, clean and cool after the warm density of the gallery. 125th Street was still alive, a restaurant across the avenue had its doors propped open, the sound of salsa music competing with the rumble of a city bus pulling away from the curb. A couple walked past holding hands, their laughter trailing behind them.

Amaya stood on the sidewalk and breathed. The evening had given her what she'd come for: a firsthand look at the museum's event operation, the dynamics between its key players, and the first direct encounter with Calvin Whitaker. It had also given her Ron Devane—an angry young artist whose grievance was real and whose presence at a private event he hadn't been invited to raised questions she'd need to answer.

But the image that stayed with her as she walked toward the subway was smaller than any of those. It was the glances between Calvin and Emily—brief, controlled, and timed to avoid overlap with anyone else's attention. Two people who knew each other's position in a crowded room without needing to look.

That was either the habit of colleagues who'd worked together often enough to develop spatial awareness.

Or it was the habit of people who'd rehearsed.

Chapter 5: The View from Riverdale

Saturday morning, and the duplex smelled like plantains.

Amaya stood at the stove in a faded Howard University t-shirt and sweatpants, turning the sweet plantain slices in the pan with the patience the process demanded—low heat, no rushing, let the sugars do their work until the edges caramelized to a deep amber. Her mother had taught her the technique before Amaya was tall enough to see over the counter, standing on a step stool in their old kitchen on Prospect Avenue, learning that the difference between good maduros and burnt ones was the willingness to wait.

Chaos sat on the kitchen floor two feet from the stove, his green eyes tracking each plantain slice with the unblinking focus of a cat who had convinced himself that this particular food, which he had never been offered and would not enjoy—was the one thing standing between him and complete happiness. His tail swept the tile in a slow metronome.

"It's a plantain. You don't want a plantain."

He blinked. The tail continued.

"You're a cat. You eat fish-flavored pellets that smell like a pier at low tide. This is not for you."

He chirped, a short, insistent sound that managed to convey both hope and moral injury.

Amaya dropped a flake of salmon from last night's leftovers onto the floor beside him. He abandoned the plantain watch instantly, all loyalty transferred to the salmon with the ruthless pragmatism she'd come to expect. Love was conditional in this household, and the conditions were protein-based.

She plated the plantains alongside scrambled eggs and a cup of coffee strong enough to peel paint, then carried everything to the dining table, which had been fully colonized by the Studio Museum case.

Three days of accumulated paperwork covered the surface: access logs, staff schedules, financial printouts, the guest lists Emily had provided, and Amaya's own notes, a growing collection of legal pad pages covered in her tight handwriting, organized by subject and connected with arrows and circled keywords. In the center sat her laptop, open to a spreadsheet she'd built mapping every staff member's location during each theft-night event, cross-referenced with their keycard entries.

Trouble occupied the chair at the head of the table, curled in a tight circle with her tail covering her nose. She'd been there since dawn, apparently having decided that proximity to the case materials constituted participation. Mayhem was somewhere in the duplex. Amaya could hear the faint, rhythmic thump of a ball being batted against a wall in the spare bedroom, a sound that would continue until either the ball was lost or the wall gave in.

Amaya ate with one hand and reviewed her notes with the other.

The background checks had come back overnight. She'd run them through a contact at a private security firm she'd used during her NYPD years, a retired detective named Pauline Chen who now operated a database service that was technically legal, occasionally gray, and reliably thorough.

Derek Osei. Born in Accra, Ghana; immigrated at fifteen. U.S. citizen since 2005. Juvenile theft conviction at seventeen—shoplifting, pled down, sealed record. No subsequent criminal history in twenty-six years. Military service, four years, Army, honorable discharge. Security certifications current. Credit report clean. Modest savings account consistent with his salary. The cash deposit Amaya had heard about. She'd asked Pauline to flag any unusual financial activity. It was $8,200, deposited six weeks ago. Source unlisted.

The deposit was a question mark. Not large enough to suggest major criminal involvement, but unusual enough to warrant an explanation. She'd need to address it, either directly with Derek or through the investigation's natural progression.

Emily Dawson. Born in Brooklyn; raised in Bed-Stuy. NYU, arts administration, graduated with honors. Employment history: two years at a Chelsea gallery, then hired by Lydia at the Studio Museum, where she'd been for seven years. No criminal record. Her credit report revealed she had aggressively paid down student loan debt over the past two years and was ahead of schedule. This either showed disciplined financial management or income beyond her salary. Social media presence was minimal and curated—professional accomplishments, museum events, the occasional book recommendation. Nothing personal. No visible relationship. A careful online footprint, the kind maintained by someone who understood that absence of information was its own form of control.

Calvin Whitaker. Born in Philadelphia. Howard University, art history. MBA from Columbia. Founded Whitaker Art Advisory eight years ago. The firm operated from a commercial space in West Harlem. Amaya noted the address and cross-referenced it with the tunnel map she'd been studying. Calvin's building sat on 131st Street, six blocks north of the museum. His client list included mid-tier galleries, private collectors, and three institutional clients in the tristate area. Financials were harder to access, the firm was a private LLC. But the public filings showed steady revenue growth over the past four years.

No criminal record. No red flags in the conventional sense. But Amaya had learned that the absence of red flags in a person whose business involved appraising and authenticating valuable art was itself a data point. The art world ran on trust and reputation, and Calvin Whitaker's reputation was conspicuously clean for someone who'd been operating in a field where conflicts of interest were as common as gallery openings.

Ron Devane. Born and raised in Harlem. No formal art education—self-taught, which in the art world could be either a liability or a selling point depending on who was buying. He'd shown work at small community galleries and pop-up exhibitions, building a modest following among neighborhood supporters. Three submissions to the Studio Museum, all rejected. No criminal record, but a civil complaint filed two years ago against a gallery in the East Village that had allegedly failed to return unsold work, the case was settled out of court.

Ron's profile fit a frustrated artist, not a criminal mastermind. But frustration was a driver, and his familiarity with the museum's public spaces—combined with the intensity she'd witnessed at the opening—meant she couldn't rule him out.

Amaya pushed her empty plate aside and pulled the laptop closer. She opened the spreadsheet and began adding the background data to her framework, color-coding each name by level of access, motive, and opportunity. The picture was clarifying but not yet resolved—like a painting viewed through frosted glass, the shapes visible but the details still soft.

Her phone rang. Not the office line, her cell. The caller ID showed a 718 number she didn't recognize.

She answered on the second ring. "Amaya Storm."

"Ms. Storm, this is Detective Alton Jackson, NYPD. Major Case Squad." The voice was a baritone with a deliberate pace—each word placed with the care of someone who'd learned that how you said things mattered as much as what you said. "I understand you've been retained by Lydia Brooks in connection with the Studio Museum thefts."

Amaya leaned back in her chair. She'd been expecting this call since her first visit to the museum; the only surprise was that it had taken this long. "That's correct."

"I'd like to meet. Compare notes, establish some ground rules so we're not tripping over each other." A pause that was professionally courteous but carried an undercurrent of something firmer. "I'm sure you understand the importance of coordination."

The word "coordination" did a lot of work in that sentence. What Jackson meant was: *I'm the detective on this case, you're a private investigator who's been poking around my case, and I'd like to know exactly how far you intend to poke.*

"I'm available Monday," Amaya said. "Name a place."

"There's a diner on 149th and Grand Concourse. Jimmy's. You know it?"

She did. A Bronx institution—good coffee, indifferent service, a place where cops and lawyers and neighborhood regulars coexisted in a détente maintained by cheap prices and a mutual understanding that nobody was there to be impressed.

"I know it. Ten o'clock?"

"Works. Bring whatever you've got."

The line went dead. No pleasantries, no small talk. Amaya appreciated that. People who wasted time on the phone usually wasted it in person too, and she had a feeling Detective Jackson was not a person who wasted much of anything.

She set the phone down and looked at Trouble, who had raised her head from her tail at the sound of the call and was watching Amaya with an expression of alert evaluation.

"New player," Amaya said.

Trouble held her gaze for a long moment, then lowered her head back to her tail. Assessment complete, apparently. Verdict pending.

Amaya returned to her notes, but her mind had split, one track continuing to build the case architecture, the other running a preliminary profile on Detective Alton Jackson. Major Case Squad meant he worked high-value theft, fraud, and complex investigations. The fact that the Studio Museum case had been assigned to Major Case rather than the local precinct's detective squad told her the department was taking the third theft seriously—half a million dollars in stolen art crossed the threshold from property crime into a case that attracted attention from above.

She pulled up the NYPD's public directory. Jackson, Alton. Detective Second Grade, Major Case Squad. Assigned to the Manhattan North bureau. No photo available through the directory, but a search of his name in connection with closed cases turned up a few mentions: a commercial fraud ring in Midtown, an insurance scam involving forged provenance documents for a private collection, and a gallery theft in Chelsea that had resulted in three arrests and the recovery of $2.3 million in stolen artwork.

Art theft experience. That explained why he'd drawn this case, and it meant he'd likely recognized some of the same patterns Amaya was seeing. It also meant he'd be less patient with a PI who was covering ground he'd already mapped.

She'd need to bring something to Monday's meeting that he didn't have. Something that justified her presence in his case and gave him a reason to share rather than compete.

The Whitaker financial thread was her best card. The NYPD could subpoena Calvin's business records, but they'd need probable cause, and consulting fees paid to an outside appraiser didn't clear that bar on their own. Amaya's access to the museum's internal financials—provided voluntarily by Lydia—gave her a faster route to the same questions. If she could identify specific discrepancies between the services invoiced and the services delivered, she could hand Jackson a lead that would save him weeks of legwork.

It was a trade, not a concession. She'd give him the financial angle; in return, she'd want access to whatever forensic evidence the department had gathered from the three theft scenes—fiber analysis, fingerprints, the cloned keycard data. Information she couldn't get on her own.

Her grandmother would have called it "trading baseball cards." You didn't give away your best card, but you didn't hoard them all either. The game worked when both sides felt like they'd gotten something worth having.

Amaya spent the rest of the morning preparing. She organized the Whitaker invoices into a timeline, flagging three payments that lacked corresponding deliverables— appraisal reports that should have existed but didn't appear in the museum's files. She compiled a summary of the access log patterns, highlighting Emily's consistent position as the last staff member in the building on theft nights. And she drafted a brief on the cloned keycard incident, including her own analysis of why the third theft's single anomaly might have been intentional rather than careless.

Mayhem appeared from the spare bedroom at noon, his ball game concluded, and announced his presence by jumping onto the dining table and walking directly across the access log printouts. His paws left faint impressions on the paper, a detail Amaya photographed before shooing him off, partly for the humor and partly because she'd once had a forensic consultant tell her that unexpected marks on documents had cracked a case. Mayhem wasn't a forensic consultant. But his paw prints were now part of the file's history, and she found that inexplicably comforting.

Chaos had spent the morning in the living room conducting what Amaya thought of as his "furniture audit", a periodic inventory of every surface in the duplex, conducted by jumping onto each one in sequence, sitting for exactly ten seconds, and moving to the next. The audit followed a fixed route (couch, armchair, bookshelf, radiator cover, kitchen counter, back to couch) and served no purpose Amaya could identify, but Chaos performed it with a seriousness that suggested he was fulfilling a contractual obligation.

By noon, she had a folder ready for Monday. Not everything she had. She'd hold back the Calvin-Emily connection she'd observed at the opening, keeping that thread for herself until she understood it better. But enough to demonstrate competence and invite reciprocity.

The afternoon opened up, and with it, the restlessness that came from working a case she couldn't yet move forward. The next steps—meeting Jackson, revisiting the museum, exploring the tunnel connection to Calvin's building, all required the week to begin. Saturday afternoon had no case to offer her, and Amaya had never been good at empty time.

She took the cat for a walk.

Not all three. Mayhem's leash manners were a work in progress that tended to involve him trying to climb every tree on the block, and Chaos's attention span made him a hazard near traffic. But Trouble tolerated the harness with regal indifference, and the two of them had developed a walking route through the neighborhood that Amaya found grounding in the way that routines become rituals when you do them long enough.

They walked south on Fieldston Road, past the stone houses and the old oaks that arched over the sidewalk like a cathedral ceiling. The afternoon was cool and bright, the October light sharp enough to give everything edges, the wrought-iron fences, the brick facades, the yellow leaves collecting in the gutters. A woman pruning roses in her front garden waved. A man walking a greyhound nodded as they passed, the dog and Trouble exchanging a glance of mutual, species-level assessment.

They turned west toward the park. Van Cortlandt Park stretched out before them, the oldest public park in the Bronx, a vast green space that contained ball fields, hiking trails, a golf course, and a freshwater lake that reflected the sky as it had been doing it for centuries. On a Saturday afternoon, the park was alive: kids on the soccer fields, joggers on the trail, a group of older men playing dominoes on a bench near the entrance with the focused intensity of people engaged in serious business.

Amaya settled on a bench overlooking the lake. Trouble sat beside her on the slats, her eyes scanning the water's edge where a few ducks navigated the shallows with purposeful indifference to human activity.

The view was one of Amaya's favorites, the lake, the tree line, the slow curve of the Bronx skyline beyond. It was a view that reminded you the borough was more than its reputation, more than the shorthand that people who'd never walked its streets used to describe it. The Bronx was parks and rivers and hills and a community that had been reinventing itself for generations.

She thought about the museum. About Lydia's exhaustion and Derek's frustration and Emily's too-fast answers and Calvin's too-easy charm. About Ron Devane's anger, which was either a motive or a mirror reflecting the museum's own failures back at it.

She thought about the glances between Calvin and Emily—brief, synchronized, disappearing the moment they occurred. Two people with spatial awareness of each other in a crowded room.

And she thought about Monday, and a detective she hadn't met whose voice on the phone suggested he wasn't interested in being charmed, impressed, or managed.

Trouble shifted on the bench, pressing her side against Amaya's thigh. The cat's warmth was solid, present, a small anchor in a landscape of open questions. Amaya rested her hand on Trouble's back and felt the slow rise and fall of breathing, steady as a metronome.

"Monday," she said quietly.

Trouble's ear rotated toward her voice, then forward again—acknowledging the word without committing to its implications.

They sat together as the afternoon light lengthened, the lake turning copper as the sun dropped toward the tree line. The dominoes players argued about a contested play. A child shrieked with delight somewhere on the soccer fields. The ducks continued their rounds, unbothered by any of it.

The case would move on Monday. For now, the bench was enough.

Chapter 6: A Harlem History Lesson

Monday came with rain, the serious kind, the kind that turned Harlem's streets into mirrors and made the subway platforms steam like bathhouses. Amaya ascended into the 1 train at 238th Street with her collar turned up and Trouble's carrier zipped against the weather, the cat's gaze watching the wet world through the mesh with an expression of profound personal offense.

The meeting with Detective Jackson was at ten. But Amaya had scheduled herself at the museum first, at eight-thirty—early enough to catch the building in its pre-public hours, when the staff operated without the performance of visitors and the institution's internal rhythms were exposed.

She arrived to find the museum's lobby dim and quiet, the overhead lights still on their low morning setting. A security guard she hadn't met—young, attentive, wearing the alert posture of someone still new enough to take the job personally—checked her name against a list and waved her through. Derek had arranged access for her; the guard's manner told her Derek had also communicated that Amaya's presence was to be accommodated without being advertised.

She took the elevator to the third floor and found Lydia's office door open. The director was at her desk, reading glasses perched low on her nose, a stack of correspondence in front of her. She looked older in the morning light than she had at the gala, the performance stripped away, the fatigue no longer hidden beneath evening makeup and social adrenaline.

"Early start," Amaya said from the doorway.

Lydia glanced up, removing her glasses with the automatic gesture of a woman who didn't like being seen in them. "I've been here since seven. Sleep hasn't been cooperative lately."

Amaya entered and sat without waiting for an invitation, a small assertion of the working relationship she needed to establish. She wasn't a guest anymore. "I need to look at the appraisal files for the past two years. Specifically, the deliverables from Whitaker Art Advisory—reports, authentication certificates, anything Calvin Whitaker produced for the fees the museum paid him."

Lydia's brow creased. "The appraisal files should be with the registrar. Thomas Yeboah maintains the collection documentation."

"I checked the records Emily provided. The invoices are there, but the corresponding reports aren't. Three payments over the last eighteen months—totaling just under fifteen thousand dollars, with no attached deliverables in the museum's files."

The crease deepened. Lydia removed her reading glasses entirely and set them on the desk with a deliberate precision that suggested she needed the extra second to process. "That's not possible. Every appraisal generates a report. It's standard procedure. We need them for insurance, for loans, for board reporting."

"I agree. Which means either the reports were filed somewhere I haven't looked, or they were never produced."

The implication hung between them. Lydia's jaw tightened. Not with anger, Amaya noted, but with the tension of someone whose faith in a system was being tested against evidence that the system had failed.

"I'll pull everything we have from Thomas's office," Lydia said. "If the reports exist, they'll be in the physical files. He's old-fashioned—keeps paper copies of everything."

"I'd like to go through those files myself, if you don't mind."

Lydia hesitated, a brief, revealing pause that told Amaya the director was calculating how much access to grant before the investigation's momentum outran her comfort. Then she nodded. "I'll take you down."

The registrar's office was on the lower level, adjacent to the storage vaults, a windowless room that smelled of archival paper and the faint chemical tang of conservation supplies. Thomas Yeboah's workspace was meticulous:

filing cabinets labeled by year and category, a drafting table covered in collection inventories, and a wall-mounted whiteboard tracking the museum's current loans and acquisitions.

Thomas himself wasn't in yet. Lydia unlocked his filing cabinet with a master key and left Amaya to it, retreating upstairs with the distracted energy of someone who'd been given a new thing to worry about on top of all the existing ones.

Amaya worked through the files methodically. The registrar's system was organized and thorough—each artwork in the museum's collection had a folder containing its provenance documentation, condition reports, exhibition history, and any appraisals or authentications performed. She pulled the folders corresponding to the three Whitaker invoices that lacked deliverables.

The first folder—for a Romare Bearden collage acquired eighteen months ago—contained a provenance chain, a condition report from the museum's conservator, and a blank space where an appraisal report should have been. A sticky note in Thomas's handwriting read: *Appraisal pending — follow up w/ Emily.*

The second folder, a Jacob Lawrence gouache on loan from a private collector—had the same gap. Another sticky note: *Whitaker report requested 3/14. Not received. Emily aware.*

The third folder, a contemporary mixed-media piece by an emerging artist—was missing entirely. The hanging file was there, labeled, but the folder inside was gone.

Amaya photographed everything, including the empty hanging file. Then she sat back in Thomas's chair and considered what she was looking at.

Three payments for appraisal services. No reports delivered. The registrar had flagged the missing deliverables and routed the follow-up through Emily, the same person who managed the invoicing. And one folder had disappeared entirely, which meant someone with access to this room had removed it.

The keycard log for the registrar's office would show who'd entered recently. Amaya made a note to pull it. But she already knew what she expected to find: Emily's card, used during hours when Thomas wasn't present, removing the evidence of a transaction that didn't add up.

The question was whether the missing reports meant Calvin had been paid for work he never did, a simple fraud, or whether the payments were compensation for something else entirely, disguised as consulting fees.

She was locking the filing cabinet when Trouble shifted in her carrier, a subtle redistribution of weight that Amaya felt against her hip. The cat had been motionless for the past forty minutes—unusual for a confined animal in an unfamiliar space. But something had caught her attention. Through the mesh, Trouble's ears were rotated toward the far wall of the office, angled with the precision of satellite dishes tracking a signal. Her nose pressed against the mesh panel, nostrils flaring in the rhythmic pattern Amaya had come to recognize as active scent processing. Not casual breathing but deliberate intake, the cat drawing air across her vomeronasal organ to analyze chemical traces invisible to the human nose.

Amaya unzipped the carrier. Trouble didn't bolt. She emerged with controlled purpose, dropping to the floor and crossing the office in a direct line to the far wall. She pressed her face against the baseboard, her whiskers fanning flat against the surface, her body lowering until her belly touched the concrete floor. Then she began to pace, three feet left, three feet right, three feet left again, her nose tracking something along the wall's base with the methodical focus of a cat who had identified a boundary and was mapping its extent.

Amaya watched. She'd seen Trouble do this once before. In the hallway of an apartment building during the Cuevas case, where the cat had traced the outline of a concealed wall safe by scenting the difference in air temperature between the safe's metal surface and the surrounding drywall. What Trouble was doing now had the same quality: precise, repetitive, investigative.

Amaya paused. She looked at the far wall—standard institutional drywall, painted a neutral gray, bearing nothing more interesting than a framed poster of the museum's inaugural exhibition from the 1960s. She listened. The building's mechanical systems hummed at the edge of hearing—ventilation, the compressor for the climate-controlled vaults. But nothing that should have drawn the cat's focus.

She walked to the wall and pressed her palm flat against it. The surface vibrated faintly. Not from the building's

HVAC, which she could feel in the floor, but from something deeper, a low resonance that traveled through the wall's structure like a pulse.

Amaya knocked. The sound was flat and solid for the first three raps. On the fourth, two feet to the left and lower, the pitch changed—higher, with a slight echo that suggested open space behind the surface.

She crouched and examined the baseboard. The building was new construction, the museum had moved into this facility only two years ago. But the lower level sat on the foundation of an older structure. Amaya remembered a detail from her initial research: the new museum had been built on the site of a previous building that dated to the early 1900s. The foundation had been partially retained and incorporated into the new construction.

She ran her fingers along the joint where the baseboard met the floor and found a seam. Not a crack, but a deliberate line where the drywall had been cut and reseated. The cut was clean, professional, invisible unless you were on your hands and knees looking for it.

Amaya sat back on her heels and looked at Trouble. The cat's amber eyes stared at the wall with unwavering intensity, her body coiled with the contained energy of an animal that had identified something behind a barrier and was waiting for the barrier to be removed.

"What's back there?" Amaya murmured.

She pulled out her phone and searched for the museum's building plans, the architectural filings would be public record, available through the city's Department of Buildings. It took several minutes of scrolling through permit documents before she found what she was looking for: the foundation survey, completed prior to construction, which mapped the footprint of the original structure beneath the new building.

The survey included a notation she'd missed during her earlier research: *Sub-grade passages identified along north and east foundation walls. Passages sealed per engineering recommendation. See addendum.*

The addendum wasn't included in the digital filing. But the notation confirmed what the hollow wall suggested: the museum's lower level sat above, or adjacent to, a network of underground passages that predated the building by a century or more.

Amaya stood, brushed off her knees, and called Lydia.

"I need to talk to you about the building's foundation."

Lydia arrived four minutes later, her expression tightening when she saw Amaya crouched near the baseboard. "What did you find?"

"Your building sits on top of underground passages. The foundation survey flagged them before construction. They were supposed to be sealed." Amaya pointed to the seam in the wall. "This section has been opened and resealed. Recently, based on the drywall compound. It hasn't fully cured."

Lydia stared at the wall as though it had betrayed her. "I knew about the passages. The architects mentioned them during the design phase—historical tunnels, part of Harlem's underground network. Some dated to the abolitionist era, some were dug during Prohibition. The engineers sealed them and we moved on. I didn't think—"

She stopped. Her hand went to her forehead, pressing against the skin as though trying to physically hold a thought in place.

"You didn't think anyone would unseal them," Amaya finished.

"No." The word came out small, heavy.

"I need to see what's behind this wall, Lydia. But I'd like to do it with Derek present, and I'd like it documented."

"Of course." Lydia was already reaching for her phone, the administrative reflex overriding the shock. "I'll get him down here now."

Derek arrived in under three minutes, which told Amaya he'd been close, probably monitoring the lower level, probably aware that Amaya was down here, probably maintaining the quiet vigilance that seemed to be his default state. He looked at the wall, listened to Amaya's explanation, and produced a utility knife from a belt pouch without being asked.

"The drywall's been cut before," he said, running the blade along the seam with practiced care. "Somebody used a good knife and patched it clean. If you weren't looking for it, you'd never notice."

The section came free in a single panel, revealing what Amaya had expected and Lydia had hoped wouldn't be there: a passage.

It wasn't dramatic. No yawning cavern, no gothic archway. It was a corridor roughly four feet wide and six feet tall, lined with old brick that had been recently cleared of debris. The floor was concrete—original, cracked, but swept clean. A string of battery-powered LED lights had been affixed to the ceiling with adhesive hooks, casting a flat white glow that extended maybe thirty feet before the passage curved to the right and disappeared.

Someone had not only unsealed this passage. They'd cleaned it, lit it, and made it usable.

"How far does this go?" Derek asked, his voice low, his professional composure barely concealing an anger that Amaya could read in the tension of his shoulders.

"I don't know yet." Amaya photographed the opening, the LED lights, and the clean floor. "But I have a preliminary map from the building survey that shows these passages extending north and east from the foundation. If the network is intact, it could connect to adjacent buildings for several blocks."

Derek turned to Lydia, and the look that passed between them was unguarded for the first time since Amaya had met them, his frustration and her guilt meeting in a space where professional distance couldn't mask the damage.

"I flagged the security vulnerabilities in this building eight months ago," Derek said. His voice was quiet and controlled, which made it worse than shouting would have. "I asked for additional cameras, restricted access protocols, and a full audit of the lower level. The memo went to your office."

"I know." Lydia's voice was barely above a whisper.

"The memo went through Emily."

The sentence landed like a stone in still water. Neither of them spoke for a moment. Derek hadn't accused Emily of anything. He'd simply stated a procedural fact. But the fact reframed everything: a security memo requesting measures that would have made the tunnel unusable had been routed through the person who, if Amaya's working theory held, had the most reason to ensure those measures were never implemented.

Amaya let the silence do its work. Then: "I need to explore this passage. Not today. I want to do it properly, with documentation and backup. But I need to know where it leads."

"I'll go with you," Derek said immediately.

"Agreed. Tomorrow, if possible. And Lydia—" Amaya turned to the director, whose face had gone ashen beneath its composure, ". I need you to act normally. Don't change Emily's access, don't alter any procedures, and don't have this conversation with anyone else. If whoever opened this tunnel realizes we've found it, they'll close whatever exit it connects to, and we'll lose the trail."

Lydia nodded, the gesture mechanical, a woman on autopilot, processing a betrayal she hadn't yet fully absorbed.

Derek replaced the drywall panel with the precision of someone who understood the assignment. He photographed his work and pocketed the utility knife. "Tomorrow morning. I'll have flashlights and a first-aid kit. Anything else?"

"Comfortable shoes," Amaya said. The faintest twitch at the corner of Derek's mouth. Not a smile, but the acknowledgment that humor, however thin, was a sign of shared ground.

Amaya left the museum with Trouble's carrier warm against her hip and a folder of photographs in her bag. The rain had eased to a drizzle, the street surfaces shimmering under a sky that couldn't decide between gray and silver. She walked north toward 149th Street, where Jimmy's Diner waited and Detective Alton Jackson would be learning, over coffee, that the Studio Museum case had just gotten significantly more complicated.

The tunnel changed everything. It explained how art could be removed from the museum without triggering the loading dock camera or the keycard system. It suggested a level of planning and infrastructure that went far beyond a single opportunistic thief. And it pointed, with increasing weight, toward someone who understood the building's history, had physical access to its lower level, and had the resources to prepare an underground corridor for regular use.

Someone who could clean a tunnel, install lights, and cut through drywall without being detected.

Someone who controlled the schedule that determined when the lower level was occupied and when it was empty.

Amaya's phone buzzed. A text from an unknown number: *Jimmy's. Booth in the back. I'm the one who looks impatient*

She almost smiled. Almost.

Chapter 7: Persons of Interest

Jimmy's Diner occupied the ground floor of a brick building on the Grand Concourse that had been many things over the decades, a barbershop, a check-cashing place, a short-lived Dominican restaurant that Amaya's grandmother still missed—before settling into its current identity as an establishment where the coffee was always hot, the booths were always available, and nobody pretended to be anything other than what they were.

Amaya pushed through the glass door and scanned the room. A row of red vinyl booths lined the wall beneath windows streaked with the morning's rain. A counter with chrome stools ran the length of the opposite side, occupied by the usual midmorning assembly: two ConEd workers studying a clipboard, a woman in hospital scrubs eating a western omelet with the efficiency of someone on a thirty-minute break, and an elderly man reading a Spanish-language newspaper.

The back booth. She spotted him.

Detective Alton Jackson sat with his back to the wall, a cop's reflex, facing the door, sightlines clear. He was broader than his voice had suggested, carrying a build that came from discipline rather than vanity—wide shoulders tapering to a trim waist, the proportions of a man who used a gym but didn't brag about it. His skin was a deep brown, smooth except for a thin scar that tracked along his left jawline from ear to chin—old, healed. His hair was cut close, showing the first threads of gray at the temples. He wore a dark sport coat over a white shirt, no tie, the collar open. His hands rested on the table on either side of a coffee cup, and Amaya noticed they were large, square-fingered, still, the hands of someone who'd trained himself out of fidgeting.

He looked up as she approached. His eyes were dark, set deep beneath a strong brow, and they performed the same rapid assessment she was performing on him—top to bottom, details cataloged, judgment reserved. The whole exchange took about two seconds.

"Ms. Storm."

"Detective Jackson."

"Alton." He gestured to the seat across from him. "We're going to be in each other's way for a while. Might as well use first names."

Amaya slid into the booth, setting Trouble's carrier on the seat beside her. Through the mesh, the cat's amber eyes found Jackson immediately and held—studying him with the unblinking focus she reserved for new variables.

Jackson's gaze dropped to the carrier. His expression didn't change, but something shifted behind his eyes—amusement, maybe, or the recalibration of a man who'd thought he knew what to expect from this meeting and had just encountered a data point that didn't fit.

"That a cat."

"That's Trouble."

"Named for what she causes, or what she finds?"

"Both."

He considered this for a moment, then returned his attention to Amaya with the faintest adjustment at the corner of his mouth. Not a smile, but the space where a smile would go. "Coffee?"

"Please."

He signaled the waitress without raising his hand, look and a nod, the communication just a of a regular who'd been coming here long enough to have compressed his orders into gestures. Two coffees appeared within a minute. Amaya wrapped her hands around the cup and let the warmth settle into her fingers.

"I'll go first," Jackson said. "Save us both the dance." He opened a thin folder on the table between them. "Three thefts at the Studio Museum over six months. First piece was a painting by Nkechi Adeyemi, valued at eighty thousand. Second was a William Edmondson bronze from the permanent collection, valued at two-twenty. Third was a Rashida Okonkwo mixed-media installation, five-thirty.

Total exposure north of eight hundred thousand, and that's just insured value—cultural value is incalculable."

"You've done your homework."

"It's what they pay me for." No irony in his voice, just fact. "Forensics gave us limited physical evidence. No prints at any of the three scenes that didn't belong to staff. No fiber evidence that held up. The cloned keycard used on theft three was a commercial-grade duplicate, the kind you can produce with a fifty-dollar reader off the internet if you have physical access to the original for ninety seconds."

"Thomas Yeboah's card."

Jackson's eyes sharpened slightly. "You've been thorough."

"It's what they pay me for."

The echo was deliberate, and Jackson registered it with a fractional tilt of his head—an acknowledgment that they were operating on the same level, which was either going to make this easier or harder depending on how much ego was involved.

Amaya decided to find out. She opened her own folder and placed it on the table. "Three payments to an outside consulting firm—Whitaker Art Advisory—totaling just under fifteen thousand dollars over eighteen months. No corresponding deliverables in the museum's files. The registrar flagged the missing reports and routed follow-ups through Emily Dawson, the director's assistant. The reports were never produced, and one of the three artwork folders has been physically removed from the registrar's filing system."

Jackson pulled the documents toward him, scanning them with the practiced speed of a detective who read financial records the way other people read box scores. His expression remained neutral, but Amaya caught the slight narrowing of his eyes when he reached the page summarizing the missing folder.

"Whitaker Art Advisory," he said. "Calvin Whitaker. I've heard the name. He's been on the periphery of a few art fraud investigations—never charged, never formally implicated, but his name circulates in the right conversations."

"What kind of conversations?"

"The kind where appraisals come in high enough to justify inflated insurance claims, and provenance documents materialize for pieces that don't have clean histories." Jackson set the documents down and leaned back, his posture shifting from assessment to something closer to engagement. "You're building toward a connection between Whitaker and the museum thefts."

"I'm building toward a connection between Whitaker and Emily Dawson. She controls the invoicing, the event schedules, the access code rotations for the storage vaults, and the guest list for every event where a theft occurred. She's the last staff member in the building after each event. And the security memo that would have closed the vulnerabilities exploited by the thief was routed through her office and never acted on."

Jackson absorbed this without visible reaction, a skill that Amaya recognized from her own NYPD years, the ability to take in significant information without showing your hand. "That's a strong circumstantial pattern. But it's still circumstantial."

"I know. That's why I'm bringing it to you instead of sitting on it."

"And in return?"

Amaya met his eyes. "The forensic reports. Whatever your lab pulled from the three theft scenes—fiber, chemical, tool marks, anything. And the full analysis of the cloned keycard, including where the duplication technology was sourced."

Jackson studied her for a long beat. The diner hummed around them—plates clattering, the coffee machine hissing, the ConEd workers debating something about a transformer on 161st. Through it all, Jackson's attention didn't waver. Amaya had the sense of being evaluated not just as a professional but as a person, his instincts measuring something that credentials and folders couldn't convey.

"Before we get into what I've got," he said, "I want to ask you something. You were on the job. Four-four precinct, then Bronx Narcotics."

It wasn't a question. He'd run her. Amaya felt the faintest prickle of surprise. Not that he'd checked, but that he'd said so openly. Most detectives who ran a background on someone they were about to negotiate with kept the results to themselves.

"Seven years patrol, one in plainclothes," she confirmed. "Left voluntarily. No disciplinary actions, no open complaints."

"I know. I also know you closed a financial fraud case last year that the DA's office couldn't crack for eighteen months. And that you've built a reputation in this borough for being thorough, discreet, and stubborn in approximately equal measure." He took a sip of coffee. "I don't work with people I haven't vetted. Nothing personal."

"I'd have done the same thing."

"I figured." He set the cup down. "Your grandmother was Eleanor Storm. Detective First Grade, four-four precinct. Retired 2018."

The mention of her grandmother in a professional context, from a man who'd clearly read Eleanor's service record with the same attention he'd read Amaya's— produced a response she didn't entirely expect. Not defensiveness, but a flicker of pride sharpened by protectiveness, the instinct of someone whose family legacy was also her foundation.

"She was."

"She cleared the Mott Haven insurance murders in '04. I was a rookie in the four-oh. That case was required reading." Jackson's tone carried no flattery, just the plain respect of a professional acknowledging excellence. "I can see where you learned to follow leads."

In the carrier beside her, Trouble shifted. The movement was small but purposeful, the cat had turned her head from Jackson to the diner's front window, her ears rotating forward with sudden focus. Amaya followed her gaze. Through the rain-streaked glass, a dark sedan had pulled to the curb across the street. It sat there, engine running, wipers sweeping. No one got out.

Amaya noted the vehicle—black Lincoln Town Car, tinted windows, no visible plates from this angle, and filed it without reacting. It was probably nothing. A car service waiting for a pickup, a driver killing time. But Trouble didn't redirect her attention for nothing, and the cat's body had gone rigid in the carrier, her gold eyes locked on the sedan with predatory stillness.

Jackson, who had been watching Amaya watch the window, glanced outside. "Something?"

"Probably not. My cat disagrees, but she's paranoid by nature."

Jackson looked at Trouble, then at the sedan, then back at Amaya. He didn't dismiss it. He didn't pursue it either. He simply adjusted, the micro-shift of a detective who'd logged the detail and moved on, exactly as Amaya had.

"The keycard was duplicated using a Proxmark device," he said, returning to the exchange. "Commercial model, available online, no serial number tracking. The duplication would require less than two minutes of physical contact with the original card. Our working theory is that the original was copied in the security office, the cabinet where cards are stored has a standard lock, not a high-security mechanism."

"Who has keys to that cabinet?"

"Derek Osei, the head of security. And Emily Dawson, who requisitions replacement cards when staff members lose theirs."

Another thread connecting to Emily. Amaya wrote nothing down. She'd memorize the details and document them later, away from Jackson's observation. "What about the theft scenes themselves?"

Jackson hesitated. It was a small thing, a breath held a fraction longer than the conversation's rhythm warranted, and Amaya recognized it as the moment where he was deciding how much to share. The trade was happening in real time, each piece of information a card played.

"The third theft scene gave us something the first two didn't," he said. "A chemical residue on the floor where the Okonkwo installation had been anchored. The lab identified it as a commercial-grade solvent used to dissolve industrial adhesive, the kind used to secure heavy installations to gallery floors. It's not a common product. It's sold through specialty suppliers, mostly to construction firms and art installation companies."

"Can you trace the purchase?"

"We're working on it. The supplier list is short, and the product requires a commercial account. If someone bought it recently in the tristate area, we'll find the receipt."

Amaya filed the information alongside everything else. A specialty solvent tied the third theft to someone with technical knowledge of art installation. Not a random thief, but someone who understood how museum-quality installations were secured and knew the specific product required to undo that security cleanly.

Calvin Whitaker's firm offered collection management and installation advisory services. It was listed on his website.

She didn't say this to Jackson. Not yet. The Whitaker connection was strengthening, but she wanted to explore the tunnel, and where it led—before she gave Jackson a direction that would trigger subpoenas and warrants. Once the NYPD moved on Calvin officially, the element of surprise would evaporate, and Amaya needed that surprise intact for a little while longer.

"There's something else," she said. "I found it this morning."

She told him about the tunnel. She described the cut drywall, the LED lights, the swept corridor, and the foundation survey notation. She watched his expression as the information landed, the careful neutral holding steady through the first details, then cracking slightly when she described the lights. Battery-powered LEDs installed in a century-old passage beneath a museum. That wasn't just a discovery. That was infrastructure.

Jackson was quiet for several seconds after she finished. He picked up his coffee, took a slow sip, and set it down with the precise placement of a man who was thinking carefully about what to say next.

"You're telling me there's a functional underground passage connecting the museum's lower level to God knows where, and someone's been maintaining it."

"That's what I'm telling you."

"And you found this how?"

"The building survey flagged it. I followed up."

Jackson's gaze moved to the carrier, where Trouble's eyes still watched him through the mesh. "The cat help?"

Amaya held his look. "She pointed me at the right wall."

Another silence. Then Jackson did something Amaya hadn't expected: he laughed. It was a short sound, more exhale than vocalization, but it was real, a genuine reaction that broke through the professional surface for half a second before he collected it.

"A cat pointed you at the right wall." He shook his head slowly. "That's a new one."

"She has a good track record."

"I'll take your word for it." He straightened, the humor folding back into focus. "I want to see that tunnel. Tomorrow—I'll bring a CSI team. We photograph everything, we test for trace evidence, and we find out where it exits."

"I planned to explore it tomorrow with Derek Osei."

"Then we do it together. My team, your access, Derek's knowledge of the building. And Ms. Storm—" He paused, and Amaya caught something in his expression that was harder to categorize than the professional assessment she'd been tracking all morning. It was direct, unguarded for a fraction of a second. "Good work. The financial thread, the tunnel—you've moved this case further in a week than my squad did in three months. I'm not too proud to say that."

The compliment landed clean, without embellishment or qualification, the statement of a man who valued competence and acknowledged it when he saw it. Amaya felt the warmth of it register somewhere behind her ribcage before her professional instincts reasserted themselves.

"You had a larger caseload and fewer cats."

The faintest smile. "That must be it."

They settled the check. Jackson insisted, with the quiet authority of someone who considered it a non-negotiable courtesy, and walked out into the drizzle together. The Grand Concourse stretched north and south, its wide boulevard and art deco facades holding the echo of a grander era while the present-day Bronx moved through it with its own energy.

Amaya glanced across the street. The dark sedan was gone. She scanned the block in both directions—nothing. But Trouble was restless in the carrier, shifting her weight in small circles, her ears swiveling between the street sounds like a radar dish searching for a signal that had dropped.

Amaya had seen Trouble act this way twice before— once outside a warehouse in Hunts Point during a fraud case, and once in the hallway of a building in Mott Haven where a witness had been followed. Both times, the cat's agitation had preceded the confirmation that someone else was watching. Trouble didn't spook at traffic noise or strangers. She spooked at attention directed at Amaya that Amaya herself hadn't detected.

She filed it. If the sedan was surveillance, the question was whose, and whether it was connected to the museum case or something else entirely.

"Tomorrow, eight a.m., the museum's lower level," Jackson said, turning up his collar against the rain. "I'll have my team ready."

"I'll let Derek know."

Jackson nodded. He started to turn away, then stopped. "Ms. Storm. Amaya." The correction was small, offered without ceremony. "One thing. Whatever you're holding back, and you're holding something back, because I would be too, just make sure you bring it to me before it becomes a problem."

He held her gaze long enough for the statement to register as both a professional warning and something closer to a request. Then he turned and walked north, his broad frame receding into the gray morning with the unhurried stride of a man who knew exactly where he was going.

Amaya watched him go. In the carrier, Trouble had settled, the sedan was gone and whatever had triggered her vigilance had passed. But the cat's attention had split: one ear tracked Jackson's retreating footsteps while the other rotated south, toward the direction the sedan had driven.

"Two things on your mind?" Amaya murmured. "Same."

Trouble's tail flicked once through the carrier's mesh, a gesture that in her vocabulary meant either *noted* or *obviously, keep up.*

Amaya turned south toward the subway, the rain cool on her face. Her mind ran three tracks now: the case, which was accelerating. The man she'd just met, who was sharper than she'd expected and more direct than she was used to. And the dark sedan that her cat had flagged and that she'd be watching for from now on.

She focused on the case. The other tracks could wait. But Trouble rarely raised a false alarm, and Amaya had learned—sometimes the hard way. That dismissing the cat's instincts was a mistake she couldn't afford to make twice.

Chapter 8: The Whitaker Gallery

The tunnel exploration happened at dawn on Tuesday, and it delivered exactly what Amaya had expected and worse than what she'd hoped.

She'd brought Trouble and Mayhem. Jackson had raised an eyebrow when she'd arrived at the museum's lower level with two cat carriers, but he'd watched Trouble work at the diner and he wasn't a man who dismissed a useful tool because it was unconventional. Derek, who'd seen Trouble find the hollow wall, simply nodded and held the drywall panel open wider.

Jackson's CSI team was efficient, two technicians who moved through the passage with the methodical patience of people accustomed to working in tight spaces. They photographed the LED lights, collected samples from the swept floor, dusted the adhesive hooks for prints, and mapped the corridor's dimensions and direction with a laser measuring device that cast thin red lines across the old brick walls like surgical incisions.

Derek walked point. He'd brought a flashlight, a first-aid kit, and the tightly controlled anger of a man seeing physical proof that his institution had been compromised. He said little, but his body communicated everything, the set of his jaw when they passed a section where fresh mortar had been applied to a crumbling wall, the sharp exhale when they found a second string of LEDs around the first curve.

Amaya stayed close to the CSI team, documenting on her phone and building a mental map as they progressed. Trouble walked beside her on a leash, her sleek black body low to the ground, ears forward, tail still—moving through the tunnel with the focused silence of a cat who understood that this was not a place for play. Her amber eyes swept the passage in slow arcs, cataloging the space with the same systematic attention Amaya applied to crime scenes.

Mayhem was different. Where Trouble read the atmosphere, Mayhem read the physical environment— pressing his nose to the base of the walls, pawing at seams in the brickwork, testing every surface with the blunt curiosity of a cat who believed all spaces contained secrets that could be extracted by force. His muscular body moved through the low passage with surprising grace, his eyes catching the LED light and reflecting it back in bright discs.

The passage ran roughly northeast from the museum's foundation, following a path that aligned with the original building survey. The brick was nineteenth-century—hand-laid, uneven, the mortar joints thick and irregular in the way of pre-industrial construction. But the modifications were recent: the LED lights, the swept floor, the occasional fresh patch of concrete filling a hole or stabilizing a section of wall.

Whoever maintained this passage treated it like a workspace, not a curiosity. There was no graffiti, no debris, no sign of casual trespass. This was operational substructure.

The passage branched once, a narrower corridor splitting west. The team marked it but didn't explore. Mayhem, however, had his own opinion. He strained toward the western branch, his leash pulling taut, his nose working the air at the junction with visible intensity. Amaya crouched beside him, watching his behavior. He wasn't just curious. He was tracking something. His nostrils flared in the rhythmic pattern of a cat processing a complex scent, and his body angled into the western passage as though drawn by an invisible current.

"Something down there," Amaya said quietly to Jackson.

Jackson looked at the cat, then at the passage, then back at Amaya. "We mark it. Come back with a full team." But he pulled out his phone and photographed the junction, including Mayhem's posture, documentation that wouldn't appear in an official report but that a smart detective kept for his own reference.

They continued northeast for approximately two hundred feet. The air was cool and still, carrying the organic smell of old stone and the faint chemical bite of fresh concrete. Amaya's footsteps echoed in the confined space, layering over the quiet sounds of the technicians working behind her.

The air here didn't just smell like old stone; it smelled like forgotten history—damp, heavy, and tasting faintly of iron. Trouble's ears were locked forward, tracking the silent shift of air that suggested a ventilation source they couldn't see. In this darkness, the cats were the only ones who truly knew where the walls ended and the secrets began.

Trouble stopped.

It wasn't gradual; the cat planted her front paws and went rigid, her body dropping into the compressed posture she adopted when something in her environment had changed significantly. Amaya halted immediately, her hand tightening on the leash. Derek, two steps ahead, turned at the sudden silence.

"What?" he asked.

Amaya scanned the passage ahead. Nothing visible had changed, the same brick walls, the same LED lights, the same clean floor. But Trouble's ears had flattened against her skull, and her gaze was fixed on a point twenty feet ahead where the passage appeared to narrow slightly.

"She's reacting to something. Air change, maybe, a draft from another opening." Amaya wet her finger and held it up. There—faint, but unmistakable, a current of air moving through the passage from ahead, carrying a different scent profile. Warmer. With a trace of something chemical again, that wasn't concrete.

Paint thinner. Or turpentine.

Amaya noted the location and they pressed forward. Ten feet past Trouble's alert point, the passage ended.

Not in a dead end. In a wall. A newer wall, cinder block rather than brick, with a steel door set into its center. The door was heavy gauge, industrial, fitted with a deadbolt lock and a keypad entry system that glowed faintly green in the tunnel's dim light. The air current Trouble had detected was seeping through the door's frame—imperfect seals around a barrier that separated the tunnel from whatever lay beyond.

Mayhem approached the door and pressed his face to the gap at its base, inhaling deeply. His body stiffened, then he sneezed—once, sharply, and backed away, shaking his head. Whatever was on the other side of that door carried a chemical signature strong enough to trigger a feline sneeze reflex. Paint thinner, solvents, the kind of materials used in art conservation. Or in art concealment.

Jackson, who had been walking behind the CSI team with the patient watchfulness of a man who preferred to let evidence accumulate before commenting, stepped forward and examined the door without touching it.

"Commercial-grade security on an underground door in a tunnel that's not supposed to be accessible." His voice was flat, the tone of a detective cataloging facts that were assembling into a picture he didn't like. "Someone spent serious money on this."

He looked at Mayhem, who was still shaking his head with feline indignation. "Your cat just identified the presence of volatile chemicals behind a locked door. In court, that wouldn't hold up. Off the record—" he glanced at Amaya, "—I've worked with K-9 units that gave me less to go on."

Derek shone his flashlight across the cinder block wall. "This isn't original construction. The block is modern—twenty years old at most. Someone built this partition to seal the passage and then installed a door to unseal it selectively."

"Can we get through?" Amaya asked.

Jackson shook his head. "Not without a warrant, and I don't know what's on the other side yet. If this connects to a private property, we need to establish whose property before we breach." He turned to one of the technicians. "Get me a GPS reading. I want to know exactly where we are relative to street level."

The technician consulted his device. "We're approximately one hundred and ninety feet northeast of the museum's foundation wall. Street level above us would be—" he checked the coordinates against his phone, "—131st Street. West side, mid-block."

Amaya felt the confirmation settle into place like a key finding its lock. 131st Street, mid-block, west side. Calvin Whitaker's gallery and storage facility sat at 247 West 131st Street.

She said nothing. Jackson caught her expression, a brief flicker of recognition that she regulated almost immediately, and held her gaze for a beat that told her he'd noticed, filed it, and would be asking about it later.

"We document and withdraw," Jackson said. "I'll get the property records for whatever's above us and start the warrant process. Nobody touches this door until I say so."

They retreated through the tunnel in silence, the CSI team collecting final samples as they went. Mayhem paused once more at the western branch junction, pulling toward it with the stubborn insistence of a cat who believed his opinion had been insufficiently respected. Amaya noted his reaction again—whatever scent the western passage carried, Mayhem considered it significant. That branch would need its own exploration.

But Mayhem wasn't finished. Twenty feet back from the junction, he dropped flat against the tunnel floor, his claws hooked into a hairline gap between two stone slabs that the swept surface had rendered nearly invisible. He wasn't playing; he was digging. Amaya crouched beside him and followed his eyes, and saw it: a small, recessed pull-ring hidden under a layer of dust and grit. She brushed it clear and tugged. Beneath the slab lay a waterproof case containing two portable hard drives, their indicator lights dark, their labels marked with alphanumeric coding she'd seen nowhere else in the passage. Digital provenance records for every piece they'd ever moved through this tunnel. Jackson's team would have walked right over it.

Derek resealed the drywall panel in the registrar's office with the same precision he'd used to open it, and the lower level returned to its ordinary appearance—climate-controlled vaults, fluorescent lighting, the faint hum of machinery. No sign that forty minutes ago, six people and two cats had walked through a century-old passage toward a locked door that shouldn't exist.

Amaya left the museum separately from Jackson, a precaution they'd agreed on without discussion—arriving and departing together would signal a law enforcement partnership to anyone watching, and the investigation's advantage depended on its targets not knowing how close the walls were closing.

She walked north on Lenox, the morning air sharp with the first real bite of November. The trees along the avenue had surrendered most of their leaves, the branches sketching dark lines against a sky that couldn't commit to blue or gray. She passed a coffee cart, a dry cleaner opening its gates, a group of women in matching track suits power-walking with the synchronized determination of a drill team.

Her phone buzzed. A text from Jackson: *Property records for 247 W 131st: commercial lease, Whitaker Art Advisory LLC. Warrant application in progress.*

Amaya read it twice, then deleted the thread. She opened a new message to Jackson: *I need 48 hours before you serve.*

His reply took less than a minute: *Why.*

I want to see the inside of that building before he knows we're coming.

A longer pause. Then: *You have 36. Don't do anything that compromises the warrant.*

She pocketed the phone and changed course, walking west toward 131st Street.

Calvin Whitaker's building was a converted warehouse, four stories of red brick with large factory windows that had been updated with modern glass. The ground floor housed the gallery's public-facing space, visible through a plate-glass storefront: white walls, track lighting, a few carefully positioned pieces that projected taste and discretion. A brass plaque beside the entrance read *Whitaker Art Advisory — By Appointment.*

Amaya had called ahead, using the pretext she'd prepared: a fictional client seeking an appraisal for a small collection inherited from a relative. Calvin's receptionist, a young man with an art-school haircut and a voice like warm honey, had offered her a Thursday morning slot. She'd taken it and spent the intervening day refining her cover and studying the building's public records.

The building had been purchased by a holding company three years ago. The holding company's registered agent was a law firm in Midtown whose client list was confidential. The purchase price—$2.1 million for a four-story commercial property in West Harlem—was below market value, suggesting either a distressed sale or a transaction between parties with a preexisting relationship. The property tax filings showed the building's assessed value had increased significantly since purchase, driven by renovations that the permits described as "interior buildout for commercial gallery and climate-controlled storage."

Climate-controlled storage. The same phrase appeared on Calvin's website. The same infrastructure required to house stolen artwork in conditions that preserved its value.

Thursday morning arrived cold and clear. Amaya dressed for the part, a structured wool coat, leather gloves, a silk scarf that suggested a woman accustomed to handling valuable things. She carried a portfolio case containing photographs of fictional artworks—prints she'd sourced from an online archive and described with enough specificity to pass casual inspection. Trouble, Chaos, and Mayhem stayed home. This visit required a different kind of camouflage, and after the tunnel, Amaya knew exactly what Calvin's building concealed beneath its polished surface. She didn't need the cats to find hidden passages today. She needed them to not give her away.

Still, as she rode the subway south, she felt the absence. It had become instinctive—consulting Trouble's reactions the way a pilot consults instruments, using Mayhem's physical responses as a secondary detection system. Without them, she was operating on her own senses alone. Her grandmother's training. Her years on the force. They were enough—they'd always been enough before the cats. But "enough" and "optimal" weren't the same thing, and she'd come to appreciate the difference.

Calvin met her in the gallery's reception area, and the transformation from gala host to professional consultant was seamless. Gone was the open collar and the amber drink; in their place was a fitted navy sweater over a dress shirt, reading glasses perched on his head, and a demeanor that projected scholarly authority. He shook her hand with the same warm, slightly prolonged grip she remembered from the museum opening.

"Ms. Mitchell." The alias she'd given. "Welcome. Let me show you the space, and then we can look at what you've brought."

The gallery's ground floor was elegant but restrained—six or seven pieces on display, each given generous wall space, the lighting calibrated to make the art glow without overwhelming. Calvin narrated as they walked, offering brief histories of each piece with the fluency of a man who genuinely loved what he sold. His knowledge was deep and specific, drawing connections between artists, movements, and market trends with an ease that was either the product of extensive education or extensive practice at appearing educated.

Amaya listened and watched. She complimented specific pieces, asked informed questions, and let Calvin enjoy the role of expert—people revealed more when they felt admired than when they felt interrogated.

As they paused in front of a Barkley Hendricks portrait, Amaya caught a scent—faint, threaded beneath the gallery's clean air. Familiar. The same solvent smell that had seeped through the tunnel door two days ago, the one that had made Mayhem sneeze. Here in the gallery, filtered through ventilation and distance, it was barely perceptible. But Amaya's nose had been calibrated by what the cats had found underground, and she recognized it like a signature.

Mayhem would have gone straight for it. He would have pressed his face to the floor vents, tracked the scent to its source, made a scene that Calvin couldn't ignore. Trouble would have stiffened, her ears flattening, her body telling Amaya that whatever lay beneath this polished surface was worth being afraid of.

Instead, Amaya smiled at the portrait and asked about the artist's market trajectory. She filed the scent and kept moving.

"Your storage facility," she said, as they paused in front of a small Alma Thomas painting whose colors seemed to vibrate on the canvas. "I've heard you offer climate-controlled vaulting. If my aunt's collection includes anything particularly sensitive, would that be an option?"

"Absolutely." Calvin's eyes brightened at the prospect of an expanded engagement. "Let me show you. We're quite proud of the facility."

He led her through a door at the back of the gallery and down a corridor that transitioned from the polished aesthetic of the public space to the functional architecture of a working storage operation. The corridor was well-lit, the walls lined with framed insurance certificates and climate-monitoring readouts. A security camera tracked their progress from a ceiling mount.

The storage area occupied the building's second and third floors—converted warehouse space with high ceilings, industrial shelving, and rows of art racks designed to hold framed works vertically without touching. Climate sensors dotted the walls at regular intervals, their digital readouts showing temperature and humidity within the ranges required for museum-quality conservation.

It was impressive. It was also, Amaya noted, significantly more storage capacity than a mid-tier art advisory firm would typically need. The racks were perhaps sixty percent occupied, which still represented dozens of artworks—paintings, prints, and framed works in various sizes, each tagged with inventory labels.

"How many pieces are you storing currently?" Amaya asked, keeping her tone casual.

"Roughly a hundred and forty across all clients. We handle private collectors, estates, and a few institutional clients who need overflow capacity." Calvin gestured toward a row of large-format racks. "These are from a collector in Connecticut who's renovating. We'll hold them for six months while the work is completed."

Amaya nodded, scanning the tags as they passed. The labels were coded—alphanumeric identifiers that didn't reveal the artworks' identities or owners. Efficient for a legitimate business. Also efficient for a business that preferred its inventory remain anonymous.

"And the basement level? I noticed the building has a sub-grade space."

The question was deliberate—precise enough to show she'd done research, casual enough to pass as the curiosity of a thorough potential client. She watched Calvin's reaction the way a card player watches the hand before the bet.

His response was smooth, delivered without hesitation. "The basement is our mechanical infrastructure —boilers, electrical, building systems. Not glamorous, I'm afraid." He smiled. "No art down there, just infrastructure."

It was a good lie. Clean, specific, delivered with the right amount of self-deprecation to forestall follow-up. A less attentive listener would have moved on.

Amaya was not a less attentive listener.

She'd watched Calvin's hands as he answered. Throughout the tour, his gestures had been open and expansive, a man comfortable in his space, eager to display it. On the basement question, his right hand had moved to his left wrist, adjusting his watch, a self-soothing gesture, unconscious, lasting less than a second. His feet, which had been angled toward her in the open stance of engagement, shifted to parallel, a subtle closing of posture that body-language research associated with concealment.

The basement was not just infrastructure. And Calvin knew she'd asked a question that mattered.

She didn't push. Pushing would alert him, and alerting him would trigger the same defensive maneuvers that had kept him ahead of law enforcement investigations for years. Instead, she returned to the appraisal pretext, opening her portfolio case and walking Calvin through the fictional collection with enough detail to justify a follow-up consultation. He quoted fees, discussed timelines, and offered to send a formal proposal, all the gestures of a legitimate business transaction.

They shook hands at the door. Calvin held the grip a beat longer than necessary, his eyes meeting hers with the same intelligent warmth she'd seen at the gala.

"I look forward to working with you, Ms. Mitchell."

"Likewise."

She walked half a block east before pulling out her phone and typing a note: *Storage facility 60% full. ~140 pieces, coded labels, no visible provenance documentation. Basement access restricted. Calvin displayed concealment response on basement question — watch adjustment, postural closing. Building connects to tunnel per GPS coordinates.*

She pocketed the phone and kept walking. The air was cold on her face, and 131st Street unfolded around her in the particular rhythm of a Harlem block transitioning from morning to midday—gates opening, deliveries arriving, the neighborhood asserting its daily identity with the confidence of a place that had been doing this for generations.

Somewhere beneath her feet, a tunnel ran south through century-old brick, connecting a gallery vault to a museum storeroom. And at one end of that tunnel, a man with a warm handshake and an easy smile had built a storage facility that held a hundred and forty pieces of art behind coded labels and climate-controlled vaults.

The question was no longer whether Calvin Whitaker was involved. It was how many of those hundred and forty pieces belonged to someone else.

Chapter 9: Cracks in the Foundation

Amaya was elbow-deep in the museum's financial records when someone knocked on her front door.

This was unusual. The duplex on Fieldston Road didn't get unannounced visitors. The building had a buzzer system at the street entrance, and anyone who made it past that was either a neighbor, or a delivery driver, neither of which improved Amaya's mood when she was working.

She saved her spreadsheet, closed the laptop, and went downstairs. Through the peephole, she saw a face she recognized but hadn't expected: Ron Devane, the artist who'd crashed the museum opening three weeks ago. He stood on her landing with his hands in the pockets of a canvas jacket, his shoulders hunched against the November cold, and an expression that was trying to be assertive but was closer to desperate.

Amaya opened the door but didn't step aside. "Mr. Devane."

"Ms. Storm." He met her eyes with the directness she remembered from the gala. No evasion, no performance. "I know you're investigating the museum thefts. I have information you need, and I didn't know where else to go."

"How did you find my address?"

"Your office is registered with the state. Your PI license lists this address as your business premises." A slight flush crept up his neck. "I looked it up. I'm not a stalker. I'm an artist who paints portraits of people he's never met based on public records and court sketches. Research is kind of my thing."

Despite herself, Amaya felt the corner of her mouth twitch. It was a good answer—honest, slightly self-deprecating, and specific enough to be verifiable. She stepped aside.

"Five minutes. And don't touch anything on the dining table."

Ron entered the duplex with the careful awareness of someone who understood he was in someone else's space uninvited. He took in the living room, the framed photos, the case files visible through the office doorway upstairs, the eclectic mix of comfort and function that defined Amaya's home. His gaze snagged briefly on the photograph of Eleanor in her dress blues, and something in his expression shifted—respect, or recognition, or the attention of an artist encountering a composition that interested him.

Chaos found him before Ron found the couch.

The ginger tabby had been asleep in a box of printer paper near the bookshelf, his current preferred napping location, chosen for reasons known only to himself, and the sound of an unfamiliar voice had launched him into full reconnaissance mode. He trotted across the room, circled Ron's ankles once, then sat directly in front of him and stared upward with unblinking intensity.

Ron looked down. "Hey, little man."

He crouched slowly, extending the back of his hand for Chaos to sniff. The gesture was unhurried, patient, the body language of someone who understood that trust was offered, not taken. Chaos investigated the hand thoroughly: the paint stains on his fingers, the charcoal residue under his nails, the faint scent of turpentine that clung to his jacket sleeve. After a thorough assessment, Chaos butted his head against Ron's knuckles and began to purr.

Amaya watched the exchange without comment. Chaos was the least discriminating of her three cats, his affection was available to most humans who demonstrated basic courtesy. But his reaction to strangers still carried data. People who were concealing hostility or deception tended to move too fast, reach too aggressively, or project tense energy that made Chaos retreat. Ron had done none of those things. His patience was genuine.

It wasn't exoneration. But it was information.

"Sit down," Amaya said, gesturing to the armchair. "Talk."

Ron settled into the chair with Chaos immediately claiming his lap, a development that seemed to surprise and please him in equal measure. Trouble, who had been observing from the top of the bookshelf, tracked the visitor but didn't descend. Mayhem was somewhere in the back of the duplex, his absence signaled by the faint sound of something being batted across a hard floor.

"My girlfriend works museum security," Ron began. "Keisha Williams. She's been on Derek Osei's team for two years—night shifts, mostly. She's good at her job, and she cares about the museum." He paused, his hand absently stroking Chaos's back. The cat's humming deepened. "Three weeks ago, she told me something that's been eating at me."

"Go on."

"On the nights when the thefts happened, all three of them—Keisha was scheduled for the overnight shift. But each time, about an hour before the event ended, she got a message from Emily Dawson telling her to stay out of the lower-level storage areas. The messages were framed as routine—'installation team needs the space cleared,' or 'VIP donor doing a private walkthrough, keep the corridors open.' But when Keisha mentioned it to Derek, he said he hadn't been apprised of any installation work or private walkthroughs on those nights."

Amaya's mind was already running the implications. Three theft nights. Three messages pulling security away from the storage areas. All routed through Emily, with justifications that didn't hold up against the actual event records.

"Did Keisha save the messages?"

"Screenshots. All three." Ron pulled his phone from his jacket and opened a photo album. He turned the screen toward Amaya. Three text messages from a contact labeled "Emily D — Museum," each one a variation on the same theme: *Can you keep your team on the upper floors tonight? We've got a sensitive walkthrough happening downstairs. Lydia's orders. Thanks!*

Lydia's orders. Amaya filed the phrase. Either Lydia had authorized the security stand-downs and lied to Amaya about not knowing how the thefts were executed, or Emily had used Lydia's name without authorization, a calculated invocation of authority designed to ensure compliance without verification.

"Why didn't Keisha report this?" Amaya asked.

Ron's jaw tightened. "Because she's a twenty-six-year-old Black woman working security at a museum where one theft has already made the news. She flagged it to Derek informally, and he told her to document everything and sit tight. But sitting tight means watching more art disappear while nobody listens to the person who actually noticed something was wrong."

The frustration in his voice was the same register as the anger he'd displayed at the gala, but directed differently. Not at the institution's curatorial choices but at the system's failure to hear the people closest to the problem.

"And you're coming to me because—"

"Because you're not part of their system. Keisha doesn't trust the police investigation. She thinks they'll look at Derek's record first and her second, and by the time they get around to actually investigating Emily, more art will be gone." He met Amaya's eyes. "And because I watched you at that opening. You weren't there to look at art. You were there to look at people. Specifically, you were watching Emily and that gallery guy—Whitaker, and you noticed something between them that made you pay attention."

Amaya kept her expression neutral, but internally she recalibrated. Ron was more observant than she'd credited. He'd caught her watching Calvin and Emily at the gala, the glances she'd noted between them, and he'd drawn the correct inference. His reputation as an artist who worked from observation and public records wasn't just a hobby; it was an analytical framework.

"You watch people for a living," she said.

"I paint them. Same thing, slower output." The ghost of a smile. "Look, I know how this looks—angry artist who got rejected shows up at a PI's door with information that conveniently points away from himself. But I'm not here because I have a grudge against the museum. I'm here because Keisha is scared, and the art that's being stolen belongs to a community that can't afford to lose it."

Chaos, still purring in Ron's lap, had begun kneading his thigh with rhythmic insistence, a behavior the cat reserved for situations where he was genuinely content. Amaya noted it the way she noted all of the cats' reactions: without interpretation, filed for context.

"I'll need to speak with Keisha directly," Amaya said. "And I'll need the original messages, not screenshots. I want the metadata."

"She'll talk to you. She's been wanting to talk to someone who'll actually listen." Ron's relief was visible, a loosening of the tension he'd carried through the door. "When?"

"Tomorrow. Somewhere private. Not the museum, not her apartment. Does she know the diner on Kingsbridge, Estrella's?"

"I'll make sure she does."

Ron stood carefully, transferring Chaos from his lap to the armchair cushion with the gentleness of someone who understood that disrupting a cat's comfort was a serious ethical breach. Chaos accepted the relocation with mild annoyance, resettling into the warm spot Ron had left behind.

At the door, Ron paused. "One more thing. Keisha told me that on the night of the third theft, the big one, the Okonkwo installation. She smelled something in the lower-level corridor. It smelled like paint thinner, but stronger. She mentioned it in her incident report, but nobody followed up."

The solvent. The same compound Jackson's lab had identified at the theft scene. The same chemical that Mayhem had detected behind the tunnel door and that Amaya had caught faintly in Calvin's gallery. Now a third source—Keisha's nose, in the museum corridor, on the night of the theft.

"Thank you, Ron."

He nodded, his expression settling into something more resolved than the desperation he'd arrived with. "Find whoever's doing this, Ms. Storm. That museum is the only institution in this city that's ever made me feel like my community's art matters. I'd rather be angry at it for rejecting my work than watch it get hollowed out from the inside."

He left. Amaya closed the door and stood in the quiet of her foyer, processing.

Ron Devane was either a genuine ally or the most sophisticated misdirection she'd encountered, a man using legitimate grievances and a sympathetic girlfriend to redirect the investigation away from him. The former was more likely. His body language, his patience with Chaos, the specific detail about the solvent smell, and his observation about the Calvin-Emily connection all pointed toward a person who was paying attention because he cared, not because he was covering tracks.

But she'd confirm before she trusted. That was the job.

She returned to the dining table, where the financial records waited. In the hour before Ron's arrival, she'd been tracing a new thread, one that had emerged from cross-referencing the museum's exhibition budgets with its actual expenditures. The discrepancy was subtle: for each of the three exhibitions where a theft occurred, the budgeted costs for installation and event production were significantly higher than the actual invoices from vendors. The difference—between $8,000 and $12,000 per event. The accountants recorded the difference under "miscellaneous production expenses" in the museum's books.

Miscellaneous production expenses that were authorized by Emily Dawson.

Amaya pulled the vendor invoices and laid them beside the budget summaries. The installation company was legitimate. She'd verified them independently. The catering firm was established and reputable. The AV company had a ten-year track record. None of them had been overpaid. Which meant the budget surplus—roughly $30,000 across three events—had been allocated to expenses that didn't correspond to any actual vendor.

Ghost invoices. Money flowing out of the museum under the cover of event production, landing somewhere that the standard financial review wouldn't catch because the line items looked routine and the totals weren't large enough to trigger an audit flag.

Where was the money going? The Whitaker consulting fees were a separate channel—those payments had corresponding (if undelivered) invoices from Calvin's firm. The ghost production expenses were something else. A second revenue stream, possibly funding the operational costs of the theft itself: the tunnel maintenance, the LED lights, the cinder block wall and steel door, the keypad system. Infrastructure didn't pay for itself.

Amaya added the new figures to her spreadsheet and drew a line connecting them to the Whitaker thread. Two financial channels, both managed by Emily, both pointing toward a planned operation that required ongoing investment.

Her phone buzzed. A text from Jackson: *Solvent purchase has been traced. Commercial account registered to Whitaker Art Advisory. Invoice dated six weeks before third theft. Enough for warrant enhancement.*

Amaya read it twice. The solvent, the specialty chemical used to dissolve the Okonkwo installation's adhesive anchors. It was purchased by Calvin's company. The physical evidence now connected directly to Whitaker Art Advisory, corroborating the tunnel, the financial irregularities, and the missing appraisal reports.

She started to type a response, then paused. Added: *Ron Devane came to me. His girlfriend works museum security. Has screenshots of Emily directing security away from storage areas on all three theft nights. Meeting her tomorrow.*

Jackson's reply came in two parts. The first: *Good. I want those messages.*

The second, arriving thirty seconds later: *Be careful with Devane. Haven't cleared him yet.*

She pocketed the phone. Jackson was right to maintain caution. Ron's convenient appearance at her door, loaded with useful information, deserved scrutiny regardless of how genuine he seemed. But Amaya's instincts were leaning toward trust, and so were the cats'.

Trouble had descended from the bookshelf at some point during Ron's visit and was now sitting on the dining table, directly on top of the budget spreadsheets, her gaze watching Amaya with an expression that managed to convey both judgment and solidarity. Chaos remained in the armchair, curled in the warm impression Ron had left, his contentment obvious from across the room. Mayhem had emerged from wherever he'd been hiding and was investigating the spot where Ron had stood by the door, his nose working the floor methodically. Not alarmed, not agitated, just cataloging the new scent with his usual thoroughness.

Three cats. Three reactions. None of them had flagged Ron Devane as a threat.

"Okay," Amaya said to the room. "We trust him provisionally. But we verify."

Trouble blinked once—slow, amber, definitive.

The spreadsheets could wait until morning. Amaya closed the laptop, poured herself a glass of wine, and sat in the armchair that Chaos had vacated for the couch. The duplex settled into its evening rhythm: Mayhem on the couch, Trouble on the back of the armchair behind Amaya's head, Chaos investigating the kitchen in case dinner had materialized in his absence.

Outside, Riverdale was dark and quiet. The streetlights on Fieldston Road cast amber pools on the sidewalk, and somewhere in the distance a train crossed the Broadway Bridge with the low rumble that Amaya had long since stopped hearing consciously but that formed part of the neighborhood's heartbeat.

She thought about Keisha Williams, a twenty-six-year-old security guard who'd noticed something wrong on three separate occasions, flagged it through channels, and been told to sit tight. She thought about Derek, who'd received the flag and done the cautious thing instead of the brave thing, and who was now watching his caution prove insufficient. She thought about the systems that were supposed to catch this, the audits, the oversight, the institutional checks, and how easily they'd been bypassed by someone who understood that systems trusted the people who operated them.

Eleanor's voice, clear as the Vegas sky: *The system isn't broken, Nhoma. It was built this way. Your job is to be better than it.*

Tomorrow, she'd meet Keisha. She'd get the original messages and their metadata. She'd cross-reference the timestamps with the access logs and the security camera footage, building the timeline that would transform circumstantial evidence into something a prosecutor could use.

And somewhere in this web of ghost invoices and underground passages and carefully directed security stand-downs, the shape of the conspiracy would finish resolving. Not with a dramatic revelation, but with the patient accumulation of details that left no room for alternative explanations.

That was how cases were built. Thread by thread, fact by fact, until the picture was complete and undeniable.

Trouble's tail brushed the back of Amaya's neck, a gesture that was either affection or a reminder that the cat considered herself the senior partner in this arrangement.

Amaya smiled in the dark and finished her wine.

Chapter 10: The Chelsea Connection

Keisha Williams was early.

Amaya arrived at Estrella's at eight-fifteen on Friday morning and found her already in a booth by the window, hands wrapped around a cup of coffee she hadn't touched. She was younger than Amaya had expected—twenty-six, Ron had said, but she looked twenty-two in the morning light, her braids pulled back in a neat bun, her posture tight with the tension of someone who'd made a decision to speak and was now waiting for the consequences to arrive.

Amaya slid into the opposite seat. She'd brought Chaos. Not for his investigative skills, but because the ginger tabby's presence had a way of softening the atmosphere in a room. Nervous witnesses talked more easily when something warm and uncomplicated sat within arm's reach. It was a technique she'd developed accidentally and now deployed intentionally.

Chaos, released from his carrier, hopped onto the booth seat beside Amaya and regarded Keisha with bright green eyes. Then, with the social instincts of a cat who'd never met a stranger he didn't want to charm, he walked across the table, stepped delicately over the salt shaker, and settled himself on the booth seat beside Keisha, pressing his flank against her arm.

Keisha's rigid posture softened by a degree. She looked down at the cat, and for the first time since Amaya had entered, something other than anxiety crossed her features. "Hey there."

"That's Chaos. He has no respect for personal space, but his intentions are good."

"I could use some of that right now." Keisha's hand found the cat's back and began to stroke—slowly, rhythmically, repetitive motion that grounded a person without them realizing it was happening. Chaos leaned into the touch and closed his eyes. His satisfaction was noticeable from across the table.

Marisol brought Amaya her usual coffee without asking and set a plate of tostones between them—unsolicited, as was Estrella's policy with anyone who looked like they needed feeding. Keisha glanced at the plate, then at Amaya.

"Eat," Amaya said. "We'll talk while you eat."

Keisha took a tostone, and the act of eating seemed to unlock something in her. She started talking—haltingly at first, then with increasing fluency as the story found its shape.

The messages from Emily had started six months ago, coinciding with the first theft. Keisha had been on the overnight shift, stationed on the lower level as part of Derek's standard post-event protocol. At 9:47 p.m., while the event was still winding down upstairs, Emily had texted: *Hey Keisha, can you keep your team on the upper floors tonight? Installation crew needs to prep the lower gallery for next week's rotation. Lydia approved it. Thanks!*

Keisha had complied. Emily was the director's assistant; her instructions carried implicit authority. When Keisha mentioned it to Derek the following week, he'd checked the installation schedule and found nothing. No crew had been authorized. No work had been done.

"He told me to document it and keep my eyes open," Keisha said, her voice dropping. "So I did. Next event, same thing—different excuse, same result. Emily asked me to pull coverage from the lower level. I flag it to Derek. He flags it." She paused. "Or he says he does."

"You're not sure he actually reported it?"

Keisha's hand stilled on Chaos's back. The cat opened one eye, assessed the situation, and nudged her fingers with his head, a gentle insistence that the petting resume. She complied absently.

"I trust Derek. He's a good man. But the third time it happened, the Okonkwo piece disappeared, and half a million dollars walked out of that building on a night when I was upstairs because Emily told me to be. Her eyes met Amaya's, revealing layered fear: she feared being blamed, feared being ignored, and feared that doing the right thing would cost her the job, the first stable employment she'd had since relocating to the city. "If I go to the police with this, what happens to me? I'm the guard who wasn't at her post."

"You were at your post. Someone who abused their authority redirected you." Amaya kept her voice level, factual, the tone she'd learned from Eleanor for moments when a witness needed steadiness more than sympathy. "The messages prove that. Can I see the originals?"

Keisha unlocked her phone and handed it across the table. Amaya opened the message thread with Emily and photographed each exchange, including the metadata: timestamps, delivery confirmations, read receipts. The messages were simple, specific, and devastating. Emily had directed security away from the storage areas on every theft night, using Lydia's name as authorization.

"One more question. On the night of the third theft, you reported smelling something in the lower-level corridor. What exactly did you smell?"

"Like paint thinner, but harsher. Industrial. It was in the corridor near the storage vaults. I noticed it when I did my walkthrough the next morning, before anyone knew the installation was gone." Keisha frowned. "I put it in my incident report. Nobody asked about it."

"I'm asking about it now."

Keisha studied her for a long moment—measuring, deciding. Then: "Ms. Storm, I don't care about my job if keeping it means watching that museum get gutted. Tell me what you need and I'll do it."

Amaya gave a slight nod. She gave Keisha her phone number, instructed her to forward the original message thread, and told her to continue her normal routine. "Don't tell Emily you've spoken to me. Don't change your behavior. If she contacts you about the next event, comply exactly as you have before."

Keisha agreed, finished the tostones, and left with the careful stride of someone who'd unburdened herself and was still adjusting to the lighter weight. Chaos watched her go from the booth seat, then turned to Amaya with an expression that seemed to ask whether they could keep her.

"I know," Amaya said. "I liked her too."

Two hours later, Amaya was in Chelsea with Jackson.

The auction house occupied the second floor of a converted warehouse on West 24th Street, a neighborhood where galleries and high-end dealers clustered like barnacles on a dock, each one projecting a combination of exclusivity and accessibility that the art market required. The building's exterior was industrial brick, softened by a frosted-glass entrance and a brass nameplate: *Barlow & Crane Fine Art Auctions.*

Jackson had gotten there first, his unmarked sedan was parked half a block east, and he stood on the sidewalk with two coffees, offering one to Amaya as she approached. The gesture was casual, unremarkable, and the first thing he'd done in their working relationship that wasn't directly connected to the case.

"Thanks," she said, taking the cup.

"You look like you've already had a morning."

"Interviewed Keisha Williams. Ron Devane's girlfriend, museum security. She has text messages from Emily Dawson directing security off the lower level on all three theft nights."

Jackson processed this in the way she'd expected. No visible reaction, the information absorbed and filed behind a steady gaze. "Originals?"

"Being forwarded to me today. Full metadata."

"Good. That's a pattern of deliberate misdirection tied to a named individual. Combined with the solvent purchase and the tunnel, we're building something a grand jury can work with." He took a sip of his coffee. "But we're not there yet. Let's see what Barlow and Crane have to say."

Cultivated taste defined the auction house's interior, with track-lit walls exhibiting current consignment pieces, glass cases housing smaller works, and a reception area appointed with chairs that conveyed a feeling of privilege. The air carried the scent of linseed oil and old money.

The director, a man named Philip Barlow—silver-haired, narrow-shouldered, wearing a three-piece suit that cost more than Amaya's monthly mortgage—met them in a private consultation room. His demeanor was cooperative in the specific way that people with expensive lawyers were cooperative: forthcoming with information that was already on the record, cautious about anything that wasn't.

"The piece in question was consigned to us approximately five weeks ago," Barlow said, sliding a file across the table. "A painting attributed to Nkechi Adeyemi—mixed media on canvas, thirty-six by forty-eight inches. The consignor provided provenance documentation that appeared legitimate at the time."

"Appeared," Jackson repeated.

"Our authentication process flagged inconsistencies after the piece was cataloged. The provenance chain included a bill of sale from a gallery that closed in 2019, which we were unable to verify independently. We suspended the listing and contacted INTERPOL's stolen art database." Barlow's composure was practiced but genuine. He was a man who took his reputation seriously and was visibly displeased that it had been compromised. "The painting matched the description of the first piece stolen from the Studio Museum."

Jackson opened the file and examined the provenance documents. Amaya leaned in beside him, close enough to read the papers, close enough to catch the faint scent of his soap. Something clean, unadorned, consistent with a man who didn't believe in cologne. She redirected her attention to the documents.

The provenance chain was three pages: a bill of sale from the defunct gallery, an authentication certificate from an unspecified appraiser, and a condition report dated two months prior. The papers were printed on heavyweight stock—cream-colored, textured, the kind of paper that conveyed legitimacy through its weight alone.

Amaya studied the authentication certificate. The appraiser's name was illegible—deliberately so, a scrawl that could be anyone's signature. But the letterhead caught her attention. It was generic—"Art Authentication Services"— with no address, no phone number, and a logo that was simply a stylized A in a circle. The kind of branding that existed only on paper, not in the world.

She ran her thumb along the edge of the certificate. The paper was distinctive. Not standard printer stock but a textured linen blend with a subtle watermark pattern. She'd handled paper like this before. Recently.

Calvin's gallery. The insurance certificates he showed her. She'd noticed the paper during her visit—heavy, linen-textured, with the same subtle watermark pattern that she was now holding in her hands.

"Detective Jackson," she said, keeping her voice neutral. "Can I borrow this for a moment?"

She held the certificate up to the consultation room's window, letting the light pass through. The watermark was faint, a repeating geometric pattern, barely visible to the naked eye, the kind of security feature that premium paper manufacturers embedded in their higher-end products.

"This paper is Crane and Company archive stock," she said. "It's a specialty product—archival quality, acid-free, used for legal documents, fine art certificates, and high-end stationery. It's not available at office supply stores. You order it through authorized dealers, and most of them require a business account."

Jackson was watching her with the focused attention of a detective recognizing a lead. "And you know this because?"

"Because I've handled this exact paper—same weight, same texture, same watermark. In Calvin Whitaker's gallery. He uses it for his insurance documentation."

Barlow looked between them, his composure cracking slightly. "Are you suggesting the provenance documents were created by—"

"I'm suggesting the paper can be traced," Amaya said. "The manufacturer will have sales records showing which business accounts have purchased this specific stock. If Whitaker Art Advisory is on that list, it connects the forged provenance documents directly to Calvin's operation."

Jackson was already on his phone, stepping into the hallway. Amaya could hear him giving instructions—terse, efficient, the controlled urgency of a detective who knew he was holding a thread that could unravel everything.

Barlow relaxed in his chair, his silver hair reflecting the light, his expression revealing the exhaustion of a man who had just seen his worst professional fears realized. "Ms. Storm, if this is what it appears to be, we will cooperate fully. My reputation depends on the integrity of every piece that passes through this house."

"I understand. We may need your records—consignment agreements, communication logs with the consignor, payment information."

"You'll have them by end of business today."

Jackson returned, pocketing his phone. "Paper manufacturer confirms the stock. Crane and Company, archive series. They're pulling the purchase records now." He looked at Amaya, and something in his expression had shifted. Not the professional respect she'd seen before, but something warmer beneath it, a recognition that went beyond competence into something harder to name. "How did you catch that? The paper?"

"I notice textures. It's an occupational habit."

"It's more than that." He held her gaze a beat longer than the conversation required, then seemed to catch himself. "Let's get back to the museum. I want those Keisha Williams messages in my hands before the end of the day."

They left the auction house together, stepping into the Chelsea afternoon. West 24th Street was alive with gallery traffic—well-dressed visitors drifting between openings, a photographer shooting a model against a graffiti-covered wall, a delivery truck double-parked while two men in white gloves unloaded a crated painting.

Jackson walked beside her, matching her pace without crowding, the spatial awareness of someone who was comfortable sharing sidewalk space without needing to fill it with conversation. They'd covered a full block in companionable silence before he spoke.

"Mott Haven."

Amaya glanced at him. "What?"

"You asked where I grew up. I grew up in Mott Haven." He didn't look at her as he said it, his eyes scanning the street in the habitual sweep of a cop who'd never fully turned off. "Different zip code from Riverdale, and a world away."

A small, intimate gift, given without obligation and with no expectation of anything back. A detail that a private man shared when he'd decided to open a door by a crack.

"My grandmother worked the four-four when Mott Haven was losing a building a week to arson," Amaya said. "She used to say the neighborhood had more courage per square foot than anywhere else in the city."

"She wasn't wrong." A pause. "Lot of that courage is still there. Just quieter now."

They reached the subway entrance. Jackson stopped, turning to face her. The afternoon light caught his jaw, and she noticed for the first time that it wasn't a straight line. It curved slightly, following the bone.

"Good work today, Amaya. The paper. That was the break we needed."

"It was a texture."

"It was a connection that nobody else would have made. Don't diminish it."

The directness of the statement—its refusal to let her deflect—landed with an unexpected weight. Amaya met his eyes and found nothing there but sincerity, which was in some way harder to hold than flattery would have been.

"Thank you, Alton."

His name in her voice. First time she'd used it. She watched it register, a small shift in his expression, a fractional softening around his eyes that was there and gone before the professional mask reasserted itself.

"Tomorrow," he said. "I'll have the paper records and the warrant timeline. We're getting close."

He descended into the subway. Amaya watched him go, then turned and walked north, her mind full of paper textures and provenance chains and the way Alton Jackson's voice had sounded when he'd said *Don't diminish it*, as if the words were meant for more than just the case.

She caught herself, the way she'd caught herself before. *Not the time.*

But the thought was getting harder to shelve, and she noticed she'd stopped trying quite as hard.

Chapter 11: Underground

The warrant for Calvin Whitaker's building came through on Monday morning, but Jackson held it. He wanted the tunnel mapped completely before they breached the door—wanted to know every exit, every branch, every possible escape route before they tipped their hand. It was cautious, methodical, and exactly what Amaya would have done.

They assembled at the museum at six a.m., before the staff arrived. Jackson, two CSI technicians, Derek, and Amaya. She'd brought all three cats this time. Trouble in her carrier, Mayhem on a reinforced leash, and Chaos in the soft-sided bag he'd come to associate with adventure. Jackson looked at the procession and said nothing, which Amaya interpreted as acceptance that had progressed beyond commentary.

Derek opened the drywall panel with the efficiency of someone who'd now done it three times and resented each occasion. The tunnel breathed its cool, air into the registrar's office, and they descended in single file. Derek on point, Jackson behind him, then Amaya with the cats, and the technicians bringing up the rear with their equipment.

The main passage was as they'd left it. The LEDs still glowed, the floor was still swept, and the locked steel door at the northeast end still hummed with the faint presence of whatever lay behind it. But today they weren't heading northeast. Today they were taking the western branch, the narrow corridor that Mayhem had strained toward on their first exploration, the one that had gone unexplored.

At the junction, Amaya unclipped Mayhem's leash.

Jackson raised an eyebrow. "You sure about that?"

"He flagged this branch two weeks ago. He knows something's down there, and he'll find it faster off-leash than on." She crouched beside the big black cat, her hand on his muscular shoulder. Mayhem's green eyes were fixed on the western passage, his body vibrating with contained energy, every line of him pointed forward like an arrow waiting for the string to release. "Go ahead."

He went.

Mayhem moved through the narrow passage with a purpose that transcended curiosity. His body was low, his paws placing with the deliberate care of a cat navigating uncertain terrain, his nose working the air in rapid bursts. The western branch was rougher than the main corridor, the walls were unfinished brick, the floor uneven, and the ceiling dropped to barely five feet in places, forcing Jackson and Derek to duck while the technicians cursed softly behind them.

There were no LEDs here. Derek's flashlight cut the darkness in a cone that swept the walls, revealing old graffiti—faded initials and dates from the 1920s and 30s, the kind of markings left by Prohibition-era runners who'd used these passages to move bootleg liquor between Harlem's speakeasies. History pressed close in these walls, layered like geological strata: abolitionists, bootleggers, and now art thieves, each generation repurposing the same hidden infrastructure for their own purposes.

Mayhem stopped. He was thirty feet ahead of the group, barely visible in the flashlight's reach, his body frozen in a crouch at the base of the left wall. His tail was rigid, his ears flat, and his head was angled downward toward something on the floor.

"Hold," Amaya said quietly. The group stopped. She moved forward alone, crouching beside Mayhem, and aimed her phone's flashlight at the spot where his attention was locked.

A footprint. Partial, pressed into a thin layer of dust that coated this section of floor—dust that the main passage's regular sweeping hadn't reached. The print was from a smooth-soled shoe, size ten or eleven, and it pointed west—deeper into the branch. It was crisp enough to be recent, no more than a few weeks old.

"Derek, bring the camera."

The CSI technician photographed the print from multiple angles while Amaya held Mayhem back, the cat was agitated now, pulling toward the passage ahead with the restless intensity of a hunter who'd caught the scent and didn't appreciate being held at the gate. Trouble, still in her carrier on Amaya's shoulder, had gone utterly still, the specific, tensed stillness that preceded her most reliable alerts.

They pressed deeper. The passage curved south, then west again, descending at a slight grade. The air grew cooler, damper, carrying a new scent beneath the stone and dust. Old wood. Damp earth. And, faintly, the chemical signature that had become the investigation's olfactory fingerprint: solvent.

Mayhem detected it before any of the humans did. He stopped mid-stride and sneezed, the same sharp, indignant reaction he'd had at the locked door two weeks ago. Then he turned his head and looked back at Amaya with an expression that communicated, as clearly as any spoken word, *I told you so.*

"He's getting the scent again," Amaya said.

Jackson moved up beside her, his flashlight sweeping the passage ahead. "How far does this go?"

"One way to find out."

Another hundred feet. The passage widened, the ceiling rising to a more comfortable height. The walls transitioned from rough brick to something older—hand-cut stone, massive blocks fitted without mortar in a style that predated the neighborhood's nineteenth-century development. They were in a deeper layer of Harlem's underground now, a section of passage that might have been part of the original infrastructure laid during the area's earliest settlement.

And then the passage opened.

Not into another corridor—into a room. A vaulted chamber roughly twenty feet square, the ceiling arched in a pattern that suggested it had once been a cellar or storage vault for a building that no longer existed above it. The stonework was old and solid, the air cool and still, and the space had been converted with the same careful, functional efficiency as the main tunnel.

Folding tables lined two walls, their surfaces covered with materials that Amaya cataloged in rapid succession: packing foam, acid-free tissue paper, bubble wrap, cardboard corner protectors, and a stack of custom-fitted wooden crates, the kind used to transport museum-quality artwork. A rack of tools hung on the far wall: utility knives, measuring tapes, a small power drill, and a heat gun used for shrink-wrapping protected surfaces. Beside the tool rack, two five-gallon containers of industrial solvent sat on the floor, their labels facing outward, the same brand and formula that Jackson's lab had identified at the Okonkwo theft scene.

A staging area. This was where the stolen artwork was received, repackaged for transport, and prepared for movement through the tunnel system to Calvin's building.

"Nobody touch anything," Jackson said, his voice carrying the compressed authority of a man who was looking at the physical confirmation of everything they'd been building toward. "Photograph the room, every surface, every item. I want prints, fiber, chemical samples. Everything."

The CSI technicians went to work. Derek stood at the room's entrance, his flashlight steady, his jaw set in the way it set when his professional composure was holding back something more volatile. He'd spent months watching his museum bleed while his security measures were systematically undermined. Now he was standing in the room where it happened, the operational heart of the conspiracy, hidden a hundred feet beneath the streets of the neighborhood he'd sworn to protect.

"Derek," Amaya said quietly.

He looked at her. In the flashlight's harsh light, the anger in his eyes was incandescent, but it was controlled—banked, directed, waiting for a legitimate target.

"We're going to get them."

He nodded once. It wasn't an expression of belief. It was a vow.

Amaya turned her attention back to the room. The staging area revealed itself in layers as the flashlights moved across its surfaces. The folding tables held more than packing materials. She cataloged a digital scale, a set of calipers, a magnifying loupe on a stand, and a stack of pre-cut foam inserts custom-shaped to hold specific artworks. Someone had measured each piece before it arrived here, prepared the packaging in advance, treated the logistics of theft with the same precision a museum registrar would bring to a legitimate loan.

On the second table, a laptop docking station sat beside a portable printer—both disconnected, their cables coiled neatly, but their presence confirmed that the operation included documentation. Provenance forgery, possibly. Authentication certificates printed on the same linen paper stock she'd identified at the Chelsea auction house. The digital infrastructure of fraud, maintained underground like everything else.

Mayhem had begun his own investigation while Amaya cataloged the tables. His nose pressed to the base of the folding legs, he worked his way along them with the systematic thoroughness of a crime scene technician who happened to weigh twenty pounds, pausing to sniff each joint where the metal met the floor, his whiskers brushing the concrete as he processed scent data invisible to every human in the room. He reached the far corner, where a canvas tarp had been thrown over a shape that rose from the floor. Something bulky, angular, approximately four feet tall.

Mayhem circled the shape once. He pressed his nose to its base, inhaled deeply, and his body stiffened, the reaction Amaya had learned to recognize as the moment his scent analysis shifted from cataloging to identifying. He knew something. Whatever was under that tarp carried a scent he'd encountered before.

He pawed at the tarp's edge. When it didn't yield, he grabbed it in his teeth and pulled. The canvas slid to the floor in a heap, and the flashlights converged on what it had concealed.

A bronze sculpture. A seated figure, abstract but unmistakably human, its surface catching the light with the deep patina of oxidized metal. Even in the harsh beam of Derek's flashlight, the piece radiated the kind of quiet authority that came from genuine artistry, the work of someone who had understood their material and their subject with equal depth. The figure's hands rested on its knees, palms upward, in a gesture that communicated both surrender and offering, a duality that a masterful sculpture could hold in a single pose.

Derek's breath caught. His flashlight wavered, then steadied. "That's the Edmondson."

The William Edmondson bronze. The second piece stolen from the Studio Museum, a sculpture from the permanent collection valued at $220,000, the work of a self-taught African American artist whose pieces were held by the Smithsonian and the Metropolitan Museum of Art. Edmondson had carved limestone, not cast bronze—this was one of the rare bronzes made from his original forms, a piece that represented not just an individual artist's genius but an entire tradition of Black American sculptural practice.

It had been missing for four months. It was sitting in an underground room beneath Harlem, covered by a tarp, waiting to be packaged and moved.

"Don't touch it," Jackson said, though no one had moved. "We photograph it in situ, document the covering, and leave it exactly where it is until forensics has processed the room." He looked at Amaya. "Your cat just found a quarter-million-dollar piece of stolen art."

"He likes to contribute."

Mayhem, having completed his revelation, sat beside the sculpture and began grooming his paw with the nonchalance of a cat who understood that dramatic moments were best followed by demonstrations of personal hygiene. His muscular body cast a shadow across the bronze figure, and for a moment, the flashlights catching both forms in the same beam, the living animal and the sculpted human seemed to share a quality: the absolute stillness of creatures at rest after effort.

Trouble, still in her carrier, had been quiet throughout the chamber's exploration. Not passive but processing, her body oriented toward the room's center, her ears rotating independently to track sounds from multiple directions. But as the technicians began their work and the flashlights swept the room in systematic passes, she vocalized. The sound was low, sustained. Not a growl, not a mew, but something between, a vibration that filled the stone chamber like a tuning fork struck against grief. It was the sound she made when the emotional atmosphere in a room reached an intensity that registered on whatever spectrum she monitored. Derek's anger. Jackson's grim resolve. The CSI team's professional detachment. Amaya's own complicated mixture of vindication and sadness. The chamber was saturated with human feeling, and Trouble processed it the way she processed everything: by acknowledging its presence without judging its content.

Amaya rested her hand on the carrier's mesh panel, and Trouble pressed her face against it, the gesture equivalent of taking someone's hand. "I know," Amaya whispered. "I feel it too."

Chaos, who had been remarkably quiet in his bag throughout the descent, chose this moment to announce his presence with a chirp of pure, uncomplicated enthusiasm. He'd wormed his way to the bag's mesh window and was watching the room with the bright-eyed wonder of a cat who'd discovered that the world contained underground chambers full of interesting things to investigate. His tail vibrated with excitement. When a CSI technician crouched near the bag to collect a floor sample, Chaos pressed his nose to the mesh and chittered at her, the sound a cat makes when something fascinating is just out of reach.

The technician glanced at Amaya. "Is he always like this?"

"He has two speeds: asleep and this."

Amaya smiled despite the weight of the moment. There was something clarifying about Chaos's reaction, his inability to assign moral weight to what he was seeing, his pure sensory engagement with a novel environment. Trouble felt the room's emotional charge. Mayhem found the evidence. And Chaos reminded her that discovery, even of terrible things, carried its own energy, the energy of moving forward, of uncovering, of refusing to be still when stillness meant looking away.

They spent two hours in the chamber. The technicians cataloged everything: the tools, the packing materials, the solvent containers, the sculpture, the docking station and printer.

Chaos, who had been vibrating with contained energy since his initial chirp, had finally been released from his bag at Amaya's discretion, the chamber was secured, the CSI team was working, and containing Chaos any longer would have produced a volume of protest that the stone walls would amplify into something approaching a car alarm. He hit the ground at full curiosity and began his exploration.

Where Mayhem worked methodically—nose to surface, systematic sweeps, a professional hunting approach. Chaos investigated the way a child investigated: everything, all at once, with no hierarchy of importance. He sniffed the folding table legs. He batted a loose screw across the floor. He attempted to climb the tool rack and was redirected by a technician who was clearly losing the battle between professional composure and the urge to pet him. He pawed at the solvent containers, recoiled from the smell, and moved on without shame.

And then he found the crack.

It was in the far corner of the chamber, where the stone wall met the concrete floor, a gap barely an inch wide, created by decades of settling in the old foundation. Chaos had wedged his face into it the way cats wedged their faces into every gap they encountered, operating on the feline principle that all openings led somewhere interesting. His paw followed his nose, reaching into the crack with the delicate, probing extension of a cat fishing for something just out of reach.

He pulled out a piece of paper.

It was small, two inches by three, crumpled and dusty, a scrap that fell from a pocket or a work surface and was carried by gravity into the nearest crevice. Amaya crouched beside him as he batted it across the floor, and she intercepted it before his teeth could add to its damage.

A shipping label. Partially torn, but the critical information was legible: a commercial shipping company's barcode, a destination address in Philadelphia, and a return address on West 131st Street. Calvin's building. The date was four months old, predating the second museum theft.

"Jackson." Amaya held up the label. "Philadelphia. Return address matches Whitaker's gallery."

Jackson crossed the chamber and took the label in a gloved hand, studying it under his flashlight. The Philadelphia address matched the city where Calvin had told her—on the Apollo bench. That one of his five non-museum acquisitions had originated. A gallery closing, its inventory sold to a developer. If this shipping label connected Calvin's operation to that acquisition, it corroborated his confession before he'd even made it and provided a paper trail linking the tunnel network to the broader trafficking operation.

"Your other cat just found a shipping manifest," Jackson said. His expression was caught between professional appreciation and something closer to bewilderment. "In a crack in the floor."

"Chaos doesn't believe in hierarchy. Every crack is worth investigating."

"I'm starting to think he's right."

Chaos, having been relieved of his discovery, had already moved on to investigating the canvas tarp that had covered the Edmondson bronze, pawing at its folds with the tireless enthusiasm of a cat who believed all fabric existed as potential bedding. The shipping label was already forgotten. The next study was underway.

The technicians also found a detail that Amaya might have missed if she hadn't been looking for it, a clipboard hanging from a nail on the wall near the entrance, containing a handwritten log.

The log was a record of dates and codes. No names, no descriptions, just alphanumeric entries that corresponded to the same coding system Amaya had seen on the inventory tags in Calvin's storage facility. Eight entries spanning six months. Three of them matched the dates of the museum thefts.

Eight entries. Three from the Studio Museum. Five from somewhere else.

The scope of the operation widened in Amaya's mind like a lens pulling back. This wasn't just about the Studio Museum. Calvin's network had been moving art from multiple sources through this staging area, the museum thefts were part of a larger trafficking operation that used the tunnel system as its logistics backbone.

She photographed the clipboard and showed it to Jackson. He studied the entries, his expression settling into the grim focus of a detective who'd just realized his case had grown.

"Five additional pieces from unknown sources," he said. "We need to cross-reference these codes against stolen art databases—INTERPOL, FBI Art Crime, the Art Loss Register."

"And against the coded inventory in Calvin's storage facility," Amaya added. "A hundred and forty pieces, all tagged with alphanumeric codes. If these codes match any of those tags, we can identify which pieces in his facility are stolen."

Jackson met her eyes. The case had escalated from museum theft to organized art trafficking, and they both knew what that meant—federal jurisdiction, multi-agency coordination, and a timeline that had just compressed from weeks to days. Calvin couldn't be allowed to move his inventory before the warrant was served.

"I'm accelerating the warrant," Jackson said. "We serve it Wednesday."

"What about the main tunnel door? The one connecting to his building?"

"We breach it when we serve the warrant. Both sides at once—entry team through the front door, a second team through the tunnel. No escape route."

Amaya looked around the chamber one last time. The stolen sculpture. The packing materials. The solvent. The log with its coded entries, each one representing a piece of art torn from someone's wall, someone's collection, someone's cultural heritage.

She thought about what Lydia had said in their first meeting: *Each one more significant than the last.* Lydia had been talking about three pieces. The truth was worse. Eight entries. Eight pieces, minimum, moving through a system that was still operating.

They retraced their path through the western branch, past the footprint that Mayhem had found, through the junction, and back up into the registrar's office. Derek sealed the panel. The museum's lower level returned to its institutional quiet, the hum of climate control and fluorescent lights reasserting the orderly surface that hid the infrastructure beneath.

Mayhem, back on his leash, walked with his head high and his chest forward, the posture of a cat who had located a something important and was not inclined to be modest about it. Trouble was quiet in her carrier, her eyes half-closed, processing. Chaos was trying to climb out of his bag to investigate the storage vaults, his curiosity already redirected toward the next unexplored space.

Three cats. Three modes of engagement. All three had contributed to the morning's work in ways that no human investigator could have replicated. Mayhem's scent-driven discovery of the footprint and the sculpture, Trouble's atmospheric reading of the chamber's emotional weight, and Chaos's irrepressible energy reminding Amaya that forward motion was its own form of courage.

Outside, Harlem was deep in its morning. The streets pulsed with the Monday energy of a neighborhood that had been resting and was now ready to work. A school bus rumbled past the museum. A vendor was setting up a table of books on the corner—African American literature, biographies, poetry collections, their covers bright against the gray November sky.

Amaya paused on the sidewalk and looked at the museum's facade. Glass and steel, modern and deliberate, built on a foundation that contained more history than its architects had bargained for. Inside, stolen art sat in climate-controlled vaults. Beneath it, a network of passages carried the evidence of crimes that extended beyond one institution.

And in two days, the warrant would come down, and the tunnels would give up the rest of their secrets.

She adjusted the carriers, gathered the leashes, and walked toward the subway. The cats rode in their various conveyances. Trouble watchful, Mayhem proud, Chaos straining toward whatever came next.

Wednesday was close. And they were ready.

Chapter 12: Trust Fractures

Amaya didn't confront Emily with the tunnel, the staging chamber, the solvent, or the Keisha Williams messages. She confronted her with a spreadsheet.

It was Tuesday afternoon, one day before the warrant. Jackson had asked her to apply pressure without tipping the operational timeline, and Amaya understood the assignment: shake the tree hard enough to see what moved, but not so hard that the tree fell before they were ready to catch what came out of it.

She'd requested a meeting at the museum under the pretext of reviewing the upcoming event budget. Emily had agreed without hesitation. She was, after all, the person who managed those budgets, and a routine review from Lydia's hired investigator was exactly the kind of oversight she would welcome to maintain her appearance of transparency.

They sat in the same staff break room where they'd first spoken. The coffee machine gurgled its perpetual cycle. Trouble was in her carrier beside Amaya's chair. Amaya had considered leaving her home—this conversation would be confrontational, and there was a risk that Emily would read the cat's presence as surveillance rather than comfort. But Trouble's reactions had become part of Amaya's investigative vocabulary, and she wasn't willing to go into this conversation without her best instrument.

Emily arrived precisely on time, a tablet tucked under her arm, her expression carrying the same composed warmth she'd projected since their first meeting. She wore a cream-colored blouse, small gold earrings, and the thin gold watch she touched when she was thinking. Her smile was calibrated for professional cooperation. Not too warm, not too guarded. Perfect pitch.

"Amaya, good to see you. I pulled the budget files for the upcoming gala. I thought we could walk through them together."

"Actually, I'd like to start with the last three events." Amaya opened her folder and placed two documents on the table: the event budgets for each theft-night exhibition and the corresponding vendor invoices. "I've been reconciling the numbers, and I've found some discrepancies I'd like to get an explanation for."

Emily's gaze dropped to the documents. Her expression didn't change, the composure held, seamless as always. But her hand moved to the tablet, adjusting its angle on the table. A micro-gesture. A recalibration.

"Of course. What are you seeing?"

"The budgets for all three events include line items classified as 'miscellaneous production expenses.' The amounts range from eight to twelve thousand dollars per event." Amaya pointed to the highlighted figures. "But when I match those budgets against the actual vendor invoices—installation, catering, AV, security, the invoiced amounts are consistently lower than the budgets. The surplus in each case corresponds almost exactly to the miscellaneous line items."

She paused, letting the numbers speak. Emily studied the documents with an expression of focused attention that could have been genuine concern or an excellent performance of it.

"In other words," Amaya continued, "roughly thirty thousand dollars across three events was budgeted, allocated, and disbursed, but it doesn't correspond to any goods or services that I can verify."

Emily's response came after a measured pause. Not the too-fast "absolutely not" of their first interview, but a careful, deliberate beat that signaled she was choosing her words. "Miscellaneous production expenses cover a range of things that don't always generate formal invoices. Last-minute supplies, emergency repairs, overtime for freelance staff—it's a catch-all category."

"Can you show me the receipts?"

Another pause. Longer this time. Emily's fingers moved to her watch, the familiar self-soothing gesture, and then to her tablet, where she opened a folder and scrolled

with the focused energy of someone searching for
something they knew wasn't there.

"I'd need to pull those from the physical files. Some of
these expenses were paid in cash, and the documentation—
"

"Cash payments of eight to twelve thousand dollars
without formal receipts or purchase orders." Amaya kept
her voice neutral, factual, the tone of an auditor rather than
an adversary. "That's outside the museum's standard
financial protocols, isn't it?"

Emily's composure shifted. Not cracked. Emily was too
disciplined for cracks. But the surface tension changed. Her
posture straightened. Her chin lifted. The warmth in her
expression cooled into something more angular, more
defensive.

"Amaya, I've managed this museum's event operations
for seven years. The budgets have always balanced. Every
dollar has been accounted for in the quarterly reports that
Lydia reviews and the board approves." Her voice carried
an edge that hadn't been there before. Not anger, exactly,
but the sharpness of a person who felt their competence
being questioned. "If there are discrepancies, they're
administrative—filing delays, documentation gaps. Not
malfeasance."

In the carrier, Trouble had gone still. Not relaxed-
still—alert-still. Her amber eyes were fixed on Emily's face
with the unbroken intensity she reserved for moments
when the emotional temperature in a room spiked. Amaya

could feel the cat's focus like a current running through the carrier's mesh panel against her leg.

"I'm not suggesting malfeasance," Amaya said. "I'm asking for the documentation that supports these expenditures. If it exists, the discrepancy resolves itself. If it doesn't—"

"It exists." Emily's voice was firm, but the firmness had a quality Amaya recognized from a hundred interrogations during her NYPD years: the insistence of someone building a wall, brick by brick, to hold back whatever was pressing from the other side. "I'll compile it and have it to you by the end of the week."

"I'd like it by tomorrow."

The request landed like a stone. Emily's eyes narrowed, a fraction, barely perceptible, but enough for Amaya to register the shift from defensive to calculating. She was reassessing. Not the financial question, the situation. Amaya's timeline, Amaya's tone, the fact that this conversation had moved from routine review to something with teeth.

"Tomorrow is ambitious. But I'll do my best." Emily stood, collecting her tablet with the smooth efficiency that characterized all her movements. Her smile returned— thinner than before, the warmth diluted by something colder underneath. "Is there anything else?"

"One thing. The appraisal reports from Whitaker Art Advisory. Three invoices over eighteen months, no corresponding reports in the registrar's files. Thomas

Yeboah flagged them months ago. He routed the follow-ups through you."

Emily's hand stopped on the tablet. The pause was brief, two seconds, maybe three. But in the controlled environment of Emily Dawson's self-presentation, it was an eternity. When she spoke, her voice was level, but the calibration had shifted. She was no longer managing an interaction; she was navigating one.

"I'll look into it. Thomas's filing system can be inconsistent."

"Thomas's filing system is meticulous. I've been through it."

Their eyes met. The staff break room hummed with the quiet tension of two people who both understood that the conversation had crossed a threshold from which there was no casual return. Emily's expression held—polished, professional, betraying nothing obvious. But Amaya had been reading people since she was eight years old on a bench in Crotona Park, and what she read now was a woman who had just realized that the investigation was further along than she'd estimated, and who was recalculating her options in real time.

"I'll get you what you need," Emily said. Her voice was perfectly steady. Her hand, as she turned to leave, trembled once against the edge of her tablet before she corrected it.

The door closed. Amaya exhaled. Trouble vocalized, a low, sustained note that filled the empty room like a tuning fork, the cat's way of acknowledging that something significant had just shifted in the air.

"Yeah," Amaya said quietly. "I saw it too."

She sat in the break room for a moment after Emily left, letting the encounter settle. In the space where Emily had been sitting, the air still carried traces of her perfume. Something clean, floral, expensive enough to be understated—mingling with the notable scent of adrenaline that the human nose couldn't detect but that Trouble, pressing her face against the carrier mesh, was cataloging with focused attention.

Amaya replayed the conversation in her mind. Emily's composure had held through the financial questions—strained, but intact. The pivot to "catch-all category" had been smooth, practiced, the response of someone who'd anticipated the question. But the Whitaker reports had broken through. The moment Amaya said "Thomas's filing system is meticulous," Emily's calibration had shifted from managing to surviving. The trembling hand on the tablet wasn't performance. It was the involuntary betrayal of a body that knew the mind was losing a fight it had been winning for years.

Trouble had tracked every shift. The cat's ears had rotated like radar dishes through the interview—toward Emily's voice when the pitch changed, toward her hands when they moved on the cup, toward the door when Emily's footsteps retreated down the hallway with a pace that was carefully measured but faster than her arrival. Trouble processed people the way seismographs processed the earth: not through understanding but through registration, the faithful recording of tremors that preceded larger events.

Amaya opened the carrier and let Trouble out. The cat jumped onto the break room table, circled the spot where Emily's tea cup had rested, and sniffed the ring of condensation left on the surface. Then she sat, her tail curled around her paws, and looked at Amaya with an expression that communicated, as clearly as language ever could: *That one is afraid.*

"I know," Amaya said. "That's what makes tomorrow dangerous."

She gathered Trouble, secured the carrier, and left the break room.

She found Lydia in the third-floor corridor.

Not in her office. In the hallway outside it, standing at the window that overlooked 125th Street, her arms crossed, her reflection ghosted in the glass against the gray afternoon. She didn't turn when Amaya approached, but she knew she was there. Her voice came flat, drained of the practiced warmth that usually animated it.

"You spoke with Emily."

"Yes."

"And?"

Amaya stood beside her at the window. Below them, Harlem moved through its afternoon, a delivery truck double-parked, a woman pushing a stroller past the museum's entrance, two teenagers sharing earbuds on a bench, their heads bobbing to a rhythm only they could hear. The world outside was doing what the world outside always did: continuing, regardless of what crumbled within the walls above it.

"Lydia, I can't share the specifics of my findings until the investigation is complete. But I need to ask you something, and I need an honest answer."

Lydia's reflection in the glass closed its eyes. The real woman, standing beside Amaya, did the same. "Ask."

"Did you ever authorize Emily to direct security personnel away from the lower-level storage areas during exhibition events?"

The silence that followed was the loudest thing Amaya had heard in weeks.

"No." The word came out cracked, split down the middle like a stone that had been bearing weight for too long. "No, I never—" Lydia's hand went to her mouth. Her composure, the professional mask she'd worn every day for nine years, the armor that had allowed her to stand in rooms full of donors and critics and board members and project confidence while her museum was being stripped from beneath her, all of it came apart.

She didn't sob. It was worse than that. She made no sound at all. Her shoulders drew inward, her hand pressed harder against her lips, and tears tracked down her face in silence, her grief would not be permitted to make noise.

Amaya stood beside her and said nothing. There was nothing to say that wouldn't diminish the moment. Lydia wasn't crying because she'd learned something new. She was crying because the thing she'd suspected and fought against believing had just been confirmed by a question whose answer she already knew.

Emily had used Lydia's name. Had invoked her authority. Had directed security away from the art using the trust that Lydia had spent seven years building and Emily had spent seven years absorbing.

After a minute, Lydia lowered her hand. Her eyes were red, her breathing controlled but ragged at the edges. She stared at the street below with an expression that had moved beyond grief into something harder, a resolve that had been tempered, not broken, by the impact.

"What do you need from me?"

"Tomorrow, I need you to act exactly as you would on any normal day. Emily will be watching for signs that the investigation has escalated. If she sees changes in your behavior—distance, coldness, anything that breaks the pattern—she'll know, and she'll act. I need her to believe that today's conversation was uncomfortable but routine."

"You want me to look her in the eye and pretend I don't know what she's done."

"I want you to protect your museum for one more day."

Lydia turned from the window. Her face was composed again. Not the practiced composure of performance but something rawer, willed into existence by the same determination that had built the institution in the first place. "One more day."

"One more day."

Lydia nodded. She straightened her blazer, touched the corners of her eyes with her fingertips, and walked toward her office. At the door, she stopped without turning.

"Amaya."

"Yes."

"When this is over—however it ends. I want to understand how I missed it. Not the financial details or the security gaps. How I missed what was happening to someone I considered family." Her voice held steady, but barely. "I owe myself that much."

She entered her office and closed the door with the quiet precision of someone determined to hold every remaining thing together.

Amaya stood in the corridor alone. Through the window, 125th Street continued its afternoon. The delivery truck pulled away. A new group of visitors entered the museum's lobby. Somewhere inside, Emily Dawson was sitting at her desk, compiling documentation that didn't exist for expenditures that had never occurred, calculating how long she had before the walls closed in.

Trouble shifted in her carrier, a small movement, almost imperceptible, the cat resettling against the mesh panel that rested against Amaya's hip. The warmth of it— steady, undemanding, present. It was the only comfort available in a building full of heartache.

Amaya rested her hand on the carrier.

Tomorrow, the warrant. Tomorrow, the breach. Tomorrow, the careful architecture of lies that Emily and Calvin had built would meet the evidence that Amaya, Jackson, Derek, and three cats had assembled over the course of weeks that felt like months.

But tonight, a woman was sitting behind a closed door in a museum she'd built, mourning a betrayal she hadn't seen coming by the person she'd trusted most.

There was no investigation protocol for that. No evidence collection. No chain of custody.

Just the quiet sound of a closed door, and the city moving on outside.

Chapter 13: The Artist's Angle

The call from Derek came at seven in the morning, before Amaya had finished her first cup of coffee.

"I need to tell you something, and I'd rather do it in person." His voice carried the weight of a man who'd spent the night deciding whether to speak and had landed on the side of exposure. "It's about the money."

The $8,200 cash deposit. The detail from his background check that had sat in Amaya's files like an unexploded device—too small to trigger the investigation's main alarm, too anomalous to ignore. She'd been waiting for it to resolve itself, either through evidence that connected it to the conspiracy or through an explanation that removed it. Derek was offering the latter, and the fact that he was offering it voluntarily told her something about the man before she heard a word.

"Estrella's. Eight-thirty."

He was there when she arrived—same booth Keisha had used, different posture. Where Keisha had been coiled with anxiety, Derek sat with the upright stillness of someone who'd made peace with a difficult decision and was prepared to execute it. He wore civilian clothes, a dark sweater, jeans, work boots, and without the security uniform, he looked both younger and more weary.

Amaya had brought Trouble. Not as an investigative instrument. Derek had already proven himself through weeks of cooperation. But because the cat's presence signaled something to witnesses that words couldn't: *this is not an interrogation. This is a conversation.*

Trouble, released from her carrier, claimed a spot on the booth seat and watched Derek with amber eyes that held no judgment, only attention.

"The deposit," Derek said, skipping pleasantries. "Eighty-two hundred dollars, six weeks ago. You saw it in my background check. I know you ran one, and I'd have done the same thing."

"I did."

"It was a loan repayment. My cousin in Accra. He borrowed money from me three years ago to start a small business. Electrical work, commercial buildings. The business took off, and he paid me back in full. He wired the money I took it in cash at pickup." Derek reached into his jacket and produced a folded document, a Western Union receipt, dated six weeks prior, showing a transfer from Accra, Ghana, to a pickup location in the Bronx. The amount was $8,200. "I didn't deposit it immediately because the wire arrived on a Friday and I don't bank on weekends. By Monday, I'd forgotten about it. I deposited it that Thursday."

The receipt was genuine. Amaya could tell from the document's condition, the printing quality, and the specific formatting of Western Union's international transfer confirmations. She photographed it and handed it back.

"Why didn't you mention this when I started the investigation?"

Derek's expression didn't waver, but his hands—resting flat on the table—pressed slightly harder against the surface. "Because I was ashamed. Not of the money—of what it looked like. I knew the deposit would raise questions. I knew my record, the juvenile conviction— would color how people read it. And I made the calculation that explaining it preemptively would draw more suspicion than letting it sit." He paused. "That was a mistake. I should have been transparent from the beginning."

Amaya studied him across the table. Derek Osei was a man who had spent twenty-six years outrunning a shoplifting conviction he'd committed as a teenager— building a military career, earning security certifications, constructing a professional identity so meticulous that a single cash deposit could threaten its credibility. The injustice of it, a man forced to justify legitimate family money because his past had made him permanently suspicious—sat in the booth between them like an uninvited guest.

"Derek, I cleared you as a suspect ten days ago."

His hands stilled. "What?"

"Your keycard logs don't support involvement. Your security memos demonstrate you identified the vulnerabilities that were exploited and tried to close them. Your behavior throughout this investigation has been consistently protective of the museum and hostile to whatever was happening beneath it." She met his eyes. "The deposit was a question mark. It's now answered. But it was never the reason you were on my board."

Something moved behind Derek's features. Not relief exactly, but the slow unclenching of a tension he'd been carrying. He looked down at the table, then at his hands, the hands of a man who'd spent twenty-six years building a professional identity on the foundation of a single teenage mistake, each year another brick in a wall between who he was and who a background check said he'd been.

Trouble, who had been resting with the patient stillness she maintained in the presence of people she'd already assessed, rose to her feet. She pressed her nose against the table facing Derek, her gold eyes level with his, and held his gaze with the quiet intensity she reserved for moments when the emotional register of a room shifted from surface to depth. Then she blinked, the slow, deliberate closure that was her highest signal of acceptance.

Derek noticed. His eyes moved from his hands to the cat, and something in his expression changed, a softening that he might not have permitted himself in the presence of another human but that he allowed in the presence of an animal whose judgment carried no institutional history, no record, no preconceptions. Trouble saw him as he was now. That was enough.

"Thank you," he said. The words were directed at Amaya, but his eyes were still on the cat, and the effort they cost was visible.

"Don't thank me. Thank your cousin's electrical business."

The ghost of a smile. First one she'd seen from Derek Osei. It changed his face—opened it, briefly, into the version of the man who existed beneath the uniform and the vigilance and the controlled anger. It was the face of someone who might, given time and trust, actually laugh.

They spent another twenty minutes reviewing the operational plan for tomorrow's warrant service. Derek would be positioned at the museum's lower level, managing the tunnel entry point and ensuring that the staff— particularly Emily—couldn't access the registrar's office or the sealed drywall panel. His knowledge of the building's layout and security systems made him essential to the operation, and Jackson had formally requested his cooperation through Lydia.

As they wrapped up, Amaya raised the last thread. "Ron Devane. What's your read?"

Derek considered the question with the same deliberate attention he applied to everything. "He's angry. He has reason to be, the museum's curatorial process has gaps, and some of those gaps have names attached. But anger isn't motive for theft, and Ron doesn't have the access, the resources, or the temperament for what's been happening."

"His girlfriend brought me Emily's text messages."

"I know. Keisha told me." Derek's jaw set. "I should have pushed her testimony harder when she first flagged the security stand-downs. Instead, I told her to document and wait. I was trying to protect her from exposure, and what I actually did was delay the investigation."

"You were trying to protect a junior employee in a vulnerable position. That's not a failure of judgment—it's a conflict between competing responsibilities."

"It felt like a failure."

"Most responsible decisions do, in hindsight." Amaya finished her coffee. "For what it's worth, Keisha's documentation was the cleanest evidence I've received in this entire case. She kept every message, every timestamp, every detail. That's because you taught her to document. Your training is the reason we have the proof."

Derek absorbed this quietly. He was not, Amaya had learned, a man who accepted compliments easily. Not because he lacked confidence but because he held himself to standards that made praise feel premature until the work was completely finished.

"Tomorrow," he said, standing. "We finish it."

"Tomorrow."

He left with the measured stride of a man who'd unburdened himself and was already redirecting his energy toward the task ahead. Trouble watched him go, then turned to Amaya and yawned, a full, unhurried yawn that exposed every tooth and communicated, in Trouble's particular vocabulary, that the morning's drama had been noted and cataloged and that breakfast was now overdue.

"You're right," Amaya said. "Let's go home."

The afternoon brought Ron.

Not to Amaya's door this time. She'd called him. They met at a coffee shop on Broadway near 231st, a place with exposed brick walls and too many plants that had opened six months ago and was either a sign of the neighborhood's gentrification or its vitality, depending on whom you asked.

Ron arrived with paint on his hands—cobalt blue in the creases of his knuckles, a smear of cadmium yellow on his forearm. He'd been working. The intensity that had radiated from him at the museum opening and at her doorstep was still present, but it had been refined—channeled into whatever he'd been painting that morning rather than dispersed as unfocused anger.

Chaos had come along for this meeting. The ginger tabby sat on the chair beside Amaya, his green eyes tracking the coffee shop's traffic with the tireless enthusiasm of a cat who found all human activity endlessly fascinating. When Ron sat down, Chaos immediately reached a paw toward the blue paint on his knuckles, drawn to the color like a magnet.

"He likes your palette," Amaya said.

Ron let Chaos investigate his hand, the cat's nose pressing against each paint-stained finger with the focused attention of a quality inspector. "Tell him I'm working on something new. A series about the museum. Not the building, the idea of it. What it means to a neighborhood when someone builds a house for your art and then someone else hollows it out."

"That sounds like something the museum should show."

"Maybe. If there's still a museum when this is done." Ron pulled his hand back gently when Chaos's investigation progressed to licking. "What did you need to tell me?"

"Two things. First—Keisha's testimony is central to our case. The messages she preserved are the strongest evidence we have connecting Emily Dawson to a pattern of deliberate interference with museum security. She should be proud of what she did."

Ron's expression softened. Not into gratitude but into a deeper recognition. "She's been carrying that weight for months. Knowing she wasn't imagining things. That it mattered—that's going to mean everything to her."

"Second thing. Tomorrow, law enforcement is executing search warrants connected to the museum theft investigation. I can't give you details, but I'm telling you because the aftermath will be public, and I want you and Keisha to hear it from me before you hear it from the news."

Ron leaned back, processing. The coffee shop buzzed around them, the hiss of the espresso machine, a couple arguing cheerfully about whether oat milk qualified as a legitimate dairy alternative, a child at the window table drawing on a napkin with a crayon while her mother worked on a laptop.

"Is it who I think it is?"

"I can't confirm that."

"You don't have to. I watched Emily work that room at the opening. I watched her manage Lydia, manage the staff, manage the guests—manage everything like a conductor who'd memorized the score. And I watched you watch her do it." He paused. "People who control that much don't do it because they love the music. They do it because they need to own the orchestra."

It was a sharp observation—an insight that came from someone who spent their life studying human behavior through the lens of representation. Ron painted people. He understood facades and what they concealed.

"When this is over," Amaya said, "the museum is going to need voices from the community. People who can speak to what the institution means and what it should become. Your voice matters, Ron. The anger you brought to that opening, the frustration about whose art gets shown and whose gets rejected—that's a conversation the museum needs to have."

Ron looked at her for a long moment. The anger was still there. It would probably always be there, woven into the fabric of a young artist's relationship with institutions that held the keys to visibility. But it had company now:

purpose, recognition, the beginning of a belief that being heard was possible.

"You know what's funny?" he said. "I came to you because I was pissed off and scared. I thought you'd take the information and shut me out. Instead, you're sitting here telling me my voice matters." He scratched Chaos behind the ears, and the cat leaned into the touch with shameless pleasure. "This one's got good instincts. He trusted me before you did."

"He trusts everyone who gives him attention. His standards are lower than mine."

Ron stood, leaving money on the table for both coffees. "Tomorrow. Whatever happens—good luck."

"Thank you, Ron."

He left the coffee shop with paint on his hands and something lighter in his stride. Through the window, Amaya watched him merge into the foot traffic on Broadway, a young artist in a neighborhood that was changing around him, carrying anger that had started to find its shape.

Chaos chirped from his chair, his attention already redirected toward a crumb on the table that demanded immediate investigation. Amaya let him have it.

Two suspects cleared. Derek's deposit explained, his integrity confirmed, his role in tomorrow's operation secured. Ron's trajectory shifted from grievance to potential advocacy, a transformation that had nothing to do with the investigation and everything to do with the kind of person he'd been all along, once someone bothered to listen.

Tomorrow, the remaining suspects, the ones whose explanations wouldn't resolve into innocence—would face the evidence. The warrant, the breach, the convergence of weeks of work into hours of action.

Amaya gathered Chaos, who protested the departure with a chirp of indignation, and walked home through Riverdale's quiet streets. The evening was coming on—early dark, November pressing its advantage, and the duplex would be warm, the cats would be waiting, and the case file on her dining table would be open for one last review before morning changed everything.

One more night of preparation. One more night of the careful, patient structure that Eleanor had taught her to build.

Tomorrow, they'd knock on the door.

Chapter 14: Dinner and Deduction

The restaurant was Alton's choice, a Dominican place on St. Nicholas Avenue in Washington Heights called La Reina, wedged between a barbershop and a shop selling quinceañera dresses. The facade was unremarkable: a hand-painted sign, a few tables visible through a steamed window, and a door that exhaled the scent of garlic, sofrito, and slow-cooked pernil into the November evening like an invitation you couldn't refuse.

Amaya arrived at seven. She'd gone home first to feed the cats, which had taken longer than expected because Chaos had discovered that the bag of dry food could be opened from the bottom if he worked at it with sufficient determination, and by the time Amaya found him, he'd emptied approximately two pounds of kibble onto the kitchen floor and was sitting in the middle of it like a ginger monarch surveying his kingdom.

Mayhem, who possessed no scruples about eating stolen food, had stationed himself at the perimeter of the spill zone and was working his way inward with the systematic efficiency of a snowplow. Trouble watched from the kitchen counter with an expression of profound contempt for both of them.

The cleanup had taken fifteen minutes. The cats were now fed, the floor was swept, and Amaya had changed into a dark green sweater and jeans that were nicer than her work jeans but not so nice that anyone—including herself—could accuse her of dressing up.

She was not dressing up. This was a working dinner.

Alton was already at a corner table when she entered, his sport coat hung on the back of his chair, his shirtsleeves rolled to the forearm. He stood as she approached, a reflex, and she caught herself noticing the way the restaurant's warm light caught the gray at his temples and the smooth brown of his forearms below the rolled cuffs.

Working dinner.

"You found it," he said.

"My grandmother would disown me if I couldn't find a Dominican restaurant in Washington Heights." She sat down, and the table between them was immediately occupied by a basket of tostones, a dish of pique sauce, and two sweating bottles of Presidente. The beer had appeared without either of them ordering it, the waitress, a woman in her sixties, had sized them up in a single glance and made executive decisions.

"She's good," Amaya said, nodding toward the retreating waitress.

"She's been here thirty years. She knows what cops eat before an operation." He took a pull from his beer. "We should talk about tomorrow."

They talked about tomorrow.

The warrant would be served simultaneously at two locations: Calvin Whitaker's gallery on 131st Street and the underground staging chamber accessed through the museum's tunnel system. Jackson's team would enter Calvin's building through the front door at 8:00 a.m., executing the search warrant while a second unit breached the tunnel's steel door from the museum side. The dual-entry strategy eliminated escape routes. If Calvin attempted to flee through the tunnel, he'd meet law enforcement coming from both directions.

Emily Dawson would be detained at the museum by officers positioned in the lobby, acting on an arrest warrant for fraud, conspiracy to commit grand larceny, and obstruction. Derek would manage the museum's internal security during the operation, ensuring that staff were accounted for and that the building's public areas were secured.

Amaya's role was advisory. She'd be at the museum, coordinating with Jackson's team via radio, available to provide real-time intelligence on the building's layout and the suspects' behavioral patterns. She wouldn't be entering Calvin's building or the tunnel during the operation. Jackson had been firm about that.

"You've given us everything we need to execute this. But when we breach, it's law enforcement only. No PIs, no consultants, and—" he'd paused, a faint smirk threatening, ". No cats."

"Mayhem will be disappointed."

"Mayhem found a quarter-million-dollar sculpture. He's earned a day off."

The operational details took forty minutes. They covered contingencies—what if Calvin wasn't at his gallery, what if Emily attempted to destroy evidence, what if the tunnel contained hazards the previous exploration hadn't revealed. Jackson's planning was thorough, layered, the work of a detective who'd run enough operations to know that the ones that went sideways were the ones where someone assumed everything would go right.

When the plans were settled and the plates arrived— mangu, stewed chicken, a mountain of rice and beans that could have fed a family of four, the conversation shifted. Not dramatically, not with a declared transition, but with the natural drift of two people whose professional obligations had been discharged and who found themselves still sitting across from each other with things left to say.

"How'd you end up with three cats?" Alton asked, breaking a tostoné in half.

"Trouble found me. Showed up on the fire escape four years ago, decided the accommodations were acceptable, and never left." Amaya took a bite of the mangu—perfectly mashed, rich with butter, the plantain's sweetness balanced by the salt of the accompanying salami. "Mayhem was a rescue. A narcotics case I consulted on, the suspect's apartment had a cat that animal control was going to take to the shelter. He was underweight, aggressive with the officers, and had apparently bitten the arresting detective twice."

"Sounds like a liability."

"He was scared. He'd been living with someone who used him as a prop—kept him around to look unassuming, didn't feed him properly, never took him to a vet. The shelter would have labeled him unadoptable." She shrugged. "I took him home. He bit me once, hid under the bed for three days, and then decided I was acceptable. He's been destroying my furniture with unreserved enthusiasm ever since."

Alton's expression had shifted during the story, the professional mask thinning, something warmer and more attentive surfacing beneath it. "And the third?"

"Chaos was the easy one. A neighbor was moving and couldn't take him. He's young, he's fearless, and he thinks everything in the world exists for his personal entertainment." She smiled. "He's also the reason I had to replace my kitchen floor last year. Don't ask."

"I'm asking."

"He figured out how to turn on the bathtub faucet. While I was at work. For six hours." She watched Alton's face cycle through calculation, horror, and reluctant amusement. "The water came through the ceiling into the kitchen. The floor buckled. My contractor was thrilled."

Alton laughed. Not the short exhale she'd heard at Jimmy's Diner but a real laugh, unguarded, the sound of someone who'd been holding professional composure for weeks and had momentarily let it go. The sound did something to the space between them—loosened it, warmed it, made the corner table at La Reina feel like a place where things could be said that wouldn't survive the return to work.

"You gave them names that describe their personalities," he said. "Or did the names come first?"

"Trouble named herself. She was trouble from the moment she walked in—knocking things off shelves, staring at me like I was a villian in my own home. Mayhem was an aspiration. I figured if I named him something chaotic, the universe would balance it out and he'd be calm." She paused. "The universe did not cooperate."

"And Chaos?"

"Chaos was already named when I got him. But it fit so perfectly I didn't have the heart to change it."

Alton shook his head, the remnants of his laugh still softening his features. "Three cats named for disorder. In a PI's house. In Riverdale."

"The irony isn't lost on me." She took a sip of her beer. "But here's the thing—they're not actually chaotic. They're perceptive. Trouble reads rooms better than most detectives I've worked with. Mayhem's nose has found evidence that forensic equipment missed. And Chaos—" she thought of the ginger tabby chirping in the underground chamber, his uncomplicated delight in discovery, ". Chaos reminds me that curiosity doesn't need a reason. Sometimes you follow a scent or pull a thread or open a door just because it's there, and what you find is worth the looking."

She hadn't meant to say that much. The words had come out with a candor that surprised her, the kind of unfiltered honesty that happened when good food and the right company dissolved the filters she usually maintained. She waited for Alton to make a joke, deflect, or redirect the conversation back to professional territory.

He didn't. He looked at her across the cluttered table, the demolished tostones, the half-finished plates, the sweating beer bottles, and said, "That's not just a philosophy about cats."

"No," she admitted. "It's not."

The moment held. Not with tension, with recognition. Two people who spent their professional lives reading others and concealing themselves, sitting in a restaurant in Washington Heights, briefly allowing the reading and the concealment to pause.

Alton broke the moment gently. "After tomorrow— once this is wrapped—I'd like to visit them. The cats."

"Trouble will judge you. Mayhem will try to sit on you. Chaos will attempt to steal your food."

"Sounds like family dinner at my mother's house." He signaled for the check. "Minus the cats. Plus three aunts who judge harder than any feline ever could."

Amaya laughed. It felt good—clean, unforced, the kind of laughter that arrived without invitation and improved everything it touched. The restaurant hummed around them, and for a moment the operation, the evidence, the warrants, and the tunnel receded into background noise, replaced by the simple warmth of an evening that had started as work and ended as something she didn't have a category for yet.

They split the check. Amaya insisted this time, overriding Alton's protest with the flat assertion that she'd been raised by Eleanor Storm and was therefore constitutionally incapable of letting someone else pay twice. He conceded with a raised eyebrow that communicated both amusement and the understanding that this particular battle wasn't worth fighting.

Outside, St. Nicholas Avenue was alive with its nighttime energy—salsa from an open window, a group of men playing dominoes under a streetlight, the distant thump of a basketball on a court somewhere in the dark. The air was cold, but the cold felt clarifying rather than punishing, an alertness that matched the focus settling into Amaya's chest.

Tomorrow morning. Eight o'clock. The warrants. The breach. The end of something that had been hollowing out a museum and a community for six months.

"Get some sleep," Alton said. He was standing close. Not inappropriately, not deliberately, but at the distance that happened when two people walked out of a restaurant together and hadn't yet separated. Close enough that she could feel the warmth radiating from him. Close enough that the conversation could have gone somewhere else if either of them chose to take it there.

Neither of them did. Not tonight. There was too much riding on tomorrow, and they were both too professional, and too careful, to compromise it.

But the distance was noted. By both of them.

"You too," she said. "And Alton—"

"Yeah?"

"Thank you. For letting me work this case alongside you. Not every detective would have."

His expression was direct, unguarded, and brief. "Not every PI would have earned it."

He turned and walked south. Amaya watched him go for three steps, then turned north toward the A train, the November air sharp against her face and the warmth of the evening still folded somewhere behind her ribs.

The subway car was mostly empty at this hour. She found a seat by the window and watched the tunnel walls streak past, the rhythmic clatter of the tracks synchronizing with the thoughts assembling in her mind. Tomorrow's operation. The evidence chain. Calvin's gallery. Emily's arrest. The tunnel breach. The coded inventory. The eight entries in the staging chamber's log.

And beneath it all, running like a bass line under a melody: the sound of Alton Jackson laughing in a Dominican restaurant, and the way he'd said *after tomorrow* as if the other side of the operation contained something he was looking forward to.

Not the time.

But the thought had stopped sounding like a warning and started sounding like a promise.

She got off at 207th and walked the remaining blocks to Fieldston Road. The duplex was dark except for the kitchen light she'd left on, casting a warm rectangle across the front steps. She could see Trouble's silhouette in the upstairs window, the cat had been watching for her, and the sight of that familiar shape against the glass produced a tenderness in Amaya's chest that caught her off guard.

Inside, the duplex was warm and close with the atmosphere of a home that had been occupied by cats in the absence of humans. Mayhem was asleep on the couch in a position that suggested he'd melted there hours ago and had no plans to resolidify. Chaos was in the bathtub. Not running water this time, just sitting in it, staring at the drain with the focus of a cat contemplating the void.

Trouble met her at the top of the stairs, gold eyes bright in the dim hallway. The cat walked beside her to the office, where the case file sat on the desk in its final form— every document, every photograph, every timeline and connection mapped and ready for tomorrow.

Amaya sat in her chair. Trouble jumped to the desk and positioned herself beside the file, one paw resting on the edge of the folder as though claiming co-authorship.

"You're not wrong," Amaya said.

She reviewed the file one final time. Then she closed it, turned off the lamp, and sat in the dark with her cat beside her, listening to the duplex settle into its nighttime sounds, the creak of old radiators, the distant murmur of traffic, and the steady, quiet breathing of three animals who had helped her build a case that would change the morning.

"Tomorrow," she said to Trouble.

The cat's purr started—low, steady, certain. Not a response to the word but to the intention behind it. Trouble knew what tomorrow meant the way she knew everything: through the rhythm of the room, the rhythm of Amaya's breathing, the subtle electrical shift that happened in a household on the eve of something consequential.

They sat together in the dark, investigator and cat, and waited for the morning to arrive.

Chapter 15: Calvin's Play

The call came at eleven-fourteen p.m., less than an hour after Amaya had turned off the lamp and settled into the dark with Trouble beside her.

She'd been drifting toward sleep. Not quite there, her mind still cycling through tomorrow's operational timeline the way an engine idles after a long drive. The cats had arranged themselves in their nighttime configuration: Trouble on the desk, Mayhem across the foot of the bed, Chaos wedged between two pillows in a nest he'd constructed by kneading the bedding into a shape that satisfied requirements only he understood.

Her phone lit up on the nightstand. Unknown number. 212 area code.

She was awake in a heartbeat. At this hour, an unknown Manhattan number was either a wrong number or a problem, and Amaya's life didn't generate many wrong numbers.

"Amaya Storm."

"Ms. Storm. Or should I say Ms. Mitchell?"

Calvin Whitaker's voice was warm, unhurried, and precisely calibrated, the same smooth baritone she'd heard at the gala and in his gallery, now carrying an undercurrent of something she hadn't heard from him before. Not fear. Calculation. The sound of a man who'd been playing a long game and had just realized the board was about to be flipped.

Amaya sat up. Trouble's head lifted from her paws, gold eyes finding Amaya in the dark with immediate, total focus. The cat's body had gone rigid. Not from the phone itself but from the change in Amaya's breathing, the spike of adrenaline that altered the room's atmosphere as surely as a shift in barometric pressure.

"Calvin." She kept her voice level. "It's late."

"It is. I apologize for the hour. But I've found myself in a reflective mood this evening, and I thought you might be the right person to share it with." A pause—theatrical, controlled, the pause of a man who understood that silence was a tool. "You see, I had an interesting visitor today. A colleague at the auction house in Chelsea—Philip Barlow, perhaps you know him—mentioned that a detective and a woman matching your description came by asking about provenance documents. A woman who looked remarkably like the one who'd toured my gallery the previous week. And then I remembered a charming woman named Mitchell who toured my gallery last week and asked unusually specific questions about my basement."

Amaya's mind was running at full speed now, but her voice stayed calm. On the bed, Mayhem had woken. He was watching her from the foot of the mattress, his eyes luminous in the phone's faint glow, his body shifting from sleeping sprawl to alert crouch. Even Chaos had extracted himself from his pillow nest and was sitting upright, ears forward, attuned to the tension radiating from Amaya in waves.

All three cats, awake and focused. At eleven at night, that meant something.

"You've been doing your homework," Amaya said.

"Research is the foundation of my profession. As, I imagine, it is of yours." Calvin's tone remained conversational, but the charm had thinned. It was still there, still operational, but beneath it Amaya could hear the undertone of a man rearranging his position. "I've been aware of you for some time, actually. Since your meeting with Detective Jackson at the diner on the Grand Concourse. A colleague of mine happened to be in the area."

The sedan. The dark Lincoln Town Car that Trouble had flagged outside Jimmy's Diner—engine running, tinted windows, no one getting out. Not a car service. Not a coincidence. Calvin had been watching her since the first week of the investigation, which meant he'd known about the police partnership before Amaya had even visited his gallery. The Mitchell alias had never fooled him. He'd played along because it suited his curiosity.

Trouble had tried to tell her. On that rainy sidewalk outside the diner, the cat's agitation, the split attention, the refusal to settle—had been the alert Amaya had filed without acting on. She'd trusted the observation but hadn't followed it to its conclusion. The cat had been right, and the delay had cost them nothing. Calvin would have been caught regardless. But it was a reminder that Trouble's instincts operated on a faster timeline than Amaya's analysis.

"I admire your work, Ms. Storm," Calvin continued. The museum investigation has been impressive. Methodical. Patient. You move through a problem the way a good restorer moves through a damaged painting—layer by layer, with respect for what you're uncovering."

"Is there a point to this call, Calvin?"

"The point is that I'd like to meet. Tonight, if you're willing. I have something to share that I believe would be of significant value to your investigation, and I'd prefer to share it on my terms rather than someone else's."

Amaya stood and walked to the window. Fieldston Road was empty. No cars, no pedestrians, the streetlights casting their amber circles on wet pavement. She scanned the block reflexively, her mind conjuring the dark sedan that Trouble had flagged outside Jimmy's Diner. Nothing.

"What kind of something?"

"Information. Context. The kind of perspective that doesn't survive the transition from conversation to courtroom." His voice dropped a register—intimate, confiding, the tone of a man drawing someone into a secret.

"I'm not a fool, Amaya. I know what's happening. I can feel the machinery turning, and I know how these things end. But I also know that the story being constructed about me, the narrative your investigation is building—is missing pieces that matter. Pieces that change the picture."

It was a pitch. A sophisticated, carefully constructed attempt to gain control of the narrative before the warrant stripped that control away. Calvin was offering to trade, his version of events in exchange for the opportunity to shape how they were understood. It was the move of a man who'd calculated that cooperation, even selective cooperation, gave him better odds than silence.

It was also, Amaya recognized, potentially the most dangerous meeting of the investigation. Calvin knew who she was, knew she'd been in his gallery under an alias, and knew, or strongly suspected. That law enforcement was preparing to move. A meeting on his terms, at his chosen location, at night, gave him every advantage she should be declining.

"Where?"

"My gallery. One hour."

"No."

The refusal landed without explanation, and Amaya let it sit. She would not walk into Calvin Whitaker's building, a building connected to an underground tunnel and a staging area full of evidence—on the night before a warrant, alone, at midnight. She wasn't reckless, and she wasn't performing bravery for an audience of one.

"Then you choose," Calvin said. His tone didn't shift. No irritation, no surprise. He'd expected the refusal and had planned past it. "Wherever you're comfortable."

She thought for three seconds. "The Apollo Theater. Corner of 125th and Frederick Douglass. There's a bench across the street, under the marquee lights. Thirty minutes."

Public space. Well-lit. Foot traffic, even at midnight on 125th Street. And close enough to the museum that Jackson's team, if she needed them, could respond in minutes.

"Poetic choice," Calvin said. "I'll be there."

The line went dead. Amaya stood in the dark of her bedroom, phone in hand, and weighed the decision. Meeting Calvin was a risk. But declining the meeting was also a risk. He'd called to negotiate, and a man who was negotiating was a man who had something to trade. If he offered information that expanded the scope of the investigation, the five additional entries in the staging chamber's log, the identities of other sources, the full extent of the network. It could be worth the exposure.

She texted Jackson: *Calvin Whitaker just called. He knows who I am. He wants to meet. I said yes. Apollo Theater, 125th and FDB, 30 minutes. I need you close but not visible.*

The response came in twelve seconds: *I'm on 135th. Be there in ten. I'll park on the north side of 125th. You see anything wrong, you walk.*

She pocketed the phone and moved. Jeans, boots, her heaviest jacket. She clipped Trouble's leash and lifted the cat from the desk. Trouble didn't protest. She flowed into Amaya's arms with the liquid compliance of a cat who understood that something was happening and had elected to be part of it.

"Just you tonight," Amaya murmured. Mayhem watched from the bed, his green eyes tracking her movements with the alert stillness of a cat who wanted to come but recognized the signals that said otherwise. Chaos had already fallen back asleep, his commitment to the crisis lasting approximately ninety seconds before the pillows reclaimed him.

The subway was out of the question at this hour—too slow. She called a car. Seven minutes later, she was heading south on the Henry Hudson Parkway, the city's lights reflected in the river below, Trouble warm on her lap.

125th Street at midnight was quieter than its daytime self but far from empty. The restaurants and bars near the Apollo were still spilling light and music onto the sidewalk. A few clusters of people moved between venues, their laughter sharp in the cold air. The Apollo's marquee blazed above it all, a Harlem landmark that had survived everything the twentieth century had thrown at it, its lights a beacon for a neighborhood that refused to stop performing.

Amaya found the bench across the street. She sat, set Trouble beside her. Trouble's eyes swept the street with the systematic focus of a surveillance operator.

Calvin arrived on foot, from the east, at precisely midnight. He was dressed for a different occasion than the cold bench across from a theater—wool overcoat, leather gloves, a scarf arranged with the deliberate elegance of a man who considered his appearance a form of communication. He spotted Amaya, adjusted his trajectory, and sat beside her on the bench with the ease of someone joining a friend at a café.

"You brought the cat."

"She doesn't sleep well without supervision."

Calvin glanced at Trouble, whose gaze had locked onto him with an intensity that was several degrees past casual observation. "I suspect the supervision runs in the other direction."

Smart. Even now, even cornered, Calvin read his environment with precision.

"Talk," Amaya said.

Calvin leaned back against the bench, his breath misting in the cold air, his gaze directed at the Apollo's marquee rather than at Amaya. When he spoke, his voice had shed some of its polish. Not all, but enough to reveal something underneath that was closer to the real person than anything she'd heard from him before.

"I built something, Amaya. Not just the advisory firm, a network. A system for moving art that had been trapped in institutions that couldn't protect it, couldn't display it properly, couldn't give it the audience it deserved." He turned his head to look at her. "Do you know how many works by Black artists sit in museum storage vaults, uncatalogued, unseen, deteriorating? Thousands. Tens of thousands. Works that should be in homes, in galleries, in the hands of collectors who would cherish them. Instead, they're filed away in climate-controlled closets by institutions that acquired them for diversity metrics and then forgot they existed."

"So you liberated them."

"I relocated them. To people who wanted them. Who would display them, care for them, ensure they survived."

"For a price."

"Everything has a price. The question is who sets it and who benefits." Calvin's voice carried conviction, the intensity of a man who'd built a justification around his actions and believed it, or had believed it long enough that the distinction no longer mattered. "The pieces I moved from the Studio Museum were being neglected. The Adeyemi painting hadn't been displayed in two years. The Edmondson bronze was in a storage vault with insufficient climate control. I documented the temperature fluctuations myself. The Okonkwo installation was scheduled to be deaccessioned."

"You're making a preservation argument for theft."

"I'm making a context argument. The narrative your investigation has constructed is: Calvin Whitaker stole art for profit. The truth is more complicated."

Calvin didn't look at her; he looked at the Apollo marquee. "You work outside the system too, Amaya. You took your skills and hung a shingle because you decided the institutions couldn't be trusted to do it right. I made the same calculation. The only difference is you charge by the hour and I charge by the canvas." He let that sit. "One bad budget cycle and everything Lydia built disappears into a warehouse. I placed those works with people whose wealth makes them permanent guardians. You and I both want the same thing, to keep the history alive. I just have the nerve to admit what it costs."

Trouble shifted in her carrier. The movement was subtle, a repositioning of weight that pressed her body against the side nearest Calvin, her nose working the air between them. In the cold, the scents were louder: his cologne, the leather of his gloves, and underneath both, the faint chemical signature that Amaya's nose had learned to recognize and Trouble's had identified weeks ago. Solvent. On his hands, in his coat, embedded in the fabric of a man who spent his days handling art with chemicals that dissolved the boundaries between ownership and theft.

"Where are the other five pieces?" Amaya asked. "The staging chamber's log showed eight entries. Three from the museum. Five from somewhere else."

Calvin's expression flickered, the first genuine surprise she'd seen from him. He hadn't known she'd found the log. "You've been thorough."

"Where are they, Calvin?"

He was quiet for a long moment. The Apollo's marquee hummed above them, its lights cycling through a pattern that cast moving shadows across the bench. A taxi passed, its headlights sweeping the street.

"Private collections," he said finally. "Estates. One from a gallery in Philadelphia that was closing and selling its inventory to a developer who planned to use the canvases as decoration for a hotel lobby." A thread of genuine anger entered his voice, the first uncontrolled emotion she'd heard from him. "A hotel lobby. Work by Charles White, by Alma Thomas, by artists who changed what American art could be. Reduced to décor."

"And you decided you had the right to intervene."

"Someone had to."

"Someone who profited from the intervention."

Calvin's jaw tightened. The charm, the philosophy, the narrative of cultural rescue, all of it compressed under the weight of a fact he couldn't reframe. He had been paid. The collectors who received the stolen pieces had paid him. The financial trail was documented, traced, and sitting in Jackson's evidence file.

"I'm not going to pretend the money doesn't exist," he said quietly. "But I want you to understand that it wasn't the reason. Not at the beginning."

Amaya studied him in the marquee light. Calvin Whitaker was not a simple villain. His passion for the art was genuine. She'd seen it in his gallery, heard it in his knowledge, felt it in the anger he expressed about neglected works. But passion without ethics was just appetite, and Calvin had fed his appetite by stealing from a community institution that existed precisely to protect the art he claimed to champion.

"Calvin, in about eight hours, law enforcement is going to arrive at your gallery with a search warrant. They're going to open the door in your basement that connects to the tunnel under 125th Street, and they're going to catalogue every piece of art in your storage facility. The coded inventory will be cross-referenced against stolen art databases. Whatever you've told yourself about preservation and relocation, the law sees theft. The community sees theft. And the museum you stole from sees betrayal."

She let the words settle. Trouble was pressed against Amaya's leg, her gaze fixed on Calvin, her body humming with the low-level awareness that preceded her most significant alerts. The cat wasn't reacting to danger. She was reacting to the collapse happening in real time, the slow-motion dismantling of a man's self-image under the pressure of facts he could no longer outrun.

Calvin looked at his hands. The leather gloves were immaculate, but Amaya knew what lay beneath them, the same solvent traces, the same paint residue, the hands that had moved art through underground passages with the care of a conservator and the ethics of a thief.

"Emily," he said. "Will she—"

"Emily will face her own consequences."

He nodded slowly. "She believed in what we were doing. She wasn't in it for money."

"She was in it because she spent seven years building an institution and watching someone else get the credit. That's not ideology. That's resentment."

The statement landed like a door closing. Calvin flinched—small, involuntary, the reaction of a man hearing a truth he'd avoided.

"Are you going to run?" Amaya asked.

The question was direct, stripped of diplomacy, the kind of question a former cop asked when she needed to know whether tomorrow morning's operation would find its target or an empty building.

Calvin stared at the Apollo for a long time. The marquee lights played across his face, illuminating and concealing in cycles, the way art illuminated and concealed the truth about the people who made it and the people who took it.

"No," he said. "I'm not a runner. I never was."

He stood, adjusted his coat, and looked down at Amaya with an expression that held too many things to catalogue—resignation, pride, regret, and something that might have been gratitude for the conversation itself, for the chance to say his piece to someone who listened without interrupting.

"Goodbye, Amaya."

"Goodbye, Calvin."

He walked east on 125th, his tall frame receding into the Harlem night with the unhurried stride of a man who had decided where he would be found in the morning. Trouble watched him go, her eyes tracking him until he disappeared around the corner of Lenox, and then she turned to Amaya with a sound. A trill and chirp. That

Amaya interpreted as the cat's version of a closing argument.

He's telling the truth about not running. He's not telling the truth about the money.

Amaya scratched Trouble behind the ear. "Yeah. I know."

She texted Jackson: *He's not running. He knows about the warrant. He'll be at his gallery in the morning.*

Jackson's reply: *Good. Get some sleep. It's going to be a long day.*

She looked at the Apollo one more time—its lights blazing against the November dark, a building that had survived every kind of storm Harlem had weathered. Tomorrow, another storm would break over this neighborhood. But the Apollo would still be standing, and so would the museum, and so would the community that had built both.

Amaya gathered Trouble's carrier and walked toward the car she'd kept waiting.

Tomorrow morning. Eight o'clock.

Chapter 16: The Breach

Amaya slept three hours and woke before the alarm.

The duplex was dark, the November morning still an hour from its first gray light. She lay in bed for thirty seconds, running the operational timeline through her mind the way a musician runs scales before a performance—each step in sequence, each contingency mapped, the whole structure held in working memory so that when the music started, the hands would know where to go.

Trouble was already awake. The cat sat at the foot of the bed, facing the door, her silhouette contrasted against the faint glow of the hallway nightlight. She'd been there for a while. Amaya could tell from the settled quality of her posture, the cat's body arranged with the stillness of a sentinel who'd taken the watch hours ago and hadn't moved since. Trouble knew what today was. She'd known since last night, since the phone call and the midnight bench and the ride home through empty streets. She knew the way she always knew—she sensed Amaya's tension, through rhythm, through the imperceptible shifts in the household's electrical field that preceded consequential days.

Mayhem was asleep on the bathroom mat, his muscular body coiled in a tight circle that made him look deceptively compact. He would wake explosively when Amaya started the coffee grinder. He always did, and his energy would fill the kitchen with the intensity of a cat who was looking for breakfast.

Chaos was in the bathtub again. Amaya could see him through the open bathroom door, a ginger comma curled against the white porcelain, his eyes open and blinking slowly in the pre-dawn quiet. He looked thoughtful. He'd found the most contained, most echo-prone space in the house and was enjoying the acoustics of his own breathing.

She got up. She dressed. She made coffee without the grinder—quietly, pour-over, the manual method she used when she wanted to think without Mayhem's six-a.m. enthusiasm. The cats would be staying home today. All three of them. The operation was law enforcement only, and even if it weren't, what waited on the other side of eight o'clock was no place for animals she loved.

She poured kibble into three bowls, refreshed the water dish, and stood in the kitchen for a moment, watching the duplex wake up around her. Mayhem materialized at the sound of kibble hitting ceramic, food was a signal he never missed. Chaos thumped out of the bathtub and trotted to the kitchen with the bright-eyed enthusiasm of a cat who believed every meal was a celebration. Trouble descended from the bed with unhurried grace, ate precisely half her portion, and returned to the bedroom to resume her watch.

Amaya crouched beside Trouble's bowl and stroked the cat's back as she passed. "Hold down the fort."

Trouble paused, turned, and pressed her forehead against Amaya's hand, a brief, deliberate gesture that the cat reserved for moments of departure. It wasn't affection in the way humans understood affection. It was acknowledgment. A transfer of something—warmth, trust, the quiet compact between two creatures who'd chosen each other and renewed that choice daily.

Amaya held the contact for three seconds, then stood. She gathered her phone, her keys, and the radio Jackson had issued her the previous afternoon, a police-band handset tuned to the operation's frequency. She put on her heaviest coat, locked the duplex behind her, and walked into the November dark.

The museum's lobby was lit but empty at seven-fifteen. Derek met her at the door, his uniform pressed, his posture carrying the coiled energy of a man who'd been waiting for this morning for six months. He'd positioned two of his guards at the building's public entrances with instructions to redirect any arriving staff to a holding area on the second floor. Emily's usual arrival time was eight-thirty, but Jackson had arranged for Derek to call her in early. She would walk into a building that looked normal and discover, within minutes, that nothing about her morning would proceed as planned.

"Jackson's team?" Amaya asked.

"Staged two blocks north. They'll move to Calvin's building at seven-fifty. The tunnel team is assembling in the registrar's office now." Derek handed her a museum keycard—full access, every door. "Lydia's in her office. She wanted to be here."

Amaya nodded. She'd expected that. Lydia Brooks was not a woman who would watch the dismantling of her museum's betrayal from a safe distance. She would be present, composed, and devastated, and Amaya respected all three.

She took the elevator to the lower level. The registrar's office had been converted into a staging area, the drywall panel was already open, the tunnel's cool air breathing into the room. Four officers in tactical gear stood in a loose formation, checking equipment and reviewing the entry plan. Their team leader, a sergeant named Reeves, was a compact woman with close-cropped hair and the focused energy of someone who'd breached more doors than she cared to count.

"Ms. Storm." Reeves acknowledged her with a nod that was professional without being warm. "Detective Jackson asked me to brief you. We enter the tunnel at oh-seven-fifty-five. Five-minute transit to the steel door. We breach at oh-eight-hundred, simultaneous with the front-door team at the gallery. You stay behind us until the space is secured."

"Understood."

"If you hear anything that sounds like a problem, you retreat to this room and seal the panel. We clear the space. You don't."

"Understood."

Reeves studied her for a beat—assessing, the way operatives assessed civilians who'd been granted access to their world. Whatever she found in Amaya's expression apparently satisfied her, because she turned back to her team without further comment.

Amaya's radio crackled. Jackson's voice, steady and clear: "All units, this is Jackson. Gallery team is in position. Tunnel team, confirm ready."

Reeves keyed her radio. "Tunnel team ready."

"Museum exterior team, confirm."

A voice Amaya didn't recognize: "Exterior ready. Two exits covered."

"Copy all. We execute at oh-eight-hundred. Seven minutes."

Amaya stood at the tunnel entrance and breathed. The passage stretched ahead into its LED-lit corridor, familiar now. She'd walked it three times, mapped it, photographed it, traced its path from a museum storeroom to a gallery basement. She knew its curves, its branches, its smells. But today it felt different. People with weapons would move through it in minutes, and on the other side, a door would open onto the physical evidence of a conspiracy that had hollowed out a community institution.

At seven-fifty-five, the tunnel team moved.

They entered in formation—Reeves on point, two officers behind her, a fourth covering the rear. Amaya followed at the prescribed distance, her radio held close, her footsteps soft on the swept concrete. The LEDs painted the passage in flat white light, stripping the tunnel of the atmospheric mystery it had carried during previous visits. In tactical lighting, with armed officers ahead of her, the passage was simply infrastructure, a corridor, a means of transit, a problem being solved.

They passed the western branch junction without pausing. The staging chamber had been sealed and guarded since the CSI team's last visit—its evidence preserved, its contents documented. Today's objective was the northeast door, the steel barrier that connected the tunnel to Calvin's building.

At seven-fifty-nine, Reeves halted the team ten feet from the door. She held up a closed fist—stop. Silence settled over the passage like a held breath. The keypad glowed its faint green, undisturbed.

Amaya's radio: Jackson's voice, counting down. "All teams stand by. Thirty seconds."

The seconds passed with the slowness of time measured against adrenaline. Amaya could hear her own heartbeat, the breathing of the officer behind her, and the faint hum of the keypad's electronics. The tunnel held its breath.

"Execute. Execute. Execute."

Reeves moved. Not to the keypad. She'd never intended to crack the code. The breaching tool was a hydraulic ram, compact and brutal, and it hit the door's locking mechanism with a sound that traveled through the tunnel like a thunderclap. The door buckled inward. A second strike and it swung open, revealing a flood of fluorescent light from the space beyond.

The officers poured through. Amaya heard the choreographed shouts—"Police! Search warrant! Hands where we can see them!", and the sounds of a space being cleared: footsteps, doors opening, the controlled chaos of a tactical entry proceeding according to plan.

Thirty seconds of shouting. Then Reeves's voice on the radio: "Tunnel side clear. Basement secured. One individual detained—male, mid-forties, no resistance."

Calvin. He'd been in his building, as he'd promised. Not running.

Amaya waited until Reeves radioed the all-clear, then stepped through the breached door into Calvin Whitaker's basement.

The space was larger than she'd expected, a finished basement that ran the full footprint of the building, divided into sections by industrial shelving units. The fluorescent lights revealed everything: a work area with a large table, chemical supplies, and conservation tools. A secondary storage area packed with flat files and vertical racks. And, occupying the far wall, a heavy steel vault door, the kind used in commercial storage facilities to protect high-value inventory.

Calvin was seated in a folding chair near the work table, his hands resting on his knees, his posture composed. Two officers flanked him. He wore the same wool overcoat he'd worn to the Apollo. He'd been waiting, dressed and ready; he had kept his word about where he would be found.

His eyes found Amaya as she entered. For a moment, the basement's harsh light stripped away the charm, the philosophy, the careful narratives he'd constructed to justify what this room represented. What remained was simpler: a man in a chair, caught, with the particular stillness of someone who'd been expecting the knock and had decided, sometime in the long hours before it came, not to run from its sound.

He said nothing. There was nothing to say that hadn't already said. But his gaze held hers for a beat longer than necessary, and in it Amaya read something she hadn't expected. Not regret for the theft, but regret for the ending. Calvin had loved the game. The planning, the execution, the intellectual satisfaction of moving art through a system no one knew existed. The end of the game was, for him, a kind of death.

Amaya held his gaze and felt nothing she needed to apologize for.

Jackson's voice on the radio: "Front-door team has the gallery secured. Upper floors being cleared. No additional individuals found."

Then, a moment later: "Museum team, confirm status on Dawson."

Derek's voice, tight and controlled: "Emily Dawson arrived at eight-twenty-two. She's been informed of the arrest warrant and is being held in the second-floor conference room. She's cooperating."

Cooperating. Amaya thought of Emily's composure, the calibrated warmth, the perfectly timed smiles, the hand that had trembled once against a tablet before she'd corrected it. She wondered what Emily's face looked like now, in a conference room surrounded by officers, the culmination of seven years' performance collapsing around her while she managed, as she always managed, the only thing left within her control: how she appeared while it fell.

For now, the basement demanded her attention. The CSI team from the tunnel entrance had followed the officers through the breached door and was already setting up—photographing, cataloging, beginning the slow, methodical processing of a crime scene into evidence. The work area on the table held tools Amaya recognized from the staging chamber: calipers, a digital scale, cutting instruments, and a heat gun. A laptop sat open beside them, its screen dark, its hard drive now evidence. Whatever records Calvin had maintained—transactions, contacts, the identities of buyers—lived on that machine.

Amaya approached the vault door. It was open. Calvin had complied with the front-door team's instructions without resistance. Inside, the vault was climate-controlled, well-lit, and immaculate. The air carried the faint chemical signature she'd come to associate with the entire operation—solvent, conservation chemicals, the carefully maintained atmosphere of a space designed to preserve things that had been taken from the spaces where they belonged.

Rows of vertical storage racks held framed works, each tagged with the same alphanumeric codes she'd seen during her gallery visit. A separate section held sculptures on padded shelving, and a flat-file cabinet contained works on paper—prints, drawings, documents.

A hundred and forty pieces. Some legitimate, the Connecticut collector's renovation storage, the estate holdings, the overflow from institutional clients. And some stolen, their coded tags concealing origins that the investigation would now trace, piece by piece, back to the museums, galleries, and collections they'd been taken from.

The Nkechi Adeyemi painting, the first piece stolen from the Studio Museum—was in the third rack from the left. Amaya recognized it from the exhibition catalogue Lydia had shown her: a mixed-media work on canvas depicting a woman's face fragmented and reassembled, the colors bold, the technique both raw and precise. Up close, the painting was more powerful than any photograph could convey, the fragments of the face weren't broken but rearranged, as though the artist had taken identity apart to understand how it held together. The colors vibrated against each other with an energy that was both joyful and defiant.

It hung in its rack, perfectly preserved, the climate controls maintaining the exact temperature and humidity its materials required. Calvin had cared for it. That was the contradiction at the heart of everything, the art was stolen and cherished simultaneously, the crime committed with the same hands that ensured the work survived.

She didn't touch it. She photographed it, noted its position, and moved on.

Jackson arrived through the front entrance twenty minutes later, having supervised the gallery-level search. He found Amaya in the vault, her phone in hand, systematically documenting the inventory.

"We've got him," Jackson said. The words were simple, factual, delivered without triumph, the statement of a detective who understood that arrests were not endings but transitions, the point where investigation became prosecution and the work changed shape.

"The coded inventory matches the staging chamber's log," Amaya said. "At least eight pieces here correspond to entries in that log. The Adeyemi painting is in rack three. I haven't located the Okonkwo installation yet, but the flat files may contain documentation that traces the remaining pieces."

Jackson nodded. "The DA's office has been briefed. They're sending an ADA to oversee the evidence processing. This is going to take days."

"What about Emily?"

"Being transported to the precinct for formal interview. She asked for a lawyer. That's her right, and it tells me she's been thinking about this moment for a while." He paused, his expression shifting from operational to something more personal. "She didn't resist. Derek said she walked out of the conference room with her head up and her hands steady. Didn't say a word to anyone."

Amaya absorbed this. Emily Dawson, who had choreographed events and managed crises and maintained composure through seven years of dual existence—performing loyalty to Lydia while systematically betraying the institution they'd built together—had walked into her arrest with the same controlled grace she brought to everything else. It was, in its terrible way, consistent. Emily didn't crack. She managed.

"And Calvin?"

"In custody. He waived his right to silence—wants to make a statement. I'm guessing he's going to tell us the same story he told you last night." Jackson looked at her. "The preservation narrative."

"It's compelling. It's also irrelevant to the charges."

"Agreed. But juries are human, and human beings like stories about people who believe they're doing the right thing." He held her gaze. "We'll need your testimony to counter that narrative. The financial trail, the tunnel infrastructure, the ghost invoices, the evidence that this was a profit-driven operation regardless of what Calvin told himself about his motives."

"You'll have it."

They stood together in the vault, surrounded by art that had been stolen, stored, and preserved with the contradictory care of a thief who loved what he took. The fluorescent lights hummed. The CSI team moved through the space with quiet efficiency. And somewhere above them, on the streets of Harlem, the morning continued—buses running, shops opening, people walking past a gallery that had, for years, hidden the infrastructure of a crime beneath its polished surface.

Amaya's radio crackled one final time. Derek's voice, stripped of its usual professional restraint, carrying instead something raw and earned: "Ms. Storm. The Edmondson bronze. It's been loaded into the museum's transport vehicle. It's coming home."

She closed her eyes. The sculpture Mayhem had found under a tarp in an underground chamber. The piece that had been missing for four months. Coming home.

"Copy that, Derek," she said. "Welcome it back."

She pocketed the radio and walked out of the vault, through the basement, past the breached door, and into the tunnel that had started everything. The LEDs still glowed. The passage still breathed its cool, stark air. But the door at the end was open now, and the light from both sides poured through, illuminating the space between in a way it had never been illuminated before.

Chapter 17: The Confession

Emily Dawson's lawyer was a woman named Grace Okafor—mid-fifties, silver-streaked locs pulled into a low bun, the quiet authority of someone who'd spent decades in rooms where the stakes were measured in years. She sat beside Emily at the interview table in the Major Case Squad's conference room, her legal pad open, her pen still. She'd already established the ground rules with Jackson: Emily would make a statement. The conversation was voluntary. It could be terminated at any time.

Amaya watched from the observation room, a narrow space separated from the conference room by a one-way mirror that reduced everything on the other side to a kind of theater. Jackson sat across from Emily, his posture open, his recorder centered on the table between them. A second detective, a woman named Pryce whom Amaya hadn't met—sat to Jackson's right, taking notes.

Emily looked different. Not diminished. That would have been too simple. But reconfigured, as though the internal architecture that had held her together for seven years had been dismantled and she was still figuring out which pieces to keep. She wore the same clothes she'd been arrested in, the cream blouse, the gold earrings, the thin watch. But the composure they'd once accessorized was gone. In its place was something raw and present, a woman sitting in a room with no exits and no audience to perform for.

She'd been in custody for four hours. She'd spoken to her lawyer for ninety minutes. And now, with the recorder running, she began.

"I want to start by saying that I loved that museum." Her voice was steady but stripped. No warmth calibration, no professional modulation, just the unadorned sound of a person speaking without a script for the first time in years. "I know that sounds absurd, given what I'm about to tell you. But it's important to me that it's on the record. I loved it."

Jackson didn't respond. He waited, the same patient silence Amaya had watched him deploy at Jimmy's Diner, the understanding that the most important information arrived in the spaces between prompted answers.

"I started working for Lydia when I was twenty-seven. The museum was still in the old building—smaller, scrappier, held together with grant money and determination. Lydia had the vision. She always had the vision. And I had—" Emily paused, her fingers touching the face of her watch, the familiar gesture now stripped of its self-soothing function and reduced to pure reflex. "I had everything else. The systems, the operations, the logistics. I built the event programming. I built the donor cultivation pipeline. I designed the workflows that allowed a staff of nine to operate like a staff of thirty."

"And Lydia got the credit," Jackson said. Not a question—an observation, delivered with the matter-of-fact neutrality of a man acknowledging something he'd already understood.

Emily's jaw tightened. "Lydia got the profile. The New York Times feature. The ArtNews interview. The Essence cover. Every article about the museum's transformation, and there were dozens—centered on Lydia's vision. My name appeared in two of them, both times in passing. 'With the support of her dedicated team.'" The words came out with a precision that suggested she'd memorized them years ago and had been carrying them ever since, like a stone in her pocket she couldn't stop reaching for.

Amaya watched through the glass. Emily's resentment wasn't a surprise. She'd sensed it in their first interview, caught it in the micro-expressions and word choices that betrayed the curated surface. But hearing it articulated was different. The resentment had a history, a consistency, a specific gravity that made it comprehensible even as it made the betrayal worse.

"I met Calvin at a gallery opening two and a half years ago," Emily continued. "He was charming—you've met him, you know how he is. But it wasn't the charm that got me. It was the way he talked about art. About what it meant, who it belonged to, what happened when institutions failed to protect it." Her eyes dropped to the table. "He understood something I'd been feeling for years. That the museum, for all its mission statements, was letting work slip through the cracks. Pieces in storage that nobody looked at. Conservation needs that got deferred because the budget prioritized exhibitions. Art that was acquired to fill a diversity quota and then forgotten."

"Was any of that true?" Jackson asked.

"Some of it. Enough to make his argument persuasive." Emily's voice carried the flatness of someone recounting a seduction. Not romantic, but intellectual, the slow process by which a reasonable premise was extended into unreasonable action. "Calvin said he could help. He said he had collectors—serious people, people who would care for the work in ways the museum couldn't. He said the pieces would be preserved, displayed, valued. All he needed was access."

"And you provided it."

"Not at first. At first, it was just information, which pieces were in storage, what their conservation status was, how the security operated during events. I told myself it was consultation. That he was helping us identify gaps in our collection management." She pressed her palms flat against the table, the gesture of someone anchoring themselves against a current. "The first theft was his idea, but I made it possible. I directed security away from the lower level. I left the storage vault code unchanged for an extra cycle so he'd have the access window. I filed the event budget with inflated line items to cover the costs of maintaining the tunnel."

"You knew about the tunnel from the beginning?"

"Calvin stumbled upon it during the building's construction phase. He was consulting on collection installation for the new facility, and the contractors uncovered the passage during foundation work. The engineers sealed it, but Calvin documented the access points before they did. When we started planning—" she caught herself on the word, her expression flickering with the recognition that "planning" was a confession in itself, "He unsealed the museum end and built out the passage to connect with his building."

The room was quiet except for the clanking of the ventilation system and the faint scratch of Detective Pryce's pen. Through the mirror, Amaya could see the toll the statement was taking. Not on Emily's composure, which had already collapsed, but on something deeper. Each sentence she spoke dismantled another section of the narrative she'd maintained for years: that she was the museum's most dedicated employee, that her work mattered, that she deserved more than she'd received. What she was speaking on now didn't contradict those feelings. It existed alongside them, two realities occupying the same space the way the tunnel existed beneath the museum— hidden, functional, corroding the foundation from below.

"The money," Jackson said. "Walk me through the financial structure."

Emily outlined it with the same organizational precision she'd brought to managing the museum's events—because, Amaya realized, this had been managed the same way. Two channels: the Whitaker Art Advisory invoices, which covered Calvin's consulting fees and provided a paper trail for legitimate-appearing services, and the ghost production expenses embedded in the event budgets, which funded the tunnel's operational costs—LED lights, construction materials, the steel door and keypad system, the solvent and packing materials in the staging chamber.

"How much?" Jackson asked.

"The invoices totaled about forty thousand. The production expenses, another thirty. Calvin's buyers paid separately—those transactions didn't flow through the museum at all. I don't know the total amounts." She paused. "I didn't want to know."

"But you received compensation."

Emily closed her eyes. When she opened them, the last trace of the woman who'd managed the Studio Museum's operations with seamless efficiency had dissolved, replaced by someone younger, more exposed, sitting in a room where the foundation of seven years' work—legitimate and criminal—had been stripped to its studs.

"Calvin paid me sixty thousand dollars over two years. Cash, in installments. I used it to pay off my student loans."

The student loans. The detail from Amaya's background check—paid down ahead of schedule, flagged as either disciplined financial management or evidence of outside income. It had been both, and neither, and the mundanity of it was somehow worse than any extravagant motive would have been. Emily Dawson hadn't betrayed Lydia Brooks for luxury or greed. She'd done it for the same reason millions of Americans made compromises they didn't feel good about: to get out from under the weight of educational debt that had been pressing on her since she was twenty-two.

Jackson let the silence extend. Emily's lawyer sat beside her, still and watchful, her pen motionless on her pad. There was nothing to object to. Emily was talking freely, and the story she was telling was the story of a crime that had begun with legitimate grievance and metastasized into something neither grievance nor ideology could justify.

"The five additional pieces," Jackson said. "The ones that didn't come from the Studio Museum."

Emily shook her head. "That was Calvin's operation. He had sources—other institutions, private collections, an estate sale in Philadelphia. I didn't participate in those acquisitions and I don't know the details. My involvement was limited to the Studio Museum." She looked up at Jackson, and for the first time, something in her expression requested rather than stated. "I need you to understand that. I know it doesn't change the charges. But the scope of what I did. It was this museum. This place. Not a network."

Jackson studied her for a long moment. "That will be for the DA to assess."

"I know."

"Is there anything else you want to add to your statement?"

Emily looked at her lawyer, who gave a barely perceptible nod. Then she turned back to Jackson and said something that Amaya, watching through the glass, hadn't expected.

"Lydia didn't know. I want that on the record, clearly and unambiguously. Lydia Brooks had no knowledge of the thefts, the tunnel, the financial manipulation, or my involvement with Calvin Whitaker. She trusted me, and I used that trust to steal from the institution she built. Whatever failures of oversight occurred, and there were failures. They were the result of her believing in me, not of her participating in what I did."

The statement was delivered with the first real emotion Emily had shown since the interview began. Not the curated warmth or the controlled edge or the calculated vulnerability, but something unprocessed, unmanaged, arriving in her voice like a wave that had been building beneath the surface for years.

It was, Amaya recognized, the closest Emily Dawson would come to an apology. Not for the crime. That would be adjudicated in court, deconstructed by lawyers, reduced to charges and sentences. But for the betrayal. For the specific, personal damage she'd done to a woman who'd called her family and meant it.

Jackson ended the interview at twelve forty-seven p.m. Emily was escorted to a holding area to await arraignment. Her lawyer packed her legal pad, exchanged a few words with Jackson about scheduling, and left. The conference room emptied with the silence that follows confession. Not the silence of a space that had been quiet, but the silence of a space that had been full.

Amaya stood in the observation room and pressed her hand flat against the one-way glass. On the other side, the table where Emily had sat still held the impression of her sweaty palms, the faint warmth of a body that had been pressed against a surface for two hours while its occupant dismantled her own life, piece by piece, with the same organizational precision she'd brought to building it.

She thought about Trouble. Not strategically. Not in the way she thought about the cat during investigations, as an instrument or a barometer. She thought about Trouble the way she thought about her on evenings when the work was done and the duplex was quiet and the cat's warm weight settled on her lap with the uncomplicated certainty of an animal that had chosen its person and intended to stay. She wanted to go home. She wanted to sit on her couch with a cat on her chest and listen to the radiator click and let the day's weight disintegrate across the hours until it became bearable.

That was what the cats gave her, she realized. Not just investigative assistance, not just domestic comedy. They gave her a place to return to. A household that persisted in its warmth and its small demands and its unshakable routines regardless of what the world outside had required of her. Trouble would be on the windowsill. Mayhem would be on the couch. Chaos would be somewhere he wasn't supposed to be. And the duplex would feel like home, and the warmth would start, and the case would begin its slow transition from present tense to past.

Jackson appeared in the doorway. He leaned against the frame, his tie loosened, the controlled energy of the morning's operation having settled into the exhaustion that followed sustained intensity. He looked at Amaya through the glass, and something in his expression told her he understood exactly what she was feeling, the depletion that came from watching someone unburden themselves of the truth.

"She protected Lydia," Amaya said.

"She did."

"That doesn't redeem what she did."

"No. It complicates it." Jackson rubbed the back of his neck, the first unguarded gesture of fatigue she'd seen from him. "Simple cases are easy. Complicated ones are the ones that are tougher."

Amaya looked at him, the loosened tie, the tired eyes, the weight of a morning that had begun with a tactical breach and ended with a woman confessing to a crime motivated by student debt and institutional invisibility. He looked like a man who'd done this enough times to know that justice and satisfaction rarely arrived in the same package.

"Buy you a coffee?" she asked.

The offer was small, practical, and contained within it nothing that either of them needed to examine too closely. A colleague offering caffeine after a long morning. That was all.

Jackson straightened from the doorframe. "There's a place around the corner that has coffee doesn't taste like precinct brew."

"That's a low bar."

"It's the bar we've got."

They walked out of the Major Case Squad's offices together, into a midday that had the thin, washed quality of November after a light rain. The city moved around them—taxis, pedestrians, a vendor selling roasted nuts from a cart whose heat shimmered in the cold air. Amaya felt the morning's adrenaline receding, replaced by something quieter and more durable: the knowledge that the case was closing, that the evidence was sound, and that the woman who'd confessed behind the one-way glass had chosen, in her final statement, to exonerate the one person she'd hurt the most.

It didn't make it right. But it made it human.

And human, Amaya had learned, was the only material the truth was ever made from.

She'd go home after the coffee. Trouble would be waiting at the window, her silhouette sleek and dark against the afternoon light. And the warmth would start before Amaya's key turned in the lock. Because Trouble heard her footsteps on the stairs, every time, and answered them the only way she knew how.

Chapter 18: Aftermath

The story broke at four p.m., and by six, it was everywhere.

Amaya watched it unfold from the couch in her Riverdale duplex, Trouble on her lap, the television tuned to NY1 with the volume low enough to follow without being assaulted. The local anchor, a woman whose professional composure reminded Amaya uncomfortably of Emily—delivered the facts with the controlled gravity that news outlets reserved for stories that were simultaneously shocking and inevitable: two arrests in connection with a series of art thefts from the Studio Museum in Harlem. A gallery owner. A museum employee. An underground tunnel. Stolen artwork valued in excess of two million dollars.

The number was larger than Amaya had calculated. Jackson's team, working through the coded inventory in Calvin's storage facility, had cross-referenced the entries against stolen art databases and identified not just the Studio Museum pieces but works from a private collection in Connecticut, an estate in Philadelphia, and a small gallery in Newark that had reported a theft nine months ago and received nothing but a case number. The scope of Calvin's operation was still expanding, and the final accounting would take weeks.

Mayhem was sprawled across the couch cushion beside her, his muscular body occupying almost half the couch, his eyes half-closed in the expression of a cat who had decided television was beneath his interest. His back paw rested against Amaya's thigh.

Chaos was in the kitchen, where he'd been for the past twenty minutes. Amaya could hear him, a series of small thuds interspersed with the crinkle of something that was probably the bread bag again. But she'd made the tactical decision to let it continue. The day had taken everything she had, and the energy required to stop the cat from disassembling a loaf of whole grain was energy she no longer possessed.

Her phone had been buzzing since the story broke. Lydia, twice. Derek, once. Ron, a text that read simply: *Saw the news. Thank you.* Two reporters she didn't know had somehow obtained her number and left voicemails requesting comment. She'd returned Lydia's call and Derek's, ignored the reporters, and sent Ron a reply: *Thank Keisha.*

The news coverage cycled through the same footage, the exterior of Calvin's gallery, the museum's facade, a stock photo of the Edmondson bronze that didn't capture a fraction of its power. Commentators speculated about the tunnel with the breathless enthusiasm of people who'd discovered that New York City contained secrets, which Amaya found both amusing and exhausting. The tunnel wasn't a marvel. It was infrastructure—old, repurposed, and maintained by people who understood that the most effective systems were the ones nobody knew existed.

She turned off the television. The duplex settled into its evening sounds: the radiators clicking, the wind pressing against the windows, Chaos's ongoing kitchen expedition, and Mayhem's breathing deepening into the slow rhythm of approaching sleep. Trouble remained awake on Amaya's lap, her gold eyes open, her body warm and still. The cat had been like this since Amaya came home. Not sleeping, not playing, just present, her weight a steady anchor against the day's turbulence.

Amaya rested her hand on Trouble's back and felt the vibration of a purr beginning—low, almost subliminal, the pitch that research suggested promoted healing in bone and tissue. Whether cats purred for their own benefit or their humans' was a question science hadn't fully answered. Amaya suspected it was both, and that the distinction mattered less than the effect.

"Long day," she murmured.

Trouble's purr deepened. Agreement, or solidarity, or the simple statement that she was here and that here was enough.

Thursday brought the board meeting.

Amaya wasn't present, the meeting was closed, board members only, held in the museum's third-floor conference room behind doors that Derek's team guarded with focused attention. But Lydia had called her that morning, her voice carrying the particular steadiness of a person who'd spent the night preparing for something she couldn't fully prepare for.

"They're going to ask me to resign," Lydia had said. "Some of them, at least. The ones who warned me about security gaps. They will rewrite the history to say they saw this coming."

"What are you going to do?"

"I'm going to sit in that room and tell the truth. About what I knew, what I missed, and what I should have done differently." A pause that held the weight of three sleepless nights. "And then I'm going to let them decide."

"Lydia—for what it's worth. You built something real. The failures were real too, but they don't erase what the museum is. What it means to that community."

"I keep hearing Emily's voice," Lydia said quietly. "Not from the confession. From before. The way she used to say 'we built this' when we were working late, hanging pieces for a new show, eating takeout on the gallery floor at midnight. She meant it then. I know she did." A breath. "That's what I can't reconcile. The person who helped me build this museum and the person who helped dismantle it—they're the same woman."

Amaya had no answer for that. Some truths didn't resolve into lessons. They just sat where they landed, heavy and permanent, and you learned to build around them.

The board meeting lasted four hours. Amaya spent them at home, working through the administrative closure of her own involvement—compiling her final report, organizing the evidence she'd hand over to the DA's office, and drafting the invoice she'd send to the museum for her services. The work was mundane and necessary, the kind of procedural attention that her grandmother had always insisted was as important as the investigation itself. "You close a case as you open it," Eleanor had said. "With discipline. Everything documented, everything filed, everything accounted for. The work isn't finished until the paperwork is done."

Trouble supervised from the desk, her paw resting on the edge of Amaya's laptop with a proprietary air; she considered all electronic devices to be furniture. Chaos had migrated from the kitchen to the office and was asleep in the paper tray of the printer, his ginger body curled into a ball. Mayhem patrolled the perimeter—desk to bookshelf to window to hallway and back, his restless energy finding expression in movement rather than destruction, for once.

At two-fifteen, Amaya's phone rang. Lydia.

"They didn't ask me to resign."

Amaya felt the tension she'd been carrying, a tightness across her shoulders she hadn't fully acknowledged—release by a fraction. "What did they decide?"

"A structured oversight plan. Independent security audit. Financial review by an outside firm. Monthly reporting to an executive committee for the next twelve months." Lydia's voice held a quality Amaya hadn't heard before. Not relief exactly, but the sound of a person who'd been bracing for worst and found the ground still beneath her feet. "Two board members pushed for my resignation. The rest voted for accountability with continuity. They said—" her voice caught, then steadied, "They said the museum needed stability, not another loss."

"They were right."

"The conditions are strict. I'll have less autonomy than I've had since the day I was hired. Every hire, every expenditure, every security decision will go through the oversight committee." A pause that carried the sound of a woman recalibrating her relationship with an institution she'd led for nearly a decade. "It's going to feel like starting over."

"Starting over with a building, a collection, a community that trusts you, and the knowledge of exactly what to watch for. Most people who start over don't get any of those."

The silence on the line was warm. Not empty but full, the quiet of a connection that had been endured under pressure and had held. Then Lydia said something that surprised Amaya.

"I'd like to hire you. Not for investigation—for consulting. Security protocols, access management, the systems that should have been in place from the beginning. I want your eyes on this building until I trust my own again."

Amaya looked at Trouble, who had lifted her head from the laptop at the sound of Lydia's voice through the phone's speaker. The cat's amber eyes held the steady, evaluative focus she brought to every new proposition— measuring not the words but the intention behind them.

"Send me a proposal," Amaya said. "We'll talk."

"Thank you, Amaya. For everything."

The call ended. Amaya sat in her office, the afternoon light slanting through the window, the sounds of Riverdale drifting in, a leaf blower somewhere on the block, a school bus grinding through its route, the distant bark of a dog who had opinions about the leaf blower.

Trouble settled her chin on the edge of the laptop and closed her eyes. Chaos shifted in the printer tray, his tail dangling over the paper output slot. Mayhem completed another patrol circuit and came to rest at Amaya's feet, his solid body a warm weight against her ankles.

The case was closed. Not fully, the legal process would grind forward for months, the DA building the prosecution while Calvin's and Emily's attorneys built their defenses. The coded inventory would take weeks to fully catalogue and trace. The five additional stolen pieces would generate their own investigations, their own victims, their own stories of loss and recovery.

But Amaya's part, the architecture she'd built from Lydia's first phone call through the tunnel exploration, the financial forensics, the interviews, the midnight bench at the Apollo, and the morning breach that brought the doors down. That part was complete.

Her phone buzzed. A text from Alton: *Evidence processing is going to take a while. But the Adeyemi painting has been authenticated and cleared for return. Lydia can have it back next week.*

Amaya smiled. The first piece stolen. The first piece coming home.

She typed back: *She'll want a ceremony. She's a museum director. They can't help themselves.*

His reply: *As long as there's no champagne. I'm still on the clock.*

There will absolutely be champagne.

Then I'll suffer through it.

She set the phone down and leaned back in her chair. Trouble's chin was still on the laptop, her breathing slow and even. The purr had returned. That low, healing frequency, vibrating through the cat's body into the desk's surface and from there into the air of the office, filling the room with a sound that was older than language and more reliable than words.

Outside, the November afternoon was fading toward early dark, the season's reminder that light was finite and that the hours between dusk and dawn were longer than most people remembered. But the duplex was warm. The cats were close. The work was done, or done enough, and the rest would keep until morning.

Amaya closed her eyes and let the purr carry her away.

The community found out the way communities always do. In pieces, through conversations at bodegas and barbershops and church lobbies, through group texts and social media threads and the telephone-game velocity of neighborhood news. By Friday, the story had moved from the television and into the streets, taking on the texture and weight of something personal.

Amaya felt it when she walked through Harlem on Friday afternoon, returning to the museum to deliver her final report. The neighborhood's response wasn't uniform. It never was. But the dominant notes were anger and pride in roughly equal measure. Anger that someone had stolen from an institution the community had built and defended through decades of neglect and gentrification. Pride that the theft had been uncovered, that the art was coming home, and that the people who'd protected the museum. Derek, Keisha, the staff who'd continued showing up every day— were being recognized.

A mural had appeared overnight on the side of a building on 126th Street, two blocks from the museum, painted in bold strokes of blue and gold. It depicted a pair of hands releasing a bird from a cage, the bird's wings spread wide, the cage dissolving into abstract fragments below. No attribution. No explanation. Just the image and, in the lower right corner, two words: *Art Returns.*

Amaya stood in front of it for a long moment. The paint was still fresh. She could smell it, sharp and alive in the cold air. Someone had climbed a scaffold in the middle of the night and put this on a wall, not for money or recognition but because the moment demanded a response and this was the response they knew how to give.

This was what Calvin's philosophy had missed. He'd talked about preserving art by removing it—relocating it to collectors who would cherish it behind closed doors. But art didn't exist in isolation. It existed in relationship, with the space it occupied, the community that surrounded it, the conversations it provoked between strangers standing on a sidewalk in November, looking up.

The mural was unsigned, and it was more valuable than anything in Calvin Whitaker's climate-controlled vault.

Amaya adjusted her collar against the cold and walked the remaining two blocks to the museum. Lydia was waiting. The report was ready. And on 126th Street, a pair of painted hands released a bird into the Harlem sky, and the neighborhood watched it fly.

Chapter 19: Homecoming

Eleanor called on Sunday at seven p.m. Eastern, as she always did, and Amaya picked up on the second ring, as she always did, and for the first thirty seconds neither of them spoke about the case, because Eleanor Storm believed in establishing the baseline of a conversation before introducing its subject.

"How are the cats?"

"Chaos opened a bag of kibble from the bottom and distributed two pounds of it across the kitchen floor."

"Resourceful. I assume Mayhem cleaned it up."

"Like a snowplow."

"And Trouble?"

"Judged them both from the counter."

"That's my girl." A pause. Not the kind that signaled a transition but the kind that held space, the way Eleanor held space in every conversation, allowing the silence to do its work before the words arrived. In the background, Amaya could hear the ambient hum of Eleanor's condo, the low murmur of a television turned to a volume that suggested it was company rather than entertainment, the occasional clink of ice in a glass.

"I watched the news," Eleanor said.

"I knew you would."

"Two arrests. An underground tunnel." Another pause, and then Eleanor's voice shifted into the lower register she reserved for conversations that mattered. "Tell me about it. Not the facts. I got those from the news. Tell me what it felt like."

Amaya was sitting on the floor of her living room, her back against the couch, Trouble pressed against her right thigh and Chaos draped across her outstretched legs like a carroty blanket. Mayhem was somewhere in the duplex. She could hear the irregular thump of him batting something down the upstairs hallway, a sound that had become so familiar it functioned as white noise. The evening was dark and quiet, and the phone was warm against her ear, and her grandmother's voice was two thousand miles away and as close as the next breath.

"The investigation was clean. The evidence was solid. The operation went exactly as planned. But the people at the center of it—" She stopped, searching for words that matched the weight. "The woman who confessed. Emily. She wasn't a monster, Grandma. She was someone who felt invisible in a place she'd helped build, and that invisibility turned into something corrosive. By the time she realized what she'd become, she was too deep to climb out."

"Most criminals are." Eleanor's voice was matter-of-fact, carrying the authority of a woman who'd spent three decades watching people arrive at the worst moments of their lives. "The ones who scare me aren't the ones with plans. It's the ones who started with grievances. Grievances fester. They'll wait years for the right opportunity, and when it comes, the person holding the grievance barely recognizes what they've become."

"She protected Lydia in her confession. Went on the record saying Lydia had no knowledge of any of it."

"Did you believe her?"

"Yes."

"Then it's the truest thing she said." Eleanor took a sip of whatever was in her glass. Amaya pictured bourbon, neat, the drink her grandmother had favored since before Amaya was born. "And the man? The gallery owner?"

"Calvin Whitaker. He's more complicated. He genuinely loves art—I've never doubted that. He has a real philosophy about preservation, about who art belongs to, about what happens when institutions fail their collections. Some of what he said was true. But he used that truth to justify stealing from a community museum that was doing exactly what he claimed institutions should do."

"Idealists make the most dangerous thieves, Nhoma. They steal with one hand and justify with the other, and by the time you catch them, they've convinced themselves the philosophy is the truth." The ice clinked again. "Did the museum survive?"

"The director kept her position. Strict oversight, independent audits, twelve months of probation essentially. But the building's standing and the collection is being recovered."

"Good. Reputations are harder to rebuild than institutions." A beat of silence that felt different from the others—warmer, more personal, carrying a warmth a grandmother about to say something she'd been saving. "I'm proud of you. Not for solving the case. You were always going to solve the case. I'm proud of how you solved it. Patient. Disciplined. You built the house right, and when you knocked on the door, the foundation held."

Amaya felt the warmth of the words spread through her chest. Not the quick heat of a compliment but the deep, slow warmth of recognition from the person whose opinion she valued most. Eleanor Storm did not distribute praise casually. She'd spent thirty-two years in the NYPD being told she was good, and she'd learned that "good" was a word people used when they meant "sufficient." When Eleanor said she was proud, she meant something specific, and that is what made it land.

"The cats helped," Amaya said, and she meant it in every sense the words could carry.

"Trouble?."

"Trouble found the wall. Mayhem found the sculpture. Chaos—" she looked down at the ginger tabby draped across her legs, his vibration moving through her kneecaps like a small engine, ". Chaos made a nervous security guard feel safe enough to talk."

Eleanor laughed, the full, rich sound that Amaya associated with her grandmother's best moments, the laugh that had survived thirty-two years of police work and the loss of a husband and the relocation to a desert city two thousand miles from everything she'd known. "You've got a good team, Nhoma. Human and otherwise."

"I do."

"Now get some rest. And tell the cats I said they earned a raise."

"They'd settle for the premium salmon."

"Then give them the premium salmon. They earned it."

They said their goodnights, the same way they always did, Eleanor's "goodnight, baby" carrying the full weight of a love that had never needed explanation, and the line went quiet. Amaya sat on the floor of her living room, the phone dark in her hand, the duplex humming its evening song around her. Trouble pressed closer against her thigh. Chaos's humming continued its steady rhythm. And upstairs, Mayhem's batting game reached its conclusion with a final thump and the sound of something rolling under a piece of furniture, followed by absolute silence, signaling the cat had lost his toy.

"It's under the dresser," Amaya called.

A pause. Then the sound of the toy bouncing around again.

She smiled in the dark.

The ceremony happened on a Wednesday, twelve days after the arrests.

Lydia had organized it with the attention to detail that defined everything she did when she was operating at full capacity—which, Amaya noted with quiet satisfaction, she was again. The board's oversight committee had approved the event, the museum's PR team had managed the media requests, and Derek's security staff had implemented a protocol so thorough that a mouse couldn't have entered the building without a background check.

The main gallery had been reconfigured for the occasion. The Nkechi Adeyemi painting, the first piece stolen, the first piece recovered—hung in the center of the primary wall, its mixed-media surface catching the track lighting and returning it in fragments of color and texture that seemed to vibrate with the energy of the room. Beside it, a placard read: *Returned to the Studio Museum through the efforts of its community, its staff, and the investigators who refused to let our heritage disappear.*

The Edmondson bronze stood on a pedestal in the gallery's center, its patina glowing under a dedicated spotlight. The sculpture had been examined, conserved, and documented by the museum's own team. Derek had personally overseen its transport from evidence storage, and the care with which he'd handled the return told Amaya everything about what this piece meant to him. Not as evidence. As heritage.

The Okonkwo installation was still in evidence—its size and complexity made it the last piece to clear the forensic process. But a photograph of the work occupied the space where it would eventually be reinstalled, accompanied by a note from the artist: *This piece was created to speak about displacement. Its theft and recovery have given it a voice I never intended but am grateful it found.*

The crowd filled the gallery and spilled into the lobby. It wasn't the black-tie assembly of the galas Amaya had attended—this was something different, something closer to the neighborhood itself. Families with children who pointed at the paintings and asked questions. Elderly residents who remembered the museum's original building and spoke about it with the proprietary affection of people who'd watched something grow. Young artists carrying sketchbooks, documenting the exhibition with the intensity of people who understood that what hung on these walls was both history and permission.

Amaya circulated with Trouble in her carrier, the cat had become a familiar presence at the museum, and several staff members greeted her by name. Derek's security team treated Trouble with the professional courtesy reserved for colleagues, which amused Amaya more than it should have.

Lydia spoke from a small podium near the Adeyemi painting. She didn't deliver a speech. She delivered an acknowledgment, brief and direct, naming the people who'd contributed to the recovery without dramatizing the process. Derek Osei, for his watchance and integrity. Keisha Williams, for her documentation and courage. The NYPD's Major Case Squad, for their partnership. And

Amaya Storm, "whose investigative skill and three remarkable cats helped bring our art home."

The crowd's laughter at the mention of the cats was warm and genuine, a response that arose when something true was also something unexpected. Amaya raised a hand in acknowledgment, and Trouble chose that precise moment to stick her head through the carrier's mesh panel and survey the room, her gaze sweeping the assembled crowd with the regal composure of a dignitary accepting applause.

The timing was coincidental. Amaya was almost certain.

Alton was there, standing near the back of the room in a dark suit that fit him better than anything she'd seen him wear during the investigation. He held a glass of champagne—suffering through it, as promised, and when Amaya's eyes found his across the crowded gallery, he raised the glass a fraction. Not a toast. An acknowledgment. A gesture that said everything.

She raised her own glass in return and turned back to the room.

Ron Devane was in the crowd. Amaya spotted him near the Edmondson bronze, his expression cycling between the awe of an artist encountering mastery and the bittersweet recognition that this space, which had rejected his work, was also the space that had given his community something to fight for. Keisha stood beside him, her arm linked through his, her posture straighter than Amaya had ever seen it. The nervous woman from Estrella's diner was gone, replaced by someone who'd found her footing.

Derek stood at his post near the gallery entrance, his uniform impeccable, his posture carrying the quiet authority of a man who'd been vindicated and didn't need anyone to say so. When the Edmondson bronze had been unveiled, Amaya had seen his expression, a momentary fracture in his professional composure, his eyes glistening, his jaw working against something that wanted out. He'd mastered it in seconds, but Amaya had caught it, and so had Trouble, whose gaze had tracked Derek's reaction with the attention she reserved for moments of genuine human emotion.

The evening wound down gently. Guests lingered, conversations deepening as the champagne flowed and the art drew people into the kind of exchanges that happened only in spaces where beauty and meaning intersected. Amaya found herself in a series of encounters, with board members who thanked her, with artists who wanted to discuss the museum's future programming, with a ten-year-old girl who asked to pet Trouble and then announced that she wanted to be a "cat detective" when she grew up.

"The field is wide open," Amaya told her. "But the cats are the ones who do the hiring."

The girl looked at Trouble, who blinked at her slowly, the feline gesture of trust, and the child's face split into a grin that could have powered the gallery's lighting system.

As the crowd thinned, Amaya found a quiet corner near the Adeyemi painting and stood before it. The work was beautiful—fragmented, reassembled, its subject's face both broken and whole, a visual argument for the persistence of identity through disruption. She thought about Nkechi Adeyemi, the emerging artist whose first major museum piece had been stolen before it could fully enter the world. She thought about what it meant to have that piece returned. Not just as property recovered but as a statement that the art mattered, the artist mattered, and the community that had built a house for both would not allow them to disappear.

Trouble shifted in the carrier, her warm body pressing against the mesh. The cat's eyes reflected the painting's colors—fragments of cobalt and gold swimming in pools of burnished amber, and for a moment, Amaya saw the work the way Trouble might see it: not as meaning or metaphor but as pattern, as light, as the arrangement of the world into something worth attending to.

That was enough. That was always enough.

She adjusted the carrier strap, finished her champagne, and walked toward the lobby, where the November evening waited with its cold air and its dark sky and its city, always its city, humming beneath the stars with the persistence of a place that never learned how to sleep.

Chapter 20: Community Canvas

December arrived in the Bronx as it always did. Not gradually but with a declaration, the temperature dropping twenty degrees in a single night. Amaya woke on the first Saturday of the month to frost on the inside of her office window and Mayhem sitting on her chest, his twenty-pound body pinning her to the mattress, his green eyes communicating with absolute clarity that the radiator had failed to meet his standards and breakfast was late

"You are too heavy for this," she informed him.

He lowered his head onto her collarbone and closed his eyes. Debate concluded.

She lay beneath him for a few minutes, listening to the duplex wake up around her. Trouble was already on the windowsill, her silhouette visible against the gray morning light, her breath misting faintly on the glass. She'd been watching the street again, the eternal watch that Amaya had never fully decoded. What did Trouble see out there every morning? What pattern held her attention through the slow transition from dark to light, from silence to sound, from the empty sidewalk to the first dog walker's appearance at six-forty-five?

Amaya suspected the answer was everything. Trouble watched because watching was who she was, the same way Amaya investigated because investigating was who she was, the same way Eleanor played poker because reading people across a table was a skill that didn't retire just because you moved to the desert. They were all, in their own ways, creatures of attention.

Chaos announced morning from the bathroom. The sound was his signature wake-up call, a yowl that combined the urgency of a fire alarm with the emotional pitch of a Shakespearean soliloquy, produced by a cat standing in an empty bathtub where the acoustics amplified his voice to a volume that the building's walls barely contained. The first time he'd done it, shortly after Amaya adopted him, she'd called the vet. The vet had listened to the recording, laughed, and said, "He's singing. Some cats are just vocalists."

Chaos had been performing his morning aria ever since, and the bathtub remained his preferred venue.

Amaya extricated herself from beneath Mayhem, a process that required negotiation, because the cat went boneless the moment she tried to move him, his muscular body converting to the approximate weight and consistency of a sandbag, and started the morning routine. Coffee. Kibble in three bowls. A check of the radiator, which had in fact stopped working overnight and which she addressed with a series of percussive adjustments to the valve that Mayhem watched with critical attention.

The radiator coughed, clanked, and kicked on. Mayhem looked unimpressed.

By nine, she was dressed and heading south on the 1 train, Trouble in her carrier, bound for Harlem. The museum had announced a community open day—free admission, workshops for children and adults, tours of the restored collection, and the public launch of a project that Lydia had been quietly developing since the board meeting: a community mural initiative that would invite local artists to create works for the museum's exterior walls.

The idea had come from the unsigned mural on 126th Street, the hands releasing the bird, the two words that had become a neighborhood rallying cry. *Art Returns*. Lydia had seen it on her walk to the museum the morning after it appeared, and something about it had cracked open a part of her thinking that the investigation and its aftermath had sealed shut. The museum had spent years bringing art into the building. What if it also brought art out—into the streets, onto the walls, into the daily visual landscape of a community that had always expressed itself through public creation?

The project needed artists. And that was how Ron Devane had gotten the call.

Amaya arrived at the museum to find 125th Street transformed. Tables had been set up along the sidewalk outside the entrance, covered with art supplies—paper, paints, brushes, crayons, chalk. Children were already working, their small hands producing the kind of art that adults spent years trying to recapture: unself-conscious, vivid, entirely present. A group of teenagers had claimed a section of sidewalk and were producing a collaborative chalk drawing that extended from the museum's entrance to the corner, a river of color flowing along the concrete.

Inside, the galleries were alive with a different kind of energy than the galas had produced. The crowd was local—Harlem residents, families, students from nearby schools, elderly couples who moved through the exhibition with the slow attentiveness of people reconnecting with something they'd missed. Docents stationed throughout the galleries offered context and conversation, and the atmosphere was more block party than black tie.

Trouble observed from her carrier with the restrained approval of a cat who appreciated organization but preferred to maintain distance. When a child of about four approached the carrier with the intense gravitational pull that young children exerted toward anything furry, Trouble submitted to the encounter with her customary grace—extending one paw through the mesh to be touched, accepting the child's delighted squeal as the cost of public engagement, and withdrawing the paw precisely when she'd had enough.

"She's very patient," the child's mother said.

"She's very strategic," Amaya corrected. "She knows exactly how much charm to deploy and when to pull it back."

The mother laughed, and the child moved on to the next exhibit, where a docent was explaining how sculptures were made to a group of first-graders whose attention spans were, optimistically, ninety seconds each. Amaya watched the scene, the docent's enthusiasm, the children's fidgeting wonder, the way one boy had stopped listening entirely and was instead studying the gallery floor with the focused intensity of someone who'd found something worth investigating.

She recognized that look. She'd worn it herself at that age.

Lydia found her in the main gallery, standing before the Adeyemi painting with Trouble's carrier at her hip. The director looked different today. Not the polished version from the galas, not the fraying version from the investigation, but something newer. Her silver-templed hair was loose rather than styled, her outfit practical—slacks, a sweater, comfortable shoes. She wore no makeup that Amaya could detect, and her face, unadorned, carried the beauty of a person who'd stopped performing and started showing up.

"It's working," Lydia said, gesturing at the crowd. "Look at them. They're here because it's theirs. Not because they were invited or because they read about it or because someone told them it was important. They're here because it's theirs."

"It always was."

"I know that now." Lydia's voice carried the specific gravity of hard-won understanding. "I spent nine years treating this museum like something I was building for the community. It took almost losing it to realize the community was always building it with me. I just wasn't listening to the right voices."

They stood together before the painting, two women connected by an investigation that had stripped away pretense and left behind something more durable. Amaya felt the warmth of an acquaintanceship that had become, through proximity to pain and recovery, something closer to friendship.

"Come with me," Lydia said. "There's someone I want you to see."

She led Amaya to the museum's community room, a large, flexible space on the ground floor that was usually configured for lectures and workshops. Today, it had been cleared and set up as a studio. Drop cloths covered the floor. Easels stood in rows. And at the center of the room, surrounded by a group of teenagers and young adults who watched him with the intensity of students witnessing mastery, Ron Devane was painting.

He worked on a canvas that was six feet wide and four feet tall, the scale alone commanding attention, but it was the image taking shape that stopped Amaya in the doorway. He was painting the museum. Not the building, the idea of it. The canvas showed the facade of the Studio Museum dissolving at its edges into the surrounding neighborhood, the building's glass and steel merging with brownstone and brick, the artwork inside flowing through the walls and into the streets where it mixed with the life already there, a woman braiding a child's hair, a man playing a saxophone, two teenagers debating over a chess board, a cat watching from a fire escape.

The cat was black, sleek, with amber eyes.

Amaya looked at Ron. He caught her gaze and shrugged, the gesture carrying the self-conscious amusement of an artist who'd been caught painting something personal into a public work.

"She's iconic," he said. "Deal with it."

"Does Trouble get royalties?"

"She gets immortality. That's better."

The students laughed. Ron returned to the painting, and Amaya watched him work, his hands sure, his strokes bold, the image emerging with the authority of an artist who'd found his subject and knew exactly what he wanted to say. This was not the angry young man who'd crashed a gala three months ago. This was the artist that anger had always been protecting—someone with vision, skill, and the fierce love for a community that his work had always expressed, even when the institutions built to recognize that love had failed to see it.

Lydia watched from beside Amaya, her expression holding the complex mixture of pride and regret that characterized every interaction Amaya had witnessed between the director and the artists she served. "I've offered Ron a solo exhibition in the spring. The curatorial committee approved it unanimously."

"How did he take it?"

"He cried. Then he told me my taste was improving. Then he got to work." Lydia smiled, a real one, unperformed, reaching her eyes. "He's going to be extraordinary. He already is, but the world is about to find out."

Ron was explaining his technique to the students now, walking them through color theory and composition with the natural fluency of a born teacher. One student, a girl of about sixteen with paint-stained fingers and the hungry expression of someone who'd found the thing they wanted to do with their life—was reproducing his brushwork on a smaller canvas, her strokes tentative but growing bolder as Ron encouraged her.

"That's it," he said, watching her work. "Don't think about it—feel the line. The brush knows what to do if you let it."

Amaya thought about Eleanor, teaching her to observe in Crotona Park. About the woman with mismatched shoes, and the lesson buried within the observation: see what's there, not what you expect. The line from grandmother to granddaughter to the work she did now—patient, attentive, built on the foundation of being taught to look—felt suddenly visible, a thread running through time and connecting the bench in the park to the bench at the Apollo to this room where a young artist was teaching the next generation to see.

Trouble shifted in her carrier. Through the mesh, her gaze was fixed on the canvas where Ron had painted her likeness, a black cat on a fire escape, watching the world with the attention that was her defining quality. Whether the cat recognized herself was unknowable. But she watched the painted version of herself with the same steady focus she brought to everything, and Amaya chose to believe it was appreciation.

The afternoon unfolded with the generous pace of an event that had no agenda beyond presence. Children painted. Adults talked. Artists demonstrated techniques and answered questions with the openness of people who understood that mystery was the enemy of community. The galleries stayed full, the workshops stayed loud, and the museum, which had been, for six months, a place defined by what had been taken from it—became, for an afternoon, a place defined by what it gave.

Amaya moved through it all with Trouble at her hip, observing the way she always observed, the dynamics between people, the energy of the spaces, the small moments that told larger stories. A grandfather explaining a painting to his granddaughter with the seriousness of a professor and the tenderness of a man sharing something precious. Two women arguing good-naturedly about whether a sculpture was beautiful or terrifying, and discovering through the argument that it was both. A security guard, one of Derek's team—crouching to help a child who'd spilled a cup of paint, his uniform absorbing a splash of blue without complaint.

Derek himself was there, not in uniform but in civilian clothes, the second time Amaya had seen him out of his professional armor. He stood near the Edmondson bronze, answering questions from visitors about the sculpture's history and significance with a knowledge that went beyond security training into genuine scholarship. When asked how the piece had been recovered, he said simply, "Good people doing careful work," and moved on to the next question.

Keisha was at his side for part of the afternoon. Not on duty, not in uniform, just present. She and Derek spoke quietly at intervals, their conversations carrying the easy rhythm of colleagues who'd been through something together and emerged with a mutual respect that didn't require explanation. When Keisha saw Amaya, she crossed the room and hugged her, a quick, fierce embrace that communicated more than any debrief could have.

"Thank you," Keisha said. "For listening."

"Thank you for documenting. Your records were the backbone of the case."

Keisha's eyes shone. "Derek says he's recommending me for a promotion. Assistant head of security. He says I've earned it."

"He's right."

As the afternoon light began to fade and the crowd thinned, Amaya found herself alone in the main gallery with the Adeyemi painting and the Edmondson bronze and the empty space where the Okonkwo installation would eventually return. The quiet settled around her like a held breath, the museum in its natural state, between visitors, between events, just a building full of art doing what art did when no one was watching: existing. Being present. Holding the accumulated weight of human expression in frames and on pedestals and against walls, waiting for the next pair of eyes to arrive and find something worth seeing.

Trouble's purr started. Low, steady, the healing frequency. The cat had been quiet all afternoon—engaged but reserved, her energy directed outward toward the crowd, the art, the shifting dynamics of a community space in full operation. Now, in the gallery's emptying silence, she was directing it inward—toward Amaya, toward the shared quiet between them, toward the peace that arrived when a case was closed and the world had been, in some small but measurable way, set right.

"Ready to go home?" Amaya asked.

Trouble blinked once. Slow. Definitive.

They walked out of the museum into the December dusk. 125th Street was settling into its twilight register, the sidewalk art supplies packed away, the chalk drawings already fading under passing feet, the storefronts lighting up for the evening rush. The temperature had dropped further, and Amaya's breath misted in the air as she turned west toward the subway.

On 126th Street, the mural still blazed against the brick, the hands, the bird, the dissolving cage. *Art Returns*. And beside it now, staked to the sidewalk on a simple wire stand, someone had placed a hand-lettered sign:

Community mural project — Studio Museum in Harlem

Applications open — all artists welcome

Your walls. Your stories. Your art.

Amaya read it twice. Then she looked at Trouble, whose eyes reflected the mural's blues and golds, and felt something settle in her chest that had been restless since Lydia Brooks's first phone call, a sense of completion, not of the case but of the circle. Art stolen, art recovered, art returned. And now, art invited—out of the building, onto the walls, into the life of a neighborhood that had always been its own greatest canvas.

The subway swallowed them into its warmth, and the train carried them north through the tunnel beneath the Bronx, a different kind of tunnel than the one that had defined the investigation, this one public, lit, carrying thousands of people home every evening with the democratic efficiency of a system that moved everyone equally, regardless of what they carried.

Amaya carried a cat and a sense of peace and the knowledge that tomorrow would bring a new case, a new tangle of lies and loyalty and human mess. But tonight, the train rocked gently, and Trouble slept in her carrier, and the city's lights streaked past the windows like brushstrokes on a canvas that was never finished and never needed to be.

Chapter 21: The Quiet Between

The week after the community open day passed with the gentleness of time reclaimed from urgency. Amaya had no active cases. The Rourke file was closed. The Cuevas case—Diana's husband, the tire shop, the car meet group—had resolved itself quietly while the museum investigation consumed her attention: Rene Cuevas had been running stolen auto parts through a buddy's garage, small-time enough to warrant a plea deal and community service rather than prison. Diana had been grateful, exhausted, and exactly as resilient as Amaya had expected. The final invoice was paid, and Amaya had moved on.

Now, for the first time in months, her corkboard was empty. No pushpins. No red thread. No photographs or timelines or names circled in marker. Just cork—blank, porous, waiting.

She found the emptiness both peaceful and faintly alarming, the way a musician might feel about silence or a surgeon about idle hands. Her grandmother had warned her about this. "The hardest part of the work isn't the work," Eleanor had said. "It's what you do with yourself when the work stops. That's where most investigators go sideways. They can't sit still, so they pick up cases they shouldn't, or they start investigating their own lives, which never ends well."

Amaya was trying to sit still. The cats were helping.

Trouble had claimed the empty corkboard as a personal territory. She'd discovered that the cork surface accepted her claws with satisfying resistance, and she spent a portion of each morning performing a slow, deliberate stretching routine against it, her body elongated to its full length, her eyes half-closed with the pleasure of a cat engaged in important maintenance. The first time she'd done it, Amaya had worried about damage to the board. By the third morning, she'd accepted that the corkboard had been reallocated.

Mayhem had entered what Amaya privately called his "retirement phase", a period that followed each completed case during which his energy levels dropped from their usual eleven to a comfortable seven, and his primary occupation shifted from patrol to sleep. He'd constructed a nest in the living room from a combination of couch cushions, a throw blanket, and what appeared to be one of Amaya's scarves, and he occupied it with territorial authority. Occasionally he emerged to eat, drink, or survey his domain from the kitchen counter, but these excursions were brief and purposeful, after which he returned to the nest and resumed his duties.

Chaos, characteristically, had responded to the absence of a case by inventing one.

He'd become fixated on a squirrel.

The squirrel lived in the oak tree outside the duplex's kitchen window, and it had committed the unforgivable crime of existing within Chaos's visual range. Every morning, the ginger tabby stationed himself on the kitchen counter, a location he was technically forbidden from occupying and from which he had never once been successfully deterred, and watched the squirrel with the concentrated fury of a cat who was absolutely certain that the glass separating them was a temporary administrative obstacle.

The squirrel, for its part, appeared to know it was being watched. It would pause on the branch closest to the window, fix Chaos with a beady black eye, and perform an elaborate tail-flicking display that Amaya interpreted as either territorial signaling or deliberate provocation. Chaos's response was a full-body vibration accompanied by a chattering sound, a rapid clicking of his jaw that cat behaviorists attributed to frustrated prey drive and that Amaya attributed to a cat who was losing his mind.

"You will never catch that squirrel," Amaya told him on Thursday morning, watching the daily standoff over her coffee.

Chaos's tail lashed. The squirrel flicked its own tail in response. The détente continued.

The squirrel had been occupying that branch since September. Their relationship had evolved from Chaos's early lunges at the glass to a ritualized standoff, each party performing its role with the committed seriousness of actors who'd been running the same show for months.

"This is not healthy for either of you," Amaya said.

Neither of them acknowledged her. The détente had its own logic, its own ecosystem, its own rules of engagement that transcended human intervention. It was, in its small and ridiculous way, the most committed relationship in the household.

These were the rhythms of a household at rest—small, repetitive, profoundly ordinary. Amaya had learned to value them the way she valued the spaces between notes in music: not as absence but as structure, the intervals that gave the melody its shape. The cats understood this instinctively. Their days had patterns—sleep, eat, patrol, play, sleep, and the patterns persisted regardless of what Amaya's caseload demanded. When she was deep in an investigation, their routines anchored her. When the investigation ended, their routines welcomed her back into a world where the most pressing question was whether Mayhem had stolen her scarf.

He'd stolen it. She was certain.

On Friday afternoon, a package arrived at the duplex. The delivery driver rang the bell and left it on the landing, a flat, rectangular box, unexpectedly heavy, with no return address. Amaya brought it inside with the mild caution of a person whose professional life occasionally generated unexpected deliveries, and opened it on the dining table while Trouble watched from the desk and Chaos investigated the packing peanuts with delight.

Inside the box was a framed certificate. The frame was simple—black wood, clean lines, and the certificate bore the Studio Museum's letterhead, Lydia's signature, and the following text:

The Studio Museum in Harlem gratefully recognizes

AMAYA STORM

For exceptional service in the protection and recovery

of the museum's collection and cultural heritage.

With particular appreciation to her investigative partners:

Trouble, Mayhem, and Chaos

December 2024

Beneath the text, in the lower right corner, was a small illustration—clearly Ron's work—depicting three cats in silhouette: one sleek and watchful, one muscular and alert, one ginger and curious. The illustration was simple, elegant, and unmistakably a portrait of her cats, rendered with the specific attention of an artist who had met his subjects and understood them.

Amaya held the certificate and felt a wave of something she didn't have a ready word for—gratitude, certainly, but also a warmth that came from being seen. Not as a PI who'd solved a case, but as a person whose life included three animals who had contributed to the work in ways that no professional credential could capture.

Trouble jumped from the desk to the dining table, a leap she executed with precision, and approached the certificate. She sniffed the frame, studied the illustration for a long moment, and then sat down directly on top of it.

"That's framed. That's an honor. You're sitting on an honor."

Trouble regarded her with an unperturbed expression; she considered all flat surfaces, regardless of their ceremonial significance, to be seating.

Amaya laughed, the real kind, the kind that started in the belly and expanded outward, and lifted Trouble off the certificate. She propped it on the bookshelf beside the photo of Eleanor in her dress blues, where it would be visible from her office chair. The cats in silhouette and the grandmother in uniform, side by side, the two sources of the instincts that had built the case and the two anchors that had kept her steady while she built it.

A second package arrived on Saturday. This one was smaller, a padded envelope containing a handwritten note and a USB drive. The note was from Derek:

Amaya—

The attached video is from the museum's security cameras, the morning the Edmondson bronze was returned to the gallery. I thought you'd want to see it.

The museum owes you more than a certificate. But I hope this is a start.

— Derek

She plugged the USB into her laptop and played the video. The footage showed the museum's main gallery, empty in the early morning light. Two staff members, one of them Derek—carefully positioned the Edmondson bronze on its pedestal, adjusting the base, checking the alignment, stepping back to assess. They worked without haste, reverent, the movements of people handling something that mattered to them beyond its monetary value.

When the sculpture was in place, Derek stood before it alone. The camera angle was wide, the image slightly grainy, but what it captured was unmistakable: Derek Osei, head of security, standing at attention before a bronze sculpture he'd helped recover, his hand rising slowly to his forehead in a gesture that was part salute, part benediction, and entirely his own.

He held the position for three seconds. Then he straightened his uniform, checked his watch, and walked out of frame, resuming his duties with the disciplined composure that defined him. The gesture had lasted three seconds. It was the most personal thing she'd ever seen him do.

Amaya closed the laptop gently. On the bookshelf, the certificate with its three cat silhouettes stood beside Eleanor's photograph. By the couch, Mayhem's nest rustled as the big cat shifted in his sleep. From the kitchen, the sound of Chaos chattering at the squirrel continued its daily cycle, the cat's frustrated hunting instincts providing a soundtrack so consistent it had become ambient.

And on the desk, Trouble sat with her eyes closed, her breathing slow, her body warm and still in the December light that fell through the office window. She wasn't sleeping. Amaya knew the difference, the particular set of Trouble's ears, the faint tension in her paws, as her whiskers angled forward even at rest. She was listening. To the duplex. To Amaya. To the quiet, steady hum of a household that had weathered something together and come out whole on the other side.

Amaya reached over and rested her hand on Trouble's back. The cat's purr started immediately. Not the low healing vibration of difficult evenings but the lighter, steadier vibration of contentment. Simple, unambiguous, the sound of a cat who was exactly where she wanted to be.

"We did good," Amaya said.

Trouble's ear rotated toward her voice, then forward again—an acknowledgment and a redirect. *Yes.*

Amaya smiled. "Let's sit with this one for a while."

The purr continued. The squirrel flicked its tail. Mayhem snored. And the duplex held them all in its familiar embrace—warm, cluttered, alive with the small sounds of creatures that had chosen each other and continued choosing, every day, through chaos and calm and everything in between.

The afternoon passed without incident, which was its own kind of gift. Amaya read. The cats slept, or watched, or conducted their private investigations into the mysteries of squirrels and scarf theft and the acoustics of empty bathtubs. The city hummed outside the windows, and the December light moved slowly across the floor, tracking time in the ancient way that light always had—patient, indifferent, beautiful.

By evening, the duplex had settled into its deepest quiet. Amaya cooked—plantains and rice and beans, the comfort food of her childhood, the smells filling the kitchen and drifting through the rooms like a welcome. Mayhem emerged from his nest, drawn by the scent, and sat beside the stove with the respectful attention of a cat who knew that proximity to cooking increased the probability of dropped food. Chaos abandoned the squirrel vigil for the first time all day, his stomach overriding his obsession. Trouble came downstairs and positioned herself in the kitchen doorway. Not begging, never begging, but present in the way that communicates expectation without lowering oneself to request.

Amaya plated the food. She dropped a flake of plantain on the floor for Mayhem, who accepted it with dignified enthusiasm. She placed a small dish of salmon beside each cat's bowl, the premium kind, as Eleanor had instructed. And she let Chaos lick the serving spoon, because some battles weren't worth fighting and the cat had been very patient about the squirrel.

She ate at the dining table, the same table that had been covered with case files for weeks, now clear except for her plate and a glass of wine and the evening light. The cats ate in their respective spots: Trouble by the window, Mayhem by the stove, Chaos wherever the serving spoon had landed.

Silence held, and it was enough.

Chapter 22: The Introductions

He brought salmon.

Not the premium canned kind that Eleanor had suggested—actual salmon, a fresh fillet from a fishmonger on Arthur Avenue, wrapped in butcher paper and tucked into a brown bag alongside a bottle of wine that Amaya recognized as a good Malbec by the label and an excellent one by the price point she glimpsed before Alton angled the bag away.

"You didn't have to bring anything," she said, holding the door open.

"The salmon is for the cats. The wine is for you. I was told there would be introductions, and I don't show up to introductions empty-handed." He stepped inside with the careful attention of a man entering someone's home for the first time. Not hesitant, but observant, his eyes performing the same sweep she'd watched him do at Jimmy's Diner, at the Chelsea auction house, at the museum. Except this time, the sweep landed on framed photographs instead of exits, on cat furniture instead of witnesses, on the particular evidence of a life assembled with intention and maintained with love.

Amaya watched him take in the duplex, the living room with its mismatched furniture and overloaded bookshelves, the dining table cleared of case files but still bearing the faint ring stains of weeks of coffee cups, the hallway lined with photographs that told the story of her life in the Bronx from childhood forward. His gaze lingered on Eleanor's academy portrait, and something in his expression shifted—recognition, respect, the silent acknowledgment of one professional paying tribute to another across generations.

"She looks like she could solve a case by staring hard," Alton said.

"She could. She frequently did."

He set the bag on the kitchen counter and turned to find that the introductions had already begun.

Trouble was on the bookcase, positioned at Alton's eye level, a vantage point she'd selected with the strategic precision of a diplomat choosing her seat at a negotiating table. She hadn't moved since his arrival. She hadn't needed to. Her gaze tracked him with the same sustained focus she'd maintained throughout the diner meeting and the museum operation, the gaze suggested she was conducting a thorough evaluation and would release her findings when she was good and ready.

Alton met her stare. He didn't reach for her, didn't extend a hand, didn't make the sounds that people who didn't understand cats made when attempting to ingratiate themselves. He simply looked at her, the way one professional regarded another at the start of a working relationship, with respect for competence and no assumptions about friendship.

"Trouble," he said. Not a greeting. An acknowledgment.

Trouble's ears rotated forward a fraction—receiving, processing. Then she blinked. Once. Slow. The deliberate, half-lidded closure that cat behaviorists called the "slow blink", which Amaya had come to understand as the highest compliment in Trouble's vocabulary: *I see you. You may stay.*

Alton's mouth moved in the direction of a smile. "I've been vetted by FBI agents who were less methodical."

"She's not done. That was preliminary clearance. Full approval takes multiple visits."

"Then I'd better make a good impression."

Mayhem's approach was less diplomatic. The big black cat had been in his nest when Alton arrived and had taken approximately forty-five seconds to assess the situation, conclude that a new human in the duplex constituted an event requiring investigation, and launch himself from the couch with the momentum of a small, furry cannonball.

He landed at Alton's feet. Not gracefully, because Mayhem's relationship with grace was complicated, and immediately began the inspection. He circled Alton's ankles twice, pressing his flank against the detective's legs with enough force to leave black fur on the dark trousers. He sniffed Alton's shoes with methodical interest, working his way from toe to heel and pausing at the left shoe's sole with the intensity that suggested something noteworthy. Then he sat back, looked up at Alton with his green eyes, and meowed.

The sound was low, resonant, and carried the specific tonal quality of a cat issuing a demand rather than making a request. Mayhem had detected the salmon. Through the butcher paper, through the brown bag. His nose had located the offering, and his patience for social formalities had reached its natural limit.

"That's Mayhem," Amaya said. "He's already smelled the salmon."

"I expected that." Alton crouched—slowly, respectfully, the way Ron had crouched for Chaos, and held the back of his hand near Mayhem's nose. The cat sniffed it with brisk efficiency, then butted his head against Alton's knuckles. Mayhem was not a cat who understood the concept of gentle. He was a cat who communicated through impact.

"He likes you," Amaya said.

"He likes the salmon."

"With Mayhem, there's no meaningful distinction."

Alton scratched behind Mayhem's ears, and the cat's purr started, a deep, rumbling vibration that Amaya could feel through the floor. Mayhem leaned into the scratching with the full weight of his muscular body, his eyes closing, his expression conveying a bliss so complete it bordered on nirvana.

"He's a solid cat," Alton said, and the admiration in his voice was genuine, the appreciation of a man who respected physical presence and found it in unexpected places.

Chaos made his entrance last, and he made it memorable.

The ginger tabby had been in the bathtub when Alton arrived, his afternoon meditation session, which he conducted daily between the hours of two and four regardless of household activity. The sound of a new voice had penetrated his contemplation, and he'd spent several minutes in the tub processing the implications before deciding that investigation outweighed serenity.

He appeared at the top of the stairs.

He assessed the scene: new human, crouching, Mayhem receiving attention, Trouble observing from the bookshelf. He processed this information at the speed of a cat whose neural pathways were wired for enthusiasm rather than caution.

And then he launched.

Chaos descended the stairs at a velocity that suggested he'd confused the staircase with a ski slope. His ginger body was a blur of motion, his paws barely touching each step, his trajectory aimed at the general vicinity of the new human with the navigational precision of a cat who trusted that the universe would sort out the details.

The universe sorted them out on Alton's lap.

Chaos arrived with the aerodynamic efficiency of a thrown pillow, all fur, no brakes, and landed squarely on Alton's thighs as the detective was still crouched beside Mayhem. The impact rocked Alton backward, and he caught himself with one hand on the floor while the other instinctively wrapped around the ginger cat who was now humming in his lap with the settled contentment of having arrived at his destination.

"That," Amaya said, watching the scene with a warmth spreading through her chest that she didn't attempt to control, "is Chaos."

Alton looked down at the cat in his lap—green eyes staring up at him with unfiltered adoration, vibrating at a volume that suggested the ginger tabby had decided, in the span of three seconds, that this human was now his favorite person. "He's, uh—"

"Enthusiastic."

"I was going to say fearless." Alton adjusted his position, shifting to sit on the floor with his back against the kitchen island, Chaos still in his lap and Mayhem now pressing against his side, the two cats claiming territory with the speed and confidence of invading forces that had encountered no resistance. "Does he do this with everyone?"

"Not everyone. He does it with people he's decided are safe." Amaya sat on the floor across from him, her back against the couch, close enough that their outstretched legs nearly touched. The kitchen island rose behind Alton, the couch behind Amaya, and between them, two cats and a space that felt both intimate and unforced, the natural geometry of people who'd chosen to be on the same level. "He has good instincts about people. Chaos reads intention. He gravitates toward people who mean well, and he avoids people who don't."

"And Trouble?" Alton glanced toward the couch, where the black cat still observed from her elevated position, her amber eyes steady, her tail draped over the shelf edge like a punctuation mark.

"Trouble reserves judgment. She watches. She waits. She'll make up her mind about you over time, based on accumulated evidence rather than first impressions." Amaya met Trouble's gaze and felt the familiar warmth of their connection, the shared wavelength between a woman who built cases from observation and a cat who'd taught her, without words, that observation was its own form of loyalty. "She's the detective of the three. Mayhem's the muscle. Chaos is the heart."

"And you?"

The question was simple, quietly asked, carrying nothing that demanded an answer and everything that invited one. Alton was looking at her. Not at the cats, not at the duplex, not at the photographs on the walls—at her. His expression was open in a way she'd seen only in flashes before: at the diner when he'd acknowledged her work, at the Chelsea sidewalk when he'd told her not to diminish it, at the museum ceremony when he'd raised his glass across the room. Each time, the openness had lasted seconds before the professional surface reasserted itself. This time, he wasn't closing it.

"I'm the one who worries," Amaya said. "About the case, the client, the cats, the outcome. I'm the one who lies awake at two a.m. running scenarios. Trouble doesn't worry. She watches. Mayhem doesn't worry. He acts. Chaos doesn't worry. He trusts. I'm the one who holds the tension so they don't have to."

"Sounds exhausting."

"It sounds like parenting."

"Or partnership."

The word settled into the space between them, a space occupied by two cats and the remnants of the afternoon light and the scent of salmon still wrapped in butcher paper on the counter above. Partnership. The word had been circling them for weeks—professional partnership, investigative partnership, the partnership of two people who'd worked a case together and discovered that their competencies complemented rather than competed. But Alton had used it now, in this context—sitting on her kitchen floor with her cats in his lap, and the word carried a weight that had nothing to do with casefiles.

Amaya didn't deflect. She didn't redirect. She sat with the word and let it breathe.

"Maybe," she said.

It was the most honest answer she had. Not yes. Not yet. But not no. A door left open, the latch undone, the lock turned but not engaged. Maybe was a word that contained time, and time was what they both needed—time away from the investigation's pressure, time to discover whether the connection that had formed under professional duress survived the return to ordinary life.

Alton seemed to understand this. He nodded, a small, single movement, and the conversation moved on without either of them needing to acknowledge the shift. They talked about the case's legal trajectory, about Jackson's squad, about the Bronx, his Mott Haven childhood versus her Riverdale present, the neighborhoods they'd both loved and watched change, the particular pride of being from a borough that the rest of the city underestimated.

He told her about his mother—still in Mott Haven, still attending Mass at St. Jerome's every Sunday, still making the sancocho that he'd been comparing every restaurant's version against for his entire adult life and finding every restaurant's version wanting. He told her about his niece, who was twelve and wanted to be a forensic scientist, and his nephew, who was nine and wanted to be a dinosaur. He told her these things without performance, without the strategic vulnerability of a man trying to appear open. He told her because she'd asked, and because her kitchen floor, occupied by cats and afternoon light, was the kind of space where truth could travel short distances without needing armor.

In return, she told him about the fire escape where Trouble had appeared, a Tuesday night in October, four years ago, the cat sitting on the iron grating like she'd been delivered there by the universe. About her mother, who lived in Florida now and called on holidays and sent birthday cards that always arrived three days late. About the years on the force, the cases that had shaped her, the frustrations that had pushed her out, and the moment she'd realized that her grandmother's skills and her own restlessness were compatible only outside the system.

They cooked the salmon together. Not the whole fillet, a portion for the cats, a portion for themselves, prepared in the kitchen while Chaos supervised from the counter and Mayhem sat at strategic distance from the stove and Trouble maintained her position on the bookshelf, declining to participate in the culinary process but reserving the right to critique the outcome.

The salmon was good. The wine was better. They ate at the dining table while the cats ate in their spots. Trouble by the window, Mayhem by the stove, Chaos on the kitchen floor where he'd positioned himself to intercept any dropped fragments. The conversation continued with the easy rhythm of people who'd discovered they could talk about things that mattered without making the conversation heavy, and talk about things that didn't matter without making it trivial.

At nine-thirty, Alton stood to leave. The evening had passed with the speed of time spent well, the hours compressed by engagement, as they expanded during surveillance or stakeouts. At the door, he paused.

"Thank you," he said. "For the introductions."

"What's your assessment?"

He considered this with the deliberate attention he brought to everything. "Trouble is exactly what you described—she's watching, she's waiting, and she'll decide on her own timeline. Mayhem is a force of nature who should probably be registered as a weapon. And Chaos—" he glanced back at the living room, where the ginger tabby had claimed the warm spot on the couch where Alton had been sitting and was already asleep in it, ". Chaos has the right idea about most things."

"He'll be in your spot for the rest of the evening. He imprints on warmth."

"There are worse legacies." Alton turned back to her. They were standing close, the doorway's geometry creating the same proximity that the restaurant exit had created weeks ago, the same unspoken acknowledgment of distance measured in inches rather than feet. "Amaya."

"Alton."

"I'd like to come back."

Five words. No subtext, no strategy, no professional framing. A man standing in a doorway, asking to return, and meaning it in every sense the words could carry.

"I'd like that too," she said.

He nodded. The smile, a real one, full, reaching his eyes and transforming the scar along his jaw from a mark of history into a line of warmth—arrived and stayed. "Goodnight, Amaya."

"Goodnight, Alton."

She closed the door behind him and stood in the foyer for a moment, listening to his footsteps descend the front stairs. Then she turned back to the living room, where

Trouble had finally descended from the couch and was sitting in the middle of the floor, watching Amaya with an expression that carried more information than any words could have conveyed.

"Don't say it," Amaya told her.

Trouble blinked. The feline equivalent of saying it anyway.

Amaya sank onto the couch beside the sleeping Chaos, who shifted to accommodate her without waking. Mayhem emerged from wherever he'd retreated after dinner and settled against her other side, his solid warmth a familiar weight. And Trouble—having made her point, registered her opinion, and confirmed through the elaborate semiotics of feline communication that the evening's visitor had passed preliminary clearance with an upgrade to provisional approval—jumped onto the couch, circled once, and settled against Amaya's chest, her purr starting before she was fully still.

The duplex was quiet. The wine was finished. The salmon was eaten. And something had started. Not with a declaration or a kiss or any of the dramatic gestures that mark the beginning of things. But with a man who brought fish for the cats and sat on the kitchen floor and asked to come back, and a woman who said yes.

Amaya closed her eyes. Trouble vibrated against her heart. Chaos dreamed in the warm spot. Mayhem anchored her from the side. And somewhere south, driving through the Bronx's December night, a man whose laugh she was beginning to memorize carried with him the warmth of an evening that had been, in every way that mattered, a homecoming of its own.

Chapter 23: New Architecture

The consulting proposal arrived on a Tuesday, delivered not by email but by courier, a manila envelope with the Studio Museum's letterhead embossed in the corner and Lydia's handwriting on the address label. Amaya carried it upstairs to her office, where Trouble had arranged herself on the desk in the precise center of the workspace, her body positioned over the keyboard with the territorial authority of a cat who had decided that productivity would proceed on her terms.

"You're going to have to move."

Trouble closed her eyes.

"That's not moving."

Trouble's tail swept once across the keyboard, producing a line of gibberish on the document Amaya had left open: *rrrrrrrrtttttttttg*.

"Great contribution. I'll add it to the report."

She lifted Trouble off the desk, the cat went limp with practiced resistance, transforming her seven pounds into what felt like thirty, and settled her at the window, where the December sun was doing its best to warm the glass. Trouble accepted the relocation with the dignified displeasure of a deposed monarch, then turned her attention to the street and began her watch as though the interruption had never occurred.

Amaya opened the envelope.

The proposal was thorough. Lydia had put real thought into it. Not the generic boilerplate of an institution checking a compliance box, but a detailed scope of work that reflected the specific vulnerabilities the investigation had exposed. The consulting engagement would cover three areas: a comprehensive security audit of the museum's physical infrastructure, including the tunnel system and all lower-level access points; a review and redesign of staff access protocols, keycard management, and financial oversight procedures; and the development of an ongoing monitoring framework that would identify anomalies in real time rather than after the damage was done.

The term was six months, renewable. The compensation was fair—generous, even, for the scope of work described. And at the bottom of the proposal, in Lydia's handwriting rather than typed, was a note:

Amaya—

I'm asking for your eyes because mine failed. Not because I couldn't see, but because I chose to look where it was comfortable instead of where it was necessary. You looked where it was necessary from your first day in my building, and you didn't stop until the truth was fully visible.

This museum needs someone who looks at hard things without flinching. I hope that can be you.

. Lydia

Amaya read the note twice. The handwriting was steady. Not the trembling script of the woman who'd stood at the third-floor window with tears tracking silently down her face, but the deliberate hand of someone who'd passed through a crisis and was rebuilding with her eyes open. Lydia wasn't asking for rescue. She was asking for accountability—specifically, the kind that came from outside the institution's own blind spots.

It was, Amaya recognized, a significant evolution. The Lydia Brooks who'd called her two months ago had been a woman seeking discretion. The Lydia Brooks who'd written this proposal was a woman seeking transparency. The distance between those two positions was the distance the investigation had traveled, measured not in evidence but in the director's willingness to confront what discretion had cost her.

Amaya set the proposal on her desk beside the certificate with Ron's cat silhouettes and Eleanor's academy portrait. Three objects on a bookshelf: a grandmother's legacy, a community's recognition, and a museum's invitation to help build something better. The progression felt deliberate, even if it hadn't been planned—each object representing a different dimension of the work she'd chosen and the life that work had built.

She picked up her phone and called Lydia.

"I read the proposal."

"And?" Lydia's voice carried the carefully neutral tone of a person prepared for either answer but hoping for one.

"I have conditions."

A pause. Not anxious, but attentive. "Tell me."

"First: I report to the oversight committee, not to you. My findings go to the board unfiltered. If I identify a vulnerability, it gets documented and addressed on a timeline I set, not one that accommodates budget cycles or institutional comfort."

"Agreed."

"Second: I bring my team."

"Your team?"

"Trouble comes with me to every on-site visit. She's better at reading your staff's emotional states than any security consultant I've ever met, and she's already familiar with the building. Non-negotiable."

The silence on Lydia's end lasted three seconds—long enough for Amaya to picture the director's expression cycling from surprise to consideration to the particular amusement of a woman who'd learned, through extraordinary circumstances, that the boundaries of professional competence were wider than she'd previously assumed.

"Does she require a separate contract?"

"She works for premium salmon. We'll keep it off the books."

Lydia laughed. It was a sound Amaya had heard only once before—at the community open day, when a child had asked the director whether the museum had a gift shop for cats. The laugh was real, warm, and carried the specific relief of a person who'd remembered, after a long period of forgetting, that life could also be funny.

"Anything else?"

"Third: Derek Osei is part of this process. Not as someone I'm auditing, as a collaborator. He identified every vulnerability I found before I found it. The only reason those vulnerabilities persisted was that his recommendations were filtered through someone who had a reason to suppress them. If you want security that works, Derek's institutional knowledge is your most valuable asset. Give him the authority to match his expertise."

"I've already begun that conversation with the oversight committee. Derek is being promoted to Director of Security Operations, with expanded authority over budget, staffing, and protocol design." Lydia's voice firmed with conviction. "He should have had that authority years ago."

"Then we're aligned." Amaya looked at the proposal on her desk, at the certificate, at Eleanor's photograph. "I'll sign the contract and start next week. But Lydia, one more thing, and this isn't a condition. It's advice."

"I'm listening."

"The next person you hire to replace Emily—whoever they are—give them credit. Publicly, specifically, by name. When the press writes about the museum's recovery, make sure the story includes the people who made it happen, not just the person at the top." She paused, feeling the weight of what she was about to say and choosing to say it anyway. "Emily's resentment was real. It grew in the gap between her contribution and her recognition. You can't control what people do with their feelings, but you can control whether those feelings have a legitimate foundation. Close the gap, Lydia."

The silence that followed was different from the others—thicker, more textured, carrying the specific gravity of a truth delivered without cruelty and received without defense. When Lydia spoke, her voice was quiet but clear.

"You're right. I know you're right. And it's one of the things I'll carry from this. Not as guilt, but as practice." A breath. "Thank you, Amaya. Not just for the advice. For saying it directly instead of letting me figure it out the hard way again."

"That's what consultants are for."

"That's what friends are for."

It arrived without fanfare—slipped into the conversation with the ease of something that had been true for a while and was only now being acknowledged. Amaya felt it land and decided not to examine it too closely. Some things were better accepted than analyzed.

"I'll see you Monday," she said.

"Monday. And Amaya—bring Trouble. The staff has been asking about her."

She brought Trouble on Monday.

Walking through the museum as a consultant felt different from walking through it as an investigator. The same hallways, the same galleries, the same climate-controlled vaults on the lower level. But the lens had shifted. Where Amaya had once looked for evidence of what had gone wrong, she now looked for the architecture of what could go right. Every camera angle, every access point, every staff rotation pattern was raw material for a system that would make the building more resistant to the next person who decided the art inside was worth more than the trust required to protect it.

Trouble seemed to feel the shift too. The cat moved through the museum with a different energy than she'd carried during the investigation—less coiled, more expansive, her gaze sweeping each room with the evaluative focus of a cat who was updating her mental map rather than searching for anomalies. She paused at the spot in the registrar's office where the drywall panel had been—now sealed permanently, the wall smooth and unmarked, and sniffed the surface once, thoroughly, before moving on. Whatever she'd detected behind that wall months ago was gone. The tunnel was filled with concrete. The passage was closed.

Derek met them on the lower level and walked the building with Amaya for two hours, pointing out structural details the architectural plans didn't capture—utility chases that created blind spots, service doors that shared keycard protocols with higher-security areas, a ventilation shaft that could theoretically be accessed from the loading dock. His knowledge of the building was encyclopedic and granular, and Amaya understood why Eleanor had always said that the best security consultants were the people who'd already been guarding the building. They knew where the cracks were because they'd been trying to cover them with insufficient resources.

Trouble walked between them like a third consultant, her attention dividing between the infrastructure Amaya was assessing and the staff they encountered along the way. A maintenance worker crouched to pet her and received the slow blink. A docent asked if she was the famous cat and was rewarded with a chin-bump against the offered hand. A young intern stared from across the hallway with the wide-eyed reverence of someone meeting a celebrity.

"She's a better ambassador than I am," Amaya said to Derek.

"She's better at most things than most people," Derek replied. It was the most generous statement she'd ever heard him make about anyone, human or otherwise.

The contract was signed that evening, at the dining table, with Mayhem acting as a paperweight on the pages she'd already reviewed and Chaos attempting to chew the corner of the signature page with an enthusiasm that required physical intervention.

"This is a legal document," Amaya told him, extracting the page from his teeth. "It has financial implications."

Chaos looked at her with the complete absence of remorse that characterized his approach to all authority figures. He was, at eleven months old, the youngest member of the household and the one least burdened by the concept of consequences. The world existed for his investigation. Documents were things to taste. Rules were things that others followed.

She signed the contract with Chaos on her lap. He'd relocated there after being denied the signature page, his body warm and his purring steady as she wrote her name on the line that formalized her relationship with the Studio Museum from investigator to consultant. It was a different kind of work than she was used to—proactive rather than reactive, building systems rather than dismantling lies. But the skills were the same: observation, analysis, the patient identification of patterns that others missed.

Eleanor's skills. Passed down through decades, from a detective's badge to a PI's license to a consulting contract signed in a Riverdale duplex with a cat on her lap and a pen that had been slightly chewed.

Amaya photographed the signed contract and texted it to Lydia. Then she texted Eleanor: *Took a consulting gig at the museum. Six months, renewable. Security and protocol design.*

Eleanor's reply arrived four minutes later—fast for a woman who typed with one finger and refused to use autocorrect on principle: *Good. Building is better than breaking. Proud of you Nhoma.*

Then, thirty seconds later: *Also your cat was right about the wall. Tell her I said so.*

Amaya laughed and set the phone down. On the windowsill, Trouble had turned from the street and was watching her—eyes catching the desk lamp's light, her silhouette framed against the December dark outside. The cat's expression was unreadable in the way that Trouble's expressions were always unreadable. Not because they contained nothing but because they contained too much to reduce to a single human word.

"Grandma says you were right about the wall."

Trouble blinked. The slow one. The one that meant everything.

"Yeah," Amaya said softly. "I know."

She stacked the contract pages, secured them in a folder, and filed the folder in the cabinet beside the closed Rourke file and the closed Cuevas file and the thick, heavy folder labeled *Studio Museum* that contained every note, photograph, timeline, and observation from the investigation that had changed the museum, the community, and, in ways she was still discovering—herself.

The cabinet drawer closed with a solid click. Case filed. New chapter beginning.

From downstairs, the sound of Mayhem dismounting the couch with a thud that rattled the ceiling fixture. From the kitchen, the clink of Chaos rattling his food bowl in case dinner had materialized early through sheer optimism. From the windowsill, the steady presence of Trouble— watching, always watching, her gold eyes carrying the accumulated intelligence of four years of partnership with a woman who'd learned, slowly and then all at once, that the best investigations were built on trust.

Amaya turned off the desk lamp and went downstairs to start dinner. The cats followed. Trouble first, then Chaos at a sprint, then Mayhem. They assembled in the kitchen in their customary positions: Trouble by the window, Chaos on the forbidden counter, Mayhem at strategic proximity to the stove.

Evening opened before them—dinner, wine, the quiet rhythm of a household that had weathered a tempest and come out the other side with its foundations. Outside, Riverdale settled into its December night, the streetlights vapor yellow, the trees bare, the sky holding the darkness of a northern city in winter, deep and close and full of the cold, clean silence that preceded snow.

Amaya cooked. The cats watched. And the duplex sustained them all, as it always had—steady, warm, and wide enough for whatever came next.

Sunday. Seven p.m. Eastern. The phone rang.

Amaya was in the bathtub, the one Chaos hadn't claimed, with a glass of wine and a paperback she'd been trying to finish since September. The water was too hot, the way she liked it, and the steam had fogged the bathroom mirror into a soft canvas that reflected nothing. Trouble was balanced on the edge of the tub with the casual defiance of gravity that only cats achieved, her body a sleek black comma against the white porcelain, her eyes half-closed in the warm humidity.

Mayhem was asleep on the bath mat. He'd positioned himself there approximately four seconds after Amaya had started the water, drawn by the warmth radiating from the bathroom the way a moth was drawn to a porch light—instinctively, immediately, and with no intention of moving until the heat source was exhausted. His muscular body rose and fell with the slow rhythm of a cat deep in the deep sleep that followed a large meal, which in Mayhem's case was every meal.

Chaos was in the other bathtub. His bathtub. The one he'd claimed through squatter's rights and daily occupation and whose porcelain walls now bore the faint paw prints of a cat who conducted his morning operas with full physical commitment. Amaya could hear him through the wall. Not singing tonight, just sitting, the occasional soft thump of his tail against the tub's interior announcing his continued presence.

The phone rang from the bedroom. Second ring. Amaya reached for it with a wet hand, nearly dropped it, caught it against her shoulder.

"Hey, Grandma."

"You're in the bath."

"How can you possibly know that."

"I can hear the echo. Tile room, water present. Also you always take a bath on Sunday evenings. You've been doing it since you were fourteen." Eleanor's voice carried the dry amusement of a woman who'd been observing people professionally for three decades and recreationally for two more. "How's the water?"

"Too hot."

"Good. Anything less is a waste of plumbing." The familiar clink of ice. Eleanor's Sunday bourbon, the weekly constant that anchored their calls the way the bath anchored Amaya's evenings. "I called to tell you something."

"Okay."

"I talked to Pauline Chen yesterday. She says you're building a reputation that's outgrowing the Bronx." Pauline. Amaya's contact at the private security firm, the retired detective who ran background checks and maintained a network of former law enforcement professionals. "She also says the cat thing is becoming a brand. Her words."

"I don't have a brand."

"Nhoma, you have a private investigation practice that's been featured in three news stories in two months, all of which mention your cats by name. Trouble has more public recognition than some celebrities. That's a brand."

Amaya sank lower in the water, the warmth covering her shoulders. Trouble adjusted her position on the tub's edge, her paws tucking more securely beneath her as the water level shifted. The cat's adaptability was reflexive. She accommodated the world's movements without surrendering her own position, a skill Amaya had spent her entire adult life trying to learn.

"I didn't plan it that way."

"The best brands are never planned. They emerge from work done well and consistently. Your grandmother didn't plan to become the detective that every rookie in the four-four wanted as a mentor. She just did the work, and the work spoke." Eleanor's voice softened. Not with sentimentality, which she distrusted, but with the tenderness she reserved for moments when she was about to say something she'd been carrying. "You've found your version of the work, Amaya. The investigation, the cats, the consulting—it's yours. It doesn't look like mine and it shouldn't. It looks like you."

Amaya closed her eyes. The steam curled around her. Trouble's purr started—low, barely audible over the water's surface, felt more than heard, a vibration that traveled through the porcelain edge and into the humid air like a frequency searching for its receiver.

"I've been thinking about what this case taught me," Amaya said. "Not the investigation skills. I had those before. But something about trust. About how it builds and how it breaks and what's left after."

"Tell me."

"Lydia trusted Emily the way you're supposed to trust someone you've worked with for seven years. Completely, instinctively, without examining the foundations. And Emily exploited that trust, which is the obvious lesson—be more careful, verify more, trust less. But that's not actually what I learned."

"What did you learn?"

"That Lydia's trust wasn't the problem. The institution's infrastructure was the problem. Lydia trusted Emily because there was no system that required trust to be verified. No independent oversight, no separation of duties, no mechanism for catching anomalies before they became patterns. Emily didn't exploit Lydia's trust. She exploited the absence of the systems that should have made trust unnecessary."

Eleanor was quiet for a moment. The bourbon glass clinked once. When she spoke, her voice held the warmth of a teacher hearing a student articulate something she'd been waiting years to hear.

"That's the lesson that takes most people an entire career to learn. Some never do. The ones who don't spend their lives blaming people for failures that belong to systems." A pause. "You learned it on your first major case.

That tells me everything I need to know about where you're headed."

"Where am I headed?"

"Wherever you point yourself, Nhoma. You've got your grandmother's eyes, your own instincts, and three cats who appear to be smarter than most of my former colleagues. The world isn't ready."

Amaya laughed, the sound bouncing off the tile walls and merging with the steam, a warmth inside a warmth. On the tub's edge, Trouble opened one eye, assessed the sound, and closed it again, the cat's version of a smile, or the closest approximation her species permitted.

"Grandma?"

"Hmm?"

"Thank you. For teaching me to look."

The silence that followed was the most comfortable silence in Amaya's life, the frequency shared by two women who'd never needed words to carry the heaviest things between them. Eleanor Storm, seventy-one years old, sitting in a Las Vegas condo with a bourbon and a television and the accumulated wisdom of a life spent in service to the truth. Amaya Storm, thirty-four years old, sitting in a Bronx bathtub with a cat on the edge and two more nearby and the beginning of a career that would be, she was starting to understand, her own kind of legacy.

"You don't thank people for giving you what was already yours," Eleanor said. "Your eyes were yours. I just showed you how to use them."

"Goodnight, Grandma."

"Goodnight, baby. Kiss Trouble for me."

"She doesn't like kisses."

"She likes mine."

The line went quiet. Amaya set the phone on the tile floor, slid deeper into the water, and let the heat dissolve the last of the day's tension. Trouble's purr continued its steady vibration against the porcelain, a sound that had become, over four years of shared life, as essential to Amaya's sense of home as the duplex itself. It wasn't background noise. It was the score.

She stayed in the bath until the water cooled, then toweled off and dressed in the sweatpants and Howard t-shirt that constituted her evening uniform. Mayhem had migrated from the bath mat to the bed during her soak, his body occupying the diagonal center of the mattress with the confidence of a cat who thought beds were invented for his personal use and humans were permitted to share at his discretion. Chaos had abandoned his bathtub and was sitting on the bedroom windowsill. Trouble's spot during the day, claimed by Chaos only at night, a timeshare arrangement the cats had negotiated through a process Amaya had never witnessed but whose terms both parties honored.

Trouble walked with Amaya through the duplex on the final circuit of the evening, a ritual they'd performed together every night for four years. Not a security check, exactly, though it functioned as one. More like a closing ceremony. The front door, locked. The kitchen, clean.

Chaos's crumbs swept, the cat's water bowls refilled, the stove off. The living room, quiet, the television dark, the bookshelves neat, the photograph of Eleanor standing guard beside the certificate with its three cat portraits. The office, still, the corkboard empty, the desk lamp off, the cabinet closed, the case filed.

Trouble moved through each room with the deliberate attention of a cat conducting an audit—pausing at doorways, testing the air, registering the household's nighttime frequencies. She checked the front door by pressing her nose to its base and inhaling deeply, a behavior Amaya had always interpreted as scent-checking for unfamiliar presences in the hallway. She inspected the kitchen by circling the room's perimeter at baseboard level, a patrol so consistent that her path had worn a faint track in the tile's finish. And she concluded in the office, where she jumped onto the desk and sat beside the darkened laptop, her gaze sweeping the room one final time before settling into the particular stillness that signaled her satisfaction.

Everything was in order. The house was secure. The household could rest.

Amaya watched her from the doorway. The cat's silhouette was sharp against the window, the same silhouette she'd seen from the street on the night she came home from the dinner with Alton, the shape that had produced a tenderness she hadn't expected. It was a simple image, a cat in a window. But it contained everything: the partnership, the trust, the shared attention to a world that rewarded patience and punished carelessness, and the quiet, irreducible fact that home was not a place but a relationship.

"Ready?" Amaya asked.

Trouble jumped from the desk and landed silently on the hardwood. She walked to Amaya, passed between her ankles with the slow, brushing contact that was her version of a hand squeeze, and continued down the hallway toward the bedroom without looking back.

Amaya followed. She turned off the hallway light. The duplex settled into its darkness—warm, close, alive with the breathing of three animals and the woman who'd chosen them, or been chosen by them, or both, the distinction having long since ceased to matter.

In the bedroom, Mayhem had grudgingly adjusted his position to allow Amaya approximately one-third of the mattress. Chaos was still on the windowsill, his ginger body catching the last amber glow from the streetlight below, his eyes reflecting the night. Trouble completed her nesting routine, three tight circles on the pillow beside Amaya's head, paws tucked, tail wrapped around her body, and closed her eyes.

The purr started last. Not Trouble's. Chaos's. From the windowsill, the youngest cat began to purr, the sound carrying across the dark room like a note held after the music stops. Then Mayhem joined, his deeper rumble rising from the foot of the bed, blending with Chaos's lighter frequency. And finally Trouble, the steadiest of the three, the frequency that research said healed bones, the sound that Amaya had come to associate with the word *home* more reliably than any other.

Three purrs. Three frequencies. A chord.

Amaya lay in the dark and listened. The case was closed. The museum was healing. Lydia was rebuilding. Derek was recognized. Ron was painting. Keisha was promoted. Calvin and Emily were awaiting trial. The art was home. And somewhere south of Riverdale, a detective named Alton Jackson was doing whatever Alton Jackson did on Sunday evenings—watching football, maybe, or calling his mother, or sitting in his own apartment thinking about a kitchen floor and three cats and a woman who'd said *maybe* in a way that sounded like the beginning of something.

The purrs continued. The darkness held. And Trouble, who knew everything that mattered about the world she inhabited—its rhythms, its dangers, its warmth, and the precise frequency at which love hummed between creatures who'd chosen each other—settled deeper into the pillow and let the night carry them all toward morning.

Epilogue: February

———————— 🐾 ————————

Seven weeks after the Studio Museum arrests, the Bronx had settled into the deep quiet of winter. Not silence—the Bronx didn't do silence—but a compression, the city drawing its noise inward, muffling itself under layers of cold and cloud. The trees on Fieldston Road were bare, their branches dark geometry against a sky the color of old concrete, and the duplex held its warmth with the determination of a building that had survived worse.

Amaya sat at her dining table on a Sunday morning in early February, the museum consulting report open on her laptop, her coffee going cold the way it always did when she was engrossed in her work. The security audit's final draft was due Friday. Derek's biometric access system had been running clean for three weeks—no anomalies, no unauthorized entries, the museum's lower level as secure as current technology allowed. The tunnel system had been sealed with reinforced concrete, the financial oversight restructured with independent quarterly audits, and Lydia's board had approved a community programming expansion that would bring twelve new artists into the exhibition calendar by spring.

The museum was safer than it had ever been. The case was closed. The work that followed—the quiet, invisible work of building systems that would outlast the people who built them—was nearly finished too.

Trouble occupied the chair at the head of the table, her body curled in a tight circle, tail over nose, amber eyes half-closed in the particular state between vigilance and rest that was her default. She'd been at the window earlier—her morning post, cataloging the dog walkers and the mail carrier and the gray squirrel that Chaos had elevated to the status of personal nemesis. Now she monitored the room from her command position, one ear rotated toward the kitchen where Chaos was conducting his morning aria in the bathtub, the acoustics producing sounds that Mayhem had long since stopped pretending to tolerate.

Mayhem was on the couch. His heated bed—Eleanor's belated Christmas gift, arrived three weeks late and claimed with the instantaneous, total commitment of an animal who'd been waiting his entire life for this specific object— sat unused for once, the couch having won the morning's territorial negotiation through force of habit. His twenty-pound body occupied the center cushion with the sprawl of a cat who considered shared furniture a contradiction in terms.

Amaya's phone buzzed. A text from Alton: *Sunday brunch? Found a Dominican spot on Jerome that does mangu that would make your ancestors weep with pride.*

She smiled. The texts had become a feature of her days—arriving at unpredictable intervals, carrying warmth, a man who communicated affection through restaurant recommendations and cat-related observations. They'd had dinner five times since the evening at the duplex. Each time, the conversation had gone deeper without either of them pushing, the way a river carved its channel not through force but through persistence. He'd been to the duplex three times. Trouble had upgraded him from provisional approval to regular clearance, which Amaya measured by the cat's willingness to sleep in his presence— a vulnerability Trouble extended to almost no one outside the household. Mayhem had adopted Alton's lap as secondary territory. Chaos had stolen his watch on the second visit, hidden it under the couch, and displayed zero remorse when it was recovered.

Mangu on Jerome sounds great, she typed back. *Noon?*

Noon works. Bringing something for the team.

He meant the cats. He always brought something for the cats. Last time, a feathered toy that Chaos had destroyed in under four minutes.

She pocketed the phone and returned to the audit report, but her mind had split—one track finishing the security protocols, the other tracing the shape of what she and Alton were building. They hadn't defined it. She wasn't sure either of them wanted to. The undefined space had its own comfort, close enough to feel the warmth without naming the fire. But the warmth was growing, and she could feel it in the small things: the way he signed texts now—just *A*, a single initial that compressed the distance between professional and personal. The way he asked about the cats before he asked about the case. The way she'd started noticing his absence from rooms he'd never been in.

Eleanor would have something to say about that. Eleanor always had something to say.

Her phone rang. Not a text—a call. She checked the screen.

Gina Alvarez.

A name she hadn't seen on her phone in four months, maybe five. Life had a way of sweeping people along, and Amaya and Gina had been swept in different directions since the fall. Their friendship was the kind that didn't require constant tending—rooted in Amaya's first year out of the academy, when Gina had been office manager at a legal aid clinic on Tremont and they'd bonded over bad coffee and strong opinions about the Bronx's future. The bond had held through career changes, relationship shifts, and the slow drift that adult friendships navigated when neither person had anything to prove.

"Gina. Hey."

"Amaya." Gina's voice carried the particular energy of a woman with news—not bad news, not urgent news, but the kind that pressed against the speaker until it found an audience. "I know it's been a minute. I have zero excuses and I'm not going to manufacture any."

"Accepted. What's going on?"

"Victor." Gina's brother. Bronx city councilman, affordable housing advocate, the man who'd given a speech at a fundraiser when Amaya was twenty-six and still in uniform that had made a roomful of cynical New Yorkers believe, briefly, that politics could be a tool for good. "He's been dating someone. Six months, apparently, and he didn't tell me until last week. Six months, Amaya. I'm his sister."

"That's very Victor."

"That's extremely Victor. But here's the thing—he says it's serious. Like, meet-the-family serious. He wants me to come to City Island next week. Valentine's Day dinner, the whole production." Gina's voice shifted, the irritation giving way to something softer, something that had been hiding behind the indignation. "He sounded nervous, Amaya. Victor doesn't get nervous. He argues housing policy against developers with three times his budget and doesn't blink. But this—whoever this person is—has him moving differently."

Amaya leaned back in her chair. Trouble had opened one eye, tracking the shift in tone the way she tracked everything—with attention that missed nothing and judgment that remained her own.

"He's happy?"

"He sounds terrified. Which, for Victor, is the same thing." Gina laughed—warm, complicated, the laugh of a woman processing the discovery that her brother had a private life she hadn't been invited into. "I just wanted to hear your voice. And maybe get your read on something."

"My read?"

"If someone hides a relationship for six months, is that about the relationship or about the world they'd have to bring it into?"

Amaya thought about that. She thought about the distance between what people protected and what they concealed, and how the line between those two things was thinner than anyone wanted to admit.

"Both," she said. "It's always both."

"That's annoyingly wise."

"I learned it the hard way."

Gina was quiet for a moment. When she spoke again, the warmth had settled into something steadier, the frequency of a friendship resuming its signal after a period of static. "Come over soon. Not for a case—for dinner. Bring the cats. Or at least bring Trouble. Mayhem last time ate half of my potted fern off my windowsill and I'm still recovering."

"That was Chaos."

"They're all guilty. It's a criminal enterprise and you're harboring them."

Amaya laughed. The sound carried through the duplex—warm, unguarded, the kind that arrived without invitation and improved everything it touched. On the chair, Trouble's tail moved once. Definitive.

The call ended. Amaya sat in the quiet that followed, holding the shape of the conversation the way she held case files—turning them, looking for angles, noting what was said and what wasn't. Victor Alvarez, nervous about a relationship. Gina, processing the discovery. Valentine's Day approaching with its freight of expectations and revelations.

She thought about calling Eleanor. Sunday morning, bourbon hour in Vegas. But the thought settled on its own. The wisdom she'd carry forward from the museum case— that trust was a system, not a feeling, and that systems needed tending—was already hers. Eleanor had given her the eyes. The rest was Amaya's own.

From the bathtub, Chaos's aria reached its crescendo— a sustained note that vibrated through the plumbing and caused Mayhem to lift his head from the couch, his patience tested to its absolute limit. Trouble's ear rotated toward the sound, assessed it, and rotated back. Her ability to ignore was higher than Mayhem's. She was not yet moved to protest.

Amaya closed her laptop. The audit would keep until tomorrow. Today was Sunday—Eleanor's call later, Alton's brunch at noon, the slow accumulation of a life that was fuller than it had been six months ago and still, somehow, entirely hers. She'd built it from the work, the way Eleanor had told her to. And the work had given her everything she'd needed: purpose, clarity, three cats who understood her better than most people, and the beginning of something with a man who sent restaurant discoveries like love letters and didn't require an answer to know he'd been heard.

The duplex held its Sunday quiet—warm, close, alive with the breathing of three cats and the woman who'd chosen them, or been chosen by them, the distinction having long since ceased to matter.

Outside, February pressed against the windows with its gray persistence. Valentine's Day was ten days away. Somewhere on City Island, a councilman was adjusting his tie and rehearsing the most important conversation of his life. And somewhere in a Riverdale duplex, a black cat with amber eyes sat on the arm of a dining chair, watching her person with the steady attention that was its own kind of love, and waited for whatever came next.

ABOUT THE AUTHOR

—————————— 🐾 ——————————

M. Tucker Cunningham writes mysteries from her home in New York City that she shares with two cats who have strong opinions about her work schedule and no respect for her keyboard. The Claw and Order series — featuring private investigator Amaya Storm and her three feline partners — is set in the Bronx neighborhoods she knows and loves, where the bodegas never close and the community never stops fighting for itself.

She holds degrees in education, psychology, and business, which means she's qualified to understand why her characters make terrible decisions and how much those decisions cost. When she's not writing, she's painting, crocheting, taking photographs, or explaining to Mayhem that the heated cat bed is not a negotiating platform. *He disagrees.*

The Claw and Order series includes *The Purrfect Crime*, *A Feline Affair*, *Murder at the Met*, and more to come.

Follow the series online

authormtucker@gmail.com

TikTok: @Author.M.Tucker
Facebook: Author M. Tucker Cunningham
mtcbooks.com